The Morning Line

"When you're at the end of your rope, tie a knot and hold on."
— Theodore Roosevelt

PROLOGUE

NEW YORK CITY - 1998

"Release the brake, Dad," the young woman instructed the white-haired man in the wheelchair.

With difficulty, William Upton turned back in the direction of his thirty-year-old daughter, Angela, the sole issue of his four marriages. There was a quizzical look on the elderly journalist's face as he cupped an ear with his hand. Angela realized that her voice had been drowned out by the standing ovation from the crowd that packed the hotel ballroom for the Metropolitan Peace Council Special Award Dinner. She leaned into her father, nearly shouting, "The hand brake, Dad. This thing won't roll with the hand brake on."

Those assembled in the glitzy room had just heard the syndicated columnist praised by the Council's chairman, Frederick Blye. His comments had ended with: "It is an inescapable conclusion that Northern Ireland is on the verge of a genuine peace thanks, in no small measure, to the brilliant, persuasive writings of Bill Upton. It is an honor to present my good friend with the Council's Peace Medal."

The brake finally released, Angela pushed the wheelchair to the center of the dais. She returned to her seat and watched with a smile as the chairman looped a white ribbon over her father's head and draped it over his shoulders. An attached oversized bronze medal rested on his chest. Blye then clipped a microphone to Upton's pin-striped lapel and patted his shoulder. "They really love you, Bill. You're a genuine hero, the real thing."

Upton raised his wrinkled hands, quieting the room, and the crowd settled back into gold-cushioned chairs. Looking out at a sea of round tables topped with white cloths and coffee cups, he noticed politicians saturated the area up front. He knew them all, as he had known virtually every New York City politician of note over his fifty-five years at the *Post*. Upton also knew some of these "public servants" despised him for the candor that was the hallmark of his twice-weekly columns. He reckoned they were present only to seek advantage from association with a long-suffering peace process they had nothing to do with, like crows circling fresh road kill on the Hudson River Parkway. He glanced upwards, in the direction of a pair of gaudy chandeliers overhanging the tables. For just a moment the craggy old newspaperman entertained an evil fantasy, but rejected it quickly. This was, after all, a night to celebrate peace and, with any luck, the return of civility to at least one spot on the globe. Fingering the bronze medal, he began to speak, his voice strong, but chafed from a half-century affair with Lucky Strikes.

"It's very nice of you to give me this handsome medal, and most folks, even those of us with ink on our hands, like to hear kind words said about them. So, I thank you, Fred, and all of you who have come out to share some rubber chicken with me tonight. But, please, remember that I was no hero, only the messenger, and a few dozen newspapers around the world helped me deliver the message. If my columns played a part in bringing about the end of this bloody war some most gently call 'the Troubles,' as my old friend Hubert used to say, 'I'm as pleased as Punch.' In fact, I had no special talent at figuring out what the hell was going on across the pond. What I had was information. Good, sound information. And insight from a young man who *was* heroic, who cared, like we all should care, about civility and honor. Insight that could be used to poke and prod both sides in the conflict, to shame some common sense into a part of the world that kicked that commodity out the door so many decades ago.

"Under certain circumstances, people who are otherwise decent can actually get involved in fostering murder and mayhem. When you say it out loud, it seems unbelievable, even bizarre, but it is surely true. Go ahead and mix politics, religion and class warfare in a big old pot, and you're sure to brew a feast for the devil." With a shaky hand, Upton managed a sip of water, and then continued.

"It is also true is that the world's stage is occasionally blessed with certain players who do what they can to even up the scales of morality, of justice. It may seem that the weights are never quite in balance, but we must be grateful for those who try to get them there. If you'll bear with this old man for just a little bit, I will tell you about one of these good guys.

"Now that the die to shape the peace in Ireland is cast, and only the dumbest sons of bitches could screw it up, I'm going to tell you about a young man I met a few years back, and how courage and sacrifice, when mixed with a bit of sleight of hand, can accomplish what most think impossible. I speak with permission, but given only with my assurance that identities will not be exposed, and that the version I report will adequately prevent the real dots from being connected. So, as they say, the names, etcetera, have been changed to protect the innocent, but the gist of my metaphor, or allegory, or whatever you may wish to call it, actually happened, just as sure as I sit here in this fancy wheelchair."

1

DERRY, NORTHERN IRELAND - MID 1980s

Early on a Sunday morning, before first light, a crooked line of five men ambled along a dark Derry road. Hooked together by arms wrapped around shoulders, they listed left, then right, while lifting their voices in discordant, booze-soaked song. Neighborhood residents were not likely to be out and about at this hour, but, if so, they'd be sure to keep a safe distance and ignore the band of carousers. If they chose to risk paying close attention, they might notice that once the men rounded the corner at an abandoned tenement, their number would be reduced to four.

British Army Sergeant Willie Tavener spent the next fifteen hours holed up in a gutted apartment on the second story of the vacant, corner building. Throughout the day he fought off boredom with an American Western paperback, writing to Welsh relatives, and nibbling on egg sandwiches and pieces of dried fruit. On the hour, he broke down and reassembled his weapons, sidearm first, then his Enfield L42 sniper rifle. When darkness returned, Tavener eased through the rear door onto an outside landing enclosed by a wood railing. He assumed a squatting position, balanced the bolt action Enfield on the railing top cap, and waited.

From the time he volunteered in 1979 in the shadow Military Reaction Force of the British Army, Tavener had taken down eleven men and one woman. MRF policy was to give their sharpshooters justification for each of the deadly sanctions, all for top players in the IRA. Tavener was convinced that his targets had been most deserving of his brilliant skill. Tonight it was Michael O'Shaughnessy, known to have led the Harrod's bombing mission two days before Christmas - eleven dead, four of them kids. A well-placed tout fingered O'Shaughnessy to be staying with his wife and son at a borrowed flat on the edge of Derry's Catholic section. The source further informed, and surveillance confirmed, that he tucked his five-year-old, Timmy, into bed each night. The youngster slept in a second-story room with an undressed window that overlooked a rear garden.

Headquarters, uneasy that a deployment on the Derry streets would alert O'Shaughnessy, had opted for a sharpshooter and kept the troops at home. If O'Shaughnessy could be taken out by a bullet, a house invasion, always accompanied by danger and likely retaliation, could be avoided. If needed, the armored muscle was tucked into a pair of troop carriers at the Ebrington Barracks, ready to roll.

Tavener's legs ached. He wanted to stand and stretch away the pain, but knew the need to minimize movement. The British Army sniper leaned back against the cold wall, his image absorbed into the darkness of the raw winter night. Gazing through a steady drizzle, he could make out a few lonesome red and green lamps strung unevenly over a doorway down the street. Bloody Catholics hate to see the Crimbo holidays go by. Then again, what with living in these hovels, who can blame them wanting a little cheer, at least for the kiddos.

Movement in an apartment across the back garden of slippery muck drew his attention. Tavener narrowed his view to the yellow light and the shapes observed through the bare window. He departed from his normal vision and bent his head, bringing his right eye to the rifle's power scope. Rhythmic puffs of breath vaporized in the cold air.

"Read it again, Ma. Read it again."

"Oh, you rascal, Timmy. It's your bedtime, and Da will be up in just a minute to tuck you in."

The youngster sat up in his bed, leaning back against a pillow. He hugged a stuffed, floppy-eared kangaroo to his pajama top. His sky-blue eyes looked pleadingly at his mother who sat at the edge of the bed, on top of a gathered up, colorful quilt. Next to the window behind Bridget

O'Shaughnessy, an open cardboard box and its ripped holiday wrapping covered the top of a bureau. She held a sheet of letter paper.

"Please! *Please.* It's from Aidan!"

"You little devil. You could take a bone from a starving wolfhound with that pretty puss of yours. Okay, but I'll have to read real fast."

"No! *Slow.* It's from Aidan!"

Timmy's mother read from the single page letter, pausing often to look up and smile at her enraptured son. "G'day - that's Aussie for Hi, Buddy. I know this kangaroo is late for Christmas, but I wanted to send it because it looked so happy and smart, just like you, my best buddy. I hope you like your new home in the North. It's for the best, you'll see. And when I get back up from this school down under, I'm bringing you a suitcase full of presents. Take good care of your ma and da. I love you more than you can ever measure. Your favorite uncle, Aidan."

Bridget smiled, picturing Aidan, her youngest brother, while carefully folding the letter. Aidan was fifteen years old when she'd left her newborn Timmy with the family in the Republic. It seemed the right decision, freeing her to stay in the North and do whatever the Army asked of her. And it kept her close to Timmy's father, Michael O'Shaughnessy, while he served out a sentence in the Maze Prison on the outskirts of Belfast.

From the day Timmy arrived in Erin Cove, Aidan looked upon his nephew as his responsibility. No one had to ask. The relationship was special. With help from his younger sister, Annie, he bore the burden willingly. As Timmy learned to crawl, walk, talk, the bond grew stronger.

In order to be there for Timmy until Bridget was able to take him back, Aidan delayed his university study. He found work with local farmers, usually tending to their animals, particularly the horses. The farmers objected at first to Timmy's constant presence, early on carried by Aidan in a backpack, tiny legs dangling through holes in the cloth sack. But they learned quickly that an Aidan McGuire, even encumbered by his little nephew, was easily worth two of anyone else.

Just a year past, Bridget married O'Shaugnessy the very day of his release from the Maze. Now Timmy lived with his ma and da in the North, where Aidan accepted he should be, but he knew his nephew would always own a huge part of his heart.

"I hear Da coming up the stairs," Bridget said and stepped to the head of the bed. She leaned over to kiss her son. "I'll keep Aidan's letter in a special place. You hold on to Rooey."

Timmy grinned and hugged the stuffed toy even closer, planting a kiss on the top of its head.

Bridget smiled at her son as Michael O'Shaughnessy filled the doorway. "Sweet dreams, my honey."

O'Shaugnessy gave a slap to his wife's bottom as she squeezed past him on her way out of the bedroom, and spoke to his son. "I guess that kangaroo has found a home, Timmy. You'll be sending a thank-you to your uncle now."

"Yup. Tomorrow, Da. Ma already said she'd help."

"That's a good big boy." O'Shaugnessy stepped to the head of the bed. "Aidan's been more of a father to you than I've been able to be. But I'll make up for it, and when he comes home from Australia, then you'll have two das, you will. Now close those eyes and go to sleep, my son."

O'Shaughnessy leaned in to kiss his son good night. As he moved toward Timmy, Sergeant Willie Tavener centered the crosshairs of his power scope on his back. Refusing to be distracted by the drip of rainwater from the edge of the roof, the marksman raised the rifle's barrel, bringing his line of sight onto the midpoint of O'Shaugnessy's curly-haired head. The semi-pointed expanding round nestled in the rifle's chamber was the boast of the armaments department. It would suffer no detour as it burst through the window glass on its way home. Tavener experienced an absolute calm and his world was silent as he moved his index finger inside the trigger guard.

"Quilt, Da, or I'll be cold."

O'Shaughnessy started to turn toward the rumpled quilt. He felt the bullet graze the back of his head on its invisible flight, which continued on a path through the kangaroo's right ear the instant before it exploded in the little heart of Timmy O'Shaughnessy.

2

DUBLIN -TWO YEARS LATER - AUTUMN

"Even down there she looks great, Pete."

Peter Cooney ripped the green rubber swim cap from his head and ran a finger across his upper lip that swelled like a miniature inner-tube. With caution, he poked his tongue into the space on the left side of his mouth that, until a few minutes ago, was occupied by a tooth. His attention to the body slinking through the water at the bottom of the pool took his mind off the throbbing pain that was building. Cooney spoke to his water polo teammate with difficulty, the words muddled. "I just hope she can find the tooth. If I can get to a dentist fast enough, maybe I'll be able to get it replanted."

The slim, fit water polo teammates stood by the side of the Trinity College swimming pool in their green speedos, green swim caps in hand. Their attention was fixed on the young woman in a white tank swimsuit canvassing the bottom of the pool in the area beneath the white team's goal. Suddenly, she turned upwards and shot through the surface of the water. Her right fist was held up in triumph, a smile lit her face. "Got the little bugger!" In just moments, a dripping Annie McGuire had hauled herself from the pool and was standing beside the two men. The pretty nineteen-year-old placed the rescued tooth in Cooney's outstretched hand. "Sorry about that," she said with a noticeable lack of conviction. Annie whipped her white cap and goggles off and unfurled a length of auburn hair. She smiled at Cooney, who, mesmerized by Annie's green eyes, barely heard her comment: "Better get your mouth to a dentist, pdq."

About five minutes earlier, the game clock was running down on the water polo match. With just seconds remaining, the Greenies and Whities were tied at seven. The Green team was making its final rush on the White goal. The keeper was out of position, well to the right of the net. Cooney had positioned himself to the left side, open to receive a pass and then a shot on goal. The ball flew in his direction. As he reached up to snag it, he opened his mouth to refill his lungs. The ball was on his fingertips when he felt an elbow smack into his face.

God! Where the hell did he come from, and how did he ever get up that high? Watching the curvaceous defender drop back into the water, Cooney realized the he was a she, and that there was blood in his mouth and a gap in his side row of teeth.

Now, he spoke to the only female on either squad, the young woman standing beside him who had first removed, then retrieved his tooth. "Thank God this was just a pickup match. If it counted for anything, I'd probably be doing the dead-man's float." Cooney looked at the tooth in the palm of his hand. "Thanks for finding it, but don't forget it was your elbow. You owe me." He attempted to smile through the pain. "Peter Cooney, College of Surgeons. Fancy a drink after I see to my mouth?"

Later in the day, Annie and her victim met at a pub near the college's main gate. They sat at a table just to the side of a small stage. Cooney gently wiped his mouth and chin with a paper napkin as he placed a glass of dark brew back on the table.

"What are you studying at the college?" he asked.

"Literature," Annie answered. "I think it's time for a great Irish woman writer. I also have to sit in for some comparative theology courses. It covers my Uncle Joe's rear end for picking me for a church stipend to help with the college costs, my being female and all. He's the pastor at St Columbkille's, back home."

"And where is back home?"

"Erin Cove. Cork. By the way," Annie ran a finger across her upper lip, "your swelling's gone down a bit."

Cooney gently massaged his face where his tooth had been replanted into his gum an hour ago. He raised his voice a few notches to be heard over a pair of banjo players who had climbed on stage and were strumming American jazz.

"Meeting you has been a mixed blessing, Annie McGuire. I came damn close to losing a tooth, and the pain's just beginning to be numbed by the Guinness, but God knows you're the most beautiful creature I've ever laid eyes on."

"You really think so?"

Cooney smiled, ignoring the effort it took. "You know it. But that's okay. I like women who are wise enough to appreciate their attributes. So, tell me, how does a nice young lady from County Cork learn such a vicious game of water polo?"

"I think I was born with fins. Erin Cove is on the coast. I used to swim off the rocks with my brother, Aidan, at all times of the year," Annie said as she raised her glass of stout.

"And the vicious part?" Cooney followed up as Annie sipped.

"I call it being competitive." Annie smiled. "Sounds better. It must come with having six older siblings, five of them brothers. Now, you tell me, why is an educated, juicy guy like yourself still available?"

"Waiting for the right girl, I guess. Speaking of available, you must have left a few broken hearts around, even at your tender age."

"Oh, I never really cared much for the boys at home. Spent most of my time with Aidan. Working with him and riding the horses he tended, and helping to care for a nephew." Annie paused a moment, her expression suggesting her thoughts were elsewhere. "Anyhow, I don't think any of the young men of Erin Cove would have dared to approach this McGuire girl. Too many brothers protecting my honor."

Cooney, his attention focused on the emerald eyes across the table, grabbed a fistful of popcorn, losing a portion as he brought it to his mouth. "What about your folks? Still at home?"

"For sure. My Da's just taking up space nowadays, collecting his scratch. Ma spends pretty much all her time caring for him. I felt more than a little guilt when I announced I was off to school in Dublin, being the last of the brood."

"Times have changed, Annie. Women have their own lives to live."

"You must be a heathen, Cooney. Say that around a Catholic priest and you'll be given ten rosaries as penance. My uncle's the exception that proves the rule."

"Are your brothers still in Erin Cove?"

"God, no. They've scattered around the world. The States, Europe, and Aidan's just finishing up at an Aussie school."

Cooney sensed a melancholy tone. "You okay, Annie?"

"Oh, sure. It's just that I miss Aidan, lots. He's closest to me in age. We were always together when we were kids. Then, a few years back, something happened that changed him." Annie produced a longing smile. "Maybe, if we become real friends some day, I'll open up. But that's for tomorrow, doctor-to-be Cooney. For tonight," Annie raised her glass of Guinness, "a few jars of the black stuff."

Cooney's eyes were riveted on Annie. He knew he was falling hard for this woman he had met so unceremoniously just a few hours ago, and he revelled in the feeling. He hoisted his glass and toasted his new friend.

"To another day, and another after that, and, I hope, after that."

Six weeks had passed since Peter Cooney's tooth had provided him with an introduction to Annie McGuire. The romance had moved swiftly. Within a month, Annie gladly agreed to move in to Cooney's flat. Their relationship seemed a natural, in the bedroom and out, and Annie began to wonder if it might well lead to the altar some day.

"How will I last the weekend without you, McGuire. I've grown used to having you around here."

Annie stuffed an oversized shoulder bag with a weekend's worth of casual clothing she had pulled from her side of the mirrored wardrobe. She spoke loudly enough for Peter to hear her in the sitting room. "You could try hanging around the library, all kinds of interesting books in there."

Peter had mentioned the possibility of accompanying Annie home for the weekend visit, but she had argued that, at least for now, their relationship should be kept under wraps from her family in Erin Cove. Imagine, she had argued, how the St Columbkille's parishioners would react if they knew she spent her time in Dublin, and their money, chasing around after a fella. And if that ever led to a discovery of their living arrangement, disaster. A shared flat could pass muster in the sophisticated capital city, but Erin Cove was a world away.

"I'll be back Sunday, by six or so," Annie said. "It's only a couple of days you'll be without my charming self."

"I'll meet you at your train. We can grab a bite. What time are you due?"

"Ah, I'm not sure."

"I'll ring you at home on Sunday and you can let me know."

"No, I don't think that's a good idea either, Peter. I haven't been home since school started. I think I should let the family know a little about you before you start phoning. I'll just plan to see you back here at the flat. That way I'll be able to drop off my bag before we head out for some food."

"Okay, whatever Annie wants, Annie gets." Peter had come into the bedroom. He placed his hands on Annie's shoulders and turned her to him. Wrapping his arms around her, he kissed her passionately, then gently pushed a strand of hair from her face. "Your taxi's waiting to take you to the station. 'Till Sunday."

A blue and white striped muffler wrapped around her neck, Annie stepped out of the taxi on Alexander Street in front of the Dublin Port Ferry Terminal. She was early for the 1:00 o'clock sailing to the Welsh port of Holyhead, across the Irish Sea. Plenty of time to purchase her ticket, and then to the 'ladies' to make herself a little less pretty. Foolish, but those were her orders. Orders. Good God, Annie thought as a shiver ran through her, what have I gotten myself into?

She had rung the Dublin number once a week since arriving in the city. Then, finally, and in a way, frighteningly, the phone was answered a fortnight ago. Her first contact was arranged at the Guinness Brewery Museum for two days later. As directed, she went to the near-empty souvenir shop. As she dawdled over some Guinness-emblazoned T-shirts, she heard a voice behind her, a quiet monotone.

"Do not turn toward me. Listen closely." The man behind the voice stepped beside Annie at the T-shirt bin. "Not Friday next, but the following, there will be a taxi at your flat at eleven in the morning. There will be an envelope and a scarf on the back seat. Carry the envelope on your person, wherever you feel it's safest. Put on the scarf and wear it so it can be seen for the whole of your trip. And muss yourself up so you're not quite the looker, drawing attention, likely to be remembered.

"The taxi will take you to the main Dublin Ferry terminal. You're to take the one o'clock boat to Holyhead, then the 6:22 train to London,

Euston Station. Go directly to the Head of Steam Public House right outside the station. Sit at the bar and buy a drink. Get up after five minutes or so. Leave the envelope on the bar. Don't worry about it, just get up and leave, don't look back.

"There's a reservation in your name at the Kennedy Hotel on Cradington. When you arrive, stay in your room till eight o'clock the next morning. Spend the better part of Saturday at the University Library at Gower Street. Have supper back at the Head of Steam and go directly back to the Kennedy. You may or may not be contacted during your visit. Sunday morning, start back to Dublin by the same route. If you've heard and understood your orders, pick up a T-shirt, look at it, and put it back down."

Before Annie looked up from putting the garment back in the bin, the man had vanished.

Now, looking up at the terminal building, the reality of her doings sunk in. She was eager, but afraid. She knew that participating, even just as a courier, could have dire consequences, but she was more than willing to take the risk. The Cause was right, oh so right. She wanted to be a player. The envelope tucked snugly in her knickers, Annie looked up at the overcast sky, took a deep breath, and walked into the terminal.

Dublin - Following Spring

Enjoying the warmth of the sun on her face, Annie strode briskly from the college yard to her flat. Her thoughts were on next week's trip to Belfast. She was pleased to have been tapped again for service, her second assignment being some four months in coming. The delay had caused her to wonder if her London task, which had seemed to go smoothly, had actually been successful. Her orders came from the same voice she had heard at the Guinness Brewery in the fall. This time, from the pew behind her in St Patrick's Cathedral. First a brief compliment on the London job, then the orders for Belfast. She skipped up the front steps of her apartment building.

The glass in the front door rattled its familiar complaint as Annie slammed it behind her. She slid her book bag off her shoulders, dropping it on a wood bench. A few steps down the hall she was greeted by Peter who gave her a quick kiss on his way to the door.

"Surprise, Annie. Company for you in the sitting room. I'm late for class."

With no idea who could be waiting, Annie poked her head around the corner. A handsome young man standing in front of the sofa stared back at her. Startled, Annie was speechless a few moments, then smiled. "Hey, Big Brother, welcome to Dublin."

Aidan's tentative look transformed into a smile. He walked across the room and hugged his sister. He kept her wrapped tightly in his arms, as if afraid to let her go. The brother and sister were silent. Tears ran down Annie's face. She said, "Oh, Aidan. Thank God. I didn't know if I'd ever see you again."

Aidan smudged one of her tears away with his thumb. "You never left my thoughts, Annie. That could never happen. Never."

In ten minutes the tea was steeped and poured. Annie placed an open package of vanilla biscuits on the kitchen table next to the pot. She pulled out a chair and joined Aidan. "I expect you won't suggest that my letters never arrived."

"No, I'll not do that. I have no excuses, Annie. It wasn't fair to you, but I had no spirit. I've just been going through the motions at school."

"It was three years February past, Aidan. The struggle goes on. To me it gets more important as time passes. I'm working with the Army now. I'm available to them for whatever they need, and they've called on me."

Aidan straightened in his chair. "Do you know the danger?"

"Of course. I've got my share of brains."

"I'd have to wonder. My God, Annie, you could end up in the Maze for years. You'd be better off in a coffin."

"It's a risk I'm glad to take. At least I've got a life. You sound like yours is over, Aidan. There's a strong, hard core in my gut. It's fed by anger, pure anger. At the Brits, at a God I don't even believe in for letting this rancid British sore fester in my country and claim its victims. Think about it, Aidan. Maybe you could do something worthwhile, and taste a little revenge while you're at it."

A few moments of silence, chewing and sipping ended as the clock in the adjacent sitting room chimed four times. Aidan stood and leaned against the stove.

"I've thought about a lot of things, Annie. When I'm finished with school next year, I'm likely to take a position with a bloodstock firm. I interviewed with them yesterday. They seemed very interested." Aidan paused, less anxious now to give his news. "They're in London. They're called Empire Breeders."

Annie's eyes widened. "Oh, that's just wonderful. Go to work for the damn Brits." Annie stood and walked to a window, her back to her brother.

"Come on, Annie. Half the country has emigrated to Britain. It's where the jobs are. Racehorses are where my interests are. In time that could change, but for now it keeps me busy. Keeps me sane. One of the reasons I find Empire attractive is because they have an important training and breeding facility in County Cork. If things go right, I could end up back home."

Annie turned back towards her brother. "Give the Cause some thought, Brother. They need all the help they can get in this war. The British bastards can't give us back our Timmy, or any of the thousands they've taken. But it's not going to end until they give us back our country, our heritage, our dignity."

Cork - One Year Later

"So, tell me, Annie, what's happened to Doctor Cooney?"

"Nothing's happened to him, Aidan. He's the same guy whose tooth I knocked out. He was uncommitted then, and he's uncommitted now. I could love him to pieces if I let myself, and I think he feels the same about me, but he's no more likely to marry than the pope, at least not until he's a licensed doc. So here I am, the ever-available Annie."

Annie's train from Dublin had arrived in Cork at noon. Aidan had flown in from London and they'd met up in the visitors' room at the Cork Regional Hospital in early afternoon. They were alone with the utilitarian furniture and dog-eared magazines. Down the corridor, just beyond an operating room, their mother lay in a recovery room. The radiography had been suggestive, but inconclusive, and the surgeon went in to see if the cancer had spread.

"Have patience, Annie. Maybe it wasn't meant to be with Cooney. Things happen for a reason."

"Oh, please, Aidan. If you don't make things happen in this world, we all just sit around and rot. It's not the occasion to get into it, but the Brits will rule the North forever if we don't keep stirring the damn pot. You might give that some thought while you're tending to their precious horses."

"Tending to those horses has paid off, Annie. I was going to call to give you the news, but then realized I'd be seeing you. I've been offered a position at Empire's farm here in County Cork. I'll have to live at the farm, so I won't exactly be at home, and there'll be quite a bit of travel involved – their clients' horses race around the world. But at least I'll be close to home."

Annie started to comment on Aidan's news when a nurse approached them. "The doctor would like to talk with you now. Please come this way."

The consultation had been short and to the point. The cancer had spread, could not be contained. With drugs they could manage the pain for the two, possibly three months she had left. "Could you please go down to administration and fill out the necessary paperwork? Sorry," the doctor said, "but sometimes the damned forms seem more important than the patients."

"Got to stick you with the paperwork and your own taxi, Brother. Irish Rail leaves in thirty."

"That's okay. I've a rental in the car park."

The brother and sister waited outside the hospital's front entrance for the taxi that would bring Annie to Friday's final train back to Dublin. They stood under a portico, protected from a steady rain.

"I'll finish up my exams in two weeks. Then I'll be the dutiful daughter. I'll be back home by the end of the month to tend to Ma and Da, then just Da. 'Till then, we'll have to count on Dot McCarthy. I guess that's what spinster neighbors are for."

"I guess so. God, it's hard to believe. How can something like this happen so fast?"

"They've just discovered it, Aidan, but it's been spreading through her for months now. We have to accept it. Cancer is cancer."

"I'll go home for the weekend and talk to Da," Aidan said as a taxi pulled up. "Ma told me by phone last week that he's not comprehending much nowadays. It's funny, but perhaps he'll miss her least of all of us."

"Except when he needs his supper. You should let him know he'll be having a new housemaid in a few weeks."

"Annie, be kind. He can't help his condition."

"I know, Aidan. I know. And, of course, I'm the only one of seven kids available to care for him."

Aidan chuckled, drawing a befuddled glance from Annie. "Can you handle a dark family secret, Little Sister?"

"Shoot."

"They were never married, Ma and Da."

A skeptical smile appeared on Annie's face. "You have to be kidding."

"Nope. According to Uncle Joe, they've been living in sin for fifty-two years. A while back he suggested a small, quiet service would solve the problem. Da said, 'What problem? Why bother? It won't change anything.' And Ma didn't think it was worth fighting over."

"My God," Annie said, "it's official. Seven McGuire bastards."

Aidan reached for the taxi door and opened it for his sister. She kissed him on the cheek and stepped into the rear seat.

3

LONDON - TWO YEARS LATER - NEW YEAR'S EVE

Hillman House, a private gentlemen's club occupying a gray stone building on St. James Street, was always exceptionally busy on the last day of the year. The increase in patronage at the comfortable bar and stately dining room had nothing to do with a New Year's Eve celebration. Not only was there no special dinner menu or relaxation of the strict guest policy, but also food and beverage service were abruptly halted at nine o'clock. Down to the overburdened pot washer, the club staff was aware of the source of the business mini-boom - when 9:00 p.m. arrived, the computing of the year's food and drink tabs would close. Those members who had not consumed sufficient amounts of lamb chops and brandy over the twelve months would be victims of the club's annual minimum tariff rule. The fact that these highly-placed industrialists and government ministers could easily suffer the loss made no difference. Since when was abundance a cure for penny-pinching?

By six-thirty darkness had overtaken the British capital. In the HiHo's second floor bar, strategic lighting accented the polished wood and brass fittings. Outside, beneath a curved window, a cream-colored canopy imprinted with a crimson HH logo stretched from the entrance of the building to the pavement. An umbrella matching the canopy and held by a footman prevented the freezing rain from assaulting members stepping out of chauffeured Bentleys and Mercedes that slipped through the slush to curbside. A pair of men in quiet conversation stood looking through the window, drinks in hand.

Tuxedo-clad Gerald Appleyard, a slightly built Londoner, had recently turned fifty and was rapidly balding. He was shorter than his companion by a half foot. The second man was just over six foot tall with a full head of dark hair. Aidan McGuire wore a blue Savile Row suit, white shirt stitched on nearby Jermyn Street, and a maroon tie. As the men spoke, they watched frozen raindrops, their descent from the black sky angled by the wind, experience instant meltdown against the warm window glass.

Across the room a collection of middle-aged men, one or two older, most wearing formal evening attire, formed a half-circle in front of a massive stone fireplace. Their conversation centered on the two men standing by the window. The tone was merrier and a little louder than usual for the club, perhaps due to the holiday spirit.

"See Appleyard's got his favorite boy with him again. Don't suppose they're..."

A portly, white-haired member spoke up, cutting off the speaker. "Hell no, Norman, at least not McGuire. May be a bachelor, but he's as randy as they come. The ladies can't get enough of him. What with those looks, he has the pick of the crop. Understand he's quite a farmer, too."

"I suspect you're right about the Mick, Harold. But I'm not too sure about little old Gerald."

When the chuckling had subsided, the eldest member in the group spoke up. "Let's be nice now and not forget that Appleyard runs the most important racehorse operation in the bloody country. Had a lot of success out of the Irish barns. Half the bloody members have a string of horses with Empire."

"I think it's about time we extended membership to McGuire. Don't care if he is a Mick. Knows more about the horses than most, and occasionally we can expect to learn something to our advantage," Harold said.

"I've no interest in the horses, Harry, but if you assure me he'll share his leftover ladies you've got my vote," an M.P. from Gloucestershire chimed in. "I'm spending too much bloody time with the wife."

A tall, grave-looking man, made taller by the upward slant of his face, joined the conversation. "Doesn't have the credentials. Nope, not at all. Graduated some veterinary college down under. Irish and all. As far as I'm concerned, they're all bloody terrorist bastards." He shook his head, "Uh, uh."

Norman accepted a whiskey and water from the waiter, placing his empty glass on the extended tray. "I agree with Harold. What the hell, McGuire's here at the club as a guest often enough. Never heard any complaints. Not all the Micks are bloodthirsty cowards. He seems good company. Hell of a horse trainer. I've a colt couldn't get one foot in front of the other until McGuire got his hands on him. In front by two lengths this past September at Newmarket." Norman looked in the direction of the front window, "They're headed this way."

The two men approached the group. "Evening, gents. I know you've all met Aidan," Appleyard said. "Mind if we join the conversation?"

"Not if you've a hot horse or two, Gerry," Harold said, moving to his left to make room for the men.

"No tips, Harry," Appleyard said, "but, as you may know, McGuire here has been general manager of Empire's facility at County Cork for about two years. He has the farm going great guns."

After five or so minutes of conversation about the business of breeding racehorses, a black-suited waiter with snow white hair approached the group. He stopped just to the rear of Appleyard. "Excuse me, sir," he whispered, barely audible over the conversation and the crackle of the fire, "My apologies. There is a gentlemen, a Mister O'Malley, on the phone from Ireland. He says it is most important, urgent actually, that he speak with your guest, Mister McGuire."

"Thank you, William." Appleyard said, turning back to the group by the fire. Aidan was praising the chairman of British Petroleum for having had the good sense to forego shipping his two-year-old colt to New York for the Champagne Stakes, with the horse coming off a foot abscess the past fall. "Beg pardon, Aidan. Georgie O'Malley's on the phone from Ireland. Urgent, he says."

Aidan responded immediately. "Where can I pick up, Mister Appleyard?" He placed his drink down on a nearby table.

"Use the phone in the small study, you know the one, next to the bar. I'll walk over with you." In a louder voice, the Empire executive apologized for taking Aidan from the group. "Excuse us, please, gentlemen. Duty calls."

Aidan smiled his apologies around the group and walked across the room with Appleyard. "Wonder what it is that would have Georgie track me down on New Year's Eve. I hope nothing's wrong."

Appleyard opened the door to the study and pointed to a desk phone, a blinking light at its base. The wood-paneled room, its three narrow windows framed by bookcases, was lit solely by a Tiffany lamp on a sideboard. Appleyard remained outside, pulling the door shut and leaving Aidan alone in the quiet of the room.

Aidan stood beside a deep blue leather easy chair and picked up the phone. "Hello, Georgie. What's so bloody important?"

"I'm sorry to be botherin' you on New Year's Eve, Aidan, but Doc Flynn was sure you'd want to know."

"Good God, man, know what?" Aidan tightened his grip on the phone.

"It's Old Lusty. She's about to foal. Been sweatin', leakin' some milk. Off by herself in the pasture today. Sometime tonight or tomorrow morning is most likely. Three weeks early, she is."

"Good God almighty!" exclaimed Aidan. "I'm on my way. If I can find the Colonel, I'll take the Lear. The estate wagon's still at the airport, right?"

The search for Empire's pilot had been successful. A call to the Retired Officers' Club in the Marylebone district was all that was required. The problem was that the former RAF fighter pilot could hardly mumble "Be right there, Mister McGuire" before the phone fell from his grasp. The din of noise and laughter made it clear that the holiday partying was in full swing. Aidan told the flyer not to bother, that he'd be able to catch the last Air Lingus flight of the year out of Heathrow.

A green BMW, its door held open by the footman, was at the curb when Aidan hurried from the club. Because Empire's business brought him to London often, the sedan, along with a flat in the Kensington section, was provided by his employer. With quiet efficiency, the luxury auto slipped away from the St. James curbside. Aidan pressed a programmed number on his phone key pad. When his call was answered, he spoke for just a few moments, then listened to the terse response from a female voice.

"You have to be bloody kidding."

"I'll make it up to you when I get back to London. More than a meal and a party hat at Grovesenor's, I promise. It will be just a day or two."

"You unromantic oaf! It's not the night on the town I'll miss. It's *you*!"

Aidan heard a clunk, followed by a disconnecting click. He slid the phone back into its cradle, experiencing a tinge of guilt. Not for the broken date, but for the situation he had let develop. Aidan had become genuinely fond of Claudia. He recognized the danger zone. Perhaps this broken date would be an opportunity to bring a halt to the relationship before she started plotting the route to the church. If there was one thing of which Aidan was certain, it was that he would never marry, never be a father. He thought of Timmy. He'd have been a happy twelve-year-old now, save the British bullet.

It seemed a daily experience, brought on by any number of ordinary observations: kids kicking a ball - Timmy had just discovered soccer - a child's bicycle in front of the grocery, a package of Timmy's favorite biscuits. Aidan's thoughts would go directly to the phone call. His roommate had answered the ring at the University of Queensland dormitory. It was February, the summer semester down under. Unusual to be sure, a phone call for the Mick. It had to be bad. Trepidation as he picked up the receiver. Da always had some sort of problem. But it wasn't about Da.

Tears flowed intermittently for days, mingled with disbelief. Then anger replaced disbelief. The tears remained, usually when he was tired, late at night, his guard down. But sometimes they came from nowhere, like now. He squeezed the teardrop from his eye with a finger. No, never again would Aidan McGuire expose his heart.

Aidan waited impatiently at the corner for the traffic signal to turn. The dashboard clock read 9:15. Concerned he might miss the final flight of the night to Cork, he decided not to head to the Kensington flat for a change of clothes, but rather to head for Cromwell Road, then straight on to Heathrow. The light changed. Aidan touched his foot to the pedal. The BMW surged around the corner.

With most of the holiday travelers settled until after the New Year, Aidan walked across a nearly empty Heathrow terminal to the Air Lingus ticketing counter. Still dressed in the suit he had worn to the Hillman House and without baggage, he approached the lone ticket agent on duty. There was a single traveler being served, a short slender man wearing glasses and with a full head of wavy brown hair. Suddenly, the man at the counter turned and stepped directly in front of Aidan, his leather grip in one hand, a ticket envelope in the other. He looked up at Aidan and hesitated. Aidan sensed recognition in the small man's eyes at the instant of contact. Quickly, the traveler glanced away and continued to step to one side, narrowly avoiding a collision.

Aidan found something about the man quite familiar. He felt sure he knew him and was about to voice a greeting, but remained silent, searching for a name. Without pocketing his ticket, the man scurried down the sparsely populated terminal, the thick heels of his shoes clicking on the lobby floor.

Aidan stepped to the counter, his eyes still fixed on the man hurrying away. "Swear I know that fellow," he said, as much to himself as to the ticket agent. "Well, maybe I'm mistaken."

"I just ticketed him for Air UK. On his way to Aberdeen. Against the regs, but I think I can help you out with his name. Let's be sure of it." As the agent typed a flight number on a keyboard and pressed the enter key, he continued talking. "Wished the little bloke a Happy Hogmanay, and he hardly reacted. Expected the opposite from a Scot, New Year's celebration being such a big deal up there and all." A short list of names appeared on his monitor. "McKinnon, Ernest, address in Arnott, Scotland." The agent turned and watched the man disappear around a corner. "And he's wearing the most obvious pair of elevator shoes I've ever seen. Can hardly keep upright in them."

"Name doesn't ring a bell, but thanks for the info." Aidan looked up at a list of flights posted behind the agent. "I'll take a seat on your ten o'clock to Cork."

Cork

Obscured by a steady drizzle, a yellow glow was barely visible in the high windows of the barn set atop a small hill. A white Range Rover with the Empire Breeders logo painted on its front doors sped up the drive leading from the county road. Aidan dragged on his cigarette as he directed the estate wagon along the curves of the blacktop. The dashboard clock glowed 11:39. Twenty-one more minutes, thought the horseman behind the wheel, and it's a full year of growing and gaining strength before he's a yearling. Perhaps a minor matter, unless it's a racehorse you're aging.

When he was a small boy, Aidan thought it stunk that all the horses had the same birthday, the first being on January 1st the year after they were foaled. As a racehorse trainer, he quickly learned that because of this administratively logical rule, the earlier in the year a foal hit the ground, the bigger and stronger it was when first raced as a two-year-old. The later in the year, the opposite. When stakes races with huge amounts of prize money can be decided by a razor's edge at the finish line, you look to every possible advantage. But perhaps this foal wouldn't be needing much help beyond his bloodlines. He was, after all, the offspring of the only encounter between Bold Roman, a legendary American sire, and Wanderlust, the most sought after date for the breeding sheds of Ireland.

The famous broodmare had a history of dropping foals early, and this anxiously awaited colt would be no different. Earlier in the day, the seventeen-year-old roan was keeping her distance from the other mares in the fields. Then, in early evening, she began breaking out in a serious sweat and Empire's veterinarian had moved her to the foaling shed. The call to Aidan, who had earlier made it clear that he wanted to be on hand when the colt arrived, was quick to follow. Aidan skidded the Rover to a halt alongside the farm's east barn. He sprang from the wagon and raced through a steady rain, into the cavernous building. As he sprinted down a corridor with stalls on either side, Aidan shouted his arrival in the direction of the foaling shed attached to the end of the barn.

The clock on the back wall of the foaling stall read ten minutes into the new year.

"Doc, I've stood up a gorgeous woman, flown across a cold dark sea, and we're beyond the magic hour. Tell her it's time." Aidan leaned against the half-wall of the large stall. He had stripped off his coat and rolled up the sleeves of his dress shirt. Although he did not expect to be needed, he would be ready to assist. He ran a hand through his hair and studied what he was confident would be the opening scene of a new chapter in racing history.

Standing in front of the mare, next to a shelf crowded with a variety of medications and a few pint bottles of whiskey, the farm's paunchy veterinarian stared at Wanderlust. With a look of anticipation on his ruddy face, Doc Flynn tugged at his braces with his left hand and scratched his red-tinged mustache with his right. He gave a belated reply to his boss's suggestion.

"I think maybe it's time you took a bride, Aidan. Learn something about patience, you would." The veterinarian reached for a pint bottle of Jameson's, took a swallow and continued. "With Lusty, we don't tell or induce. She does things her own way. You know that."

"You're right, of course, Doc. Does it pretty well, too," Aidan replied.

"She's the best by anyone's definition," Doc said. "This colt will top the mark if he's half what he should be."

"Bloodlines, bloodlines," Aidan said.

"Are you sure we have to let this one get away, Aidan?" Georgie O'Malley, the farm's assistant manager, asked from a crouched position as he smoothed the straw in front of the mare, even though he knew the answer.

"Afraid so, Georgie. The American owner shipped Kentucky's top sire over here to service old Lusty. Only time they ever let him leave home. The story is that Mister Logan won the stud rights in some sort of wager. This colt may be owned by a Yank, but at least he's Irish bred, and Mister Logan has said he wants him raised and trained right here in County Cork. So, Georgie, in a way we'll still have him."

On a bed of straw, Wanderlust lay on her right side. The broodmare's huge gray belly began to move.

"I think she's about ready," Georgie said. Quickly, he stood and backed away from the mare, catching himself as he began to trip over a discarded bucket. "She's moving the colt."

"Here he comes." Doc Flynn squatted down beside the mare. The foal's front feet moved out of the birth canal, quickly followed by the head. The process stopped momentarily and Flynn reached over with bare hands to take hold of the spindly forelegs. "Nice and easy, Lusty. Easy does it old girl." Doc gently tugged on the foal's legs. The small hump of the withers appeared, quickly followed by the slippery midsection and rear legs.

Aidan started walking toward Wanderlust and her colt, slowly, in small steps, as if he were afraid of disturbing a solemn occasion. He had observed foals being born before, including champions out of this mare, but this birth seemed a special experience. It was a good-sized colt, and perfectly formed, its brown snout distinctively marked with a white diamond down the center.

While the trio of Irishmen looked on in silent admiration, the dam licked her freshly born colt, his brown coat shimmering under the lights illuminating the stall. Unexpectedly, the colt stood. There wasn't a tremble in any leg. He moved his head in an arcing motion, as if examining the three witnesses to his birth.

"Wow." Aidan whispered. "No doubt about who's the boss with this one. I'll be needing to call Mister R. Jack Logan. If he's been saying any prayers, they have surely been answered this New Year's Day."

A brilliant flash of lightning was followed in an instant by a deafening, prolonged crack of thunder. The barn lighting flickered, then disappeared, leaving the men and horses in pitch black.

"Jaysus, Mary and Joseph," Georgie O'Malley whispered.

4

CORK - THREE YEARS LATER

"They just called your flight, Aidan. Better head for the gate."

A somber Aidan McGuire, just returned from the men's room, bent to pick up his carry-on bag. "Well, thanks for the lift, Annie. I wish this were a friendlier departure."

"That's two of us. Funny, even when I'm in a mood to kick your ass all the way to London, I have to wait for your damn flight to leave so I can be sure you're safely off."

"It's said that politics should never be discussed around an open bottle. Look what happens, even to family, when we forget that."

"You mean what's left of family."

Aidan leaned over to kiss his younger sister's cheek, effectively ending the conversation. "I'll call mid-week. Be back in Cork the weekend. I love you, like always."

Annie walked back to the car park where she would sit and wait for Air Lingus flight 540 to lift off. God, what was wrong with her brother? Couldn't he understand that there was nothing other than blood the Brits understood? That nothing else would even get their attention? But he was right about mixing booze and politics. Guaranteed to set the fur flying. She started in on him just after Da had been awakened from his chair and put to bed.

"It's really kind of crazy, Aidan. I spend the better part of my life tending after him, and I'm not even sure he knows who I am. Thinks you're just wonderful for showing up for dinner twice a month." Annie joined her brother at the kitchen table and filled her glass from a large bottle of ale.

"I've never said it's fair, Annie. What would you suggest, that I don't visit my father?"

"No. Of course not. It's just that I'd like to be able to do more for the Cause, but my being stuck here with Da stops me from that. But you could get more involved. God knows you have as good, if not greater, reason than I. With your traveling about the globe half the year for Empire's damn horses, you've plenty of opportunity to be more active."

"I've helped out when asked, Annie. No, I don't have your enthusiasm. I've never been convinced it makes a hell of a lot of difference what we do. Hasn't done much of anything yet." Aidan sipped from a tumbler of whiskey. "Last I checked, the British still call the shots up North."

"And the bastards will keep us in a virtual prison as long as we let them get away with it! God, Aidan, where were you when they passed out the brains... and the guts?"

It went on for another half hour before an angry Aidan headed for the door for the drive back to his flat at the Empire farm, some ten miles from Erin Cove.

"Oh, for God's sake, Aidan, you'll wrap yourself around a post, and I'll feel guilty for the rest of my days. Stay the night. I'll follow you back to your damn farm in the morning, and then drive you to the airport."

Now, with Aidan safely aboard, Annie looked up, toward the roar of the Air Lingus passenger jet as it rose in the gray winter sky.

Erin Cove - Late Winter

The husky teenager was pissed. "Dammit, Billy! Get back in the boat and grab the end of the fuckin' box! Who do you think I am, fuckin' Hercules?"

"Shit!" Billy exclaimed as he placed his slight, 140-pound body into the stern of the 38-foot fishing boat named "Finnegan's Wake." He barely maintained his balance as the vessel rocked against the dock. "I'll be in the fuckin' harbor any second."

"Both of you shut your damn mouths and get the crates on to the dock. The van will be here any minute," Annie McGuire barked into the wind. She pointed the narrow beam from her flashlight at the wooden crates waiting to be moved from the fishing boat.

An hour earlier, Annie and the two young IRA soldiers from Donegal had taken the boat, borrowed from Michael Finnegan, a sympathetic fisherman, out of Erin Cove's cozy harbor and into the open Celtic Sea. After tying up to and boarding a high-seas trawler, Annie had inspected and accepted the goods. Once the arms were transferred to the fishing boat, she handed over the American dollars.

By luck, the shipment of side arms and ammunition that began its sea voyage in a Moroccan fishing port arrived off the Erin Cove coast on a Friday night. Villagers who were not in their beds at this hour, close to eleven, were tucked into the Purple Goose Pub. There'd be no one wandering down to the quiet harbor on this cool night. Annie stood on the narrow dock, her jacket, sweater and jeans soaked through from the wind-driven ocean spray. Hair plastered against her face, adrenaline racing, she turned to an approaching van and waved her flashlight.

Within fifteen minutes, the van was making its way up a small rise on the north side of the harbor. Annie sat in front with the driver, whose jacket collar and cap obscured his profile and mane of white hair from the young men settled in the back of the van with the crates. Circling to the rear of the white clapboard church at the crest of the hill, the van pulled in tight to a cellar entrance.

Without a word, the driver stepped out of the van and disappeared. Annie hopped out of the passenger door and pulled open the van's rear doors. In minutes all four crates were in a corner of a musty cellar, covered with a tarp behind a half dozen rubbish bins.

Cargo delivered, the van pulled around to the front of St Columbkille's Church carrying ginger-haired Billy, now at the wheel, his fellow soldier beside him and Annie in the back section. As soon as the van halted, Annie hopped out the rear, slammed the door and trotted across the grass to the rear door of the rectory that stood next to the church. She walked through the unlit kitchen into the front room. Father Joseph Ignatius Mulligan, tall and thin, stood at a front window. He was still in his black car coat, the collar up. The white-haired priest watched a small burst of light illuminate a face in the van - a cigarette for one of the boys. As the van turned onto the road and sped away its headlamps burst to life. By sunrise it and its two occupants would be halfway back to Donegal.

Annie stood beside the priest. She shivered, suddenly aware of her cold, soaked clothing. "It went well, Uncle."

The priest turned to his niece. "God, Annie, I didn't notice your condition in the van. You didn't say you were swimming out to meet the ship."

"I'd have been more comfortable stark naked."

"That would have ignited some teenage hormones. I'm sure your helpers found you distracting enough with clothes on. What's next?"

"The guns are to be picked up within the month. I don't know when, and they'll not tell us ahead of time. You'll have to leave the cellar door to the church unlocked."

"That's no problem. Why would anyone even think of breaking into our poor little church? God knows, we have to threaten the faithful with eternal damnation to get them here once a week."

5

ERIN COVE - ONE WEEK LATER

Supper dishes were washed, wiped and stacked back into the cabinet at the McGuire home. Annie and Aidan sat at the kitchen table with a pot of tea.

"One of the boys down from Donegal for our water-logged mission last week was bragging about being part of an execution team for a tout in Belfast. A Dermot McGinnis was sent to the hereafter."

"Quiet, Annie. Da's likely to overhear you," Aidan scolded.

Annie glanced across the kitchen and into the adjoining room. Cornelius McGuire's head had sunk into his gray cardigan, his corncob pipe finally cooled, resting in the nearby ashtray. "He's out like a light, Aidan. Finished dribbling his food down his chin and fiddling with that damn pipe. He'll sleep until I wake him for bed. He's mostly deaf anyhow."

"Be easy on him. You'll be old yourself some day."

"Maybe, maybe not."

"Everything went okay last week?" Aidan asked.

Annie smiled, then boasted, "It was my little mission. Of course it went smoothly. There'll be a few more guns and bullets up North in a week or two."

"Uncle's as enthusiastic as ever to be involved?"

"Of course he'll help out, but I think he's getting a little tired. He's not a young man. Any assignment wears on him." Annie fiddled with her cup. "I've been wondering, Aidan. Do you think the Brits could be on to us here in our little corner of the world?"

"Do you know something I don't?"

"No, but they know our family history, the blood that's been spilled. It wouldn't surprise me if we're being watched. I just wonder how long we can run our little club out here in the country before they wise up, that's all."

"It seems unlikely that they're on to anything. They mostly contain their investigations to the North and Dublin. I don't think they'd be snooping around in Erin Cove."

"I'm not so sure. They seem to know everything about everything. Keeps me from sleeping soundly, I'll tell you that."

"I often wonder why we keep this ball in the air, Annie. Nothing ever seems to change. Is there any sense to it?"

"There's a grave marker in our little cemetery. It reads *Timothy O'Shaugnessy – Five Years Young*. Maybe you should leave some flowers."

Aidan drained his cup of tea and stood from the table. He looked into the adjoining room and confirmed that his father was sleeping. "You know I've never shared your enthusiasm to be directly involved. But I've had a change of heart, in a way, at least. I've come up with a scheme to raise a lot of money for the Army. Once I've crossed the T's and dotted the I's, I'll be needing to get my idea to the ear of the decision makers. Can you arrange that, Annie?"

A smile brightened Annie's face. "Of course I can, Aidan. Just let me know when." She stood from the table and hugged her brother.

Palm Sunday

The morning was warm and pleasant on the southwest coast of Ireland, ushering out the winter chill in time for Easter Week. The sun-filled morning eased the burden for the St Columbkille's parishioners as they climbed the worn wooden steps of the old church. Some at the eight o'clock Mass would rather have stayed in their beds, particularly those who had closed the Purple Goose the previous night. The conversation between two of the worshippers echoed the thoughts of many.

"Do you think Father will spare us a long-winded sermon this mornin' and just wish us a happy day?"

"It's not the amount of time he spends at the pulpit, it's the damned words he speaks. He should be wearin' orange vestments. And to think he's a Mulligan, with his two younger brothers slaughtered by the Brits."

An altar boy's hearty shake of a cluster of bells signaled the beginning of Mass.

"Praise to You, Lord Jesus Christ," the congregation intoned after Father Mulligan concluded his reading and informed them that they had been listening to the gospel of the Lord. With the constant but fragile hope that the celebrant would overlook a sermon, the congregation hesitated, staying on their feet until instructed by the priest to sit down, deflating that possibility.

With those in attendance settled onto the hard pews, Father Mulligan launched into his usual homily. At the same time, at the end of the dirt drive that wound around to the back of the small church, a young man hastily made room in the back of a dairy truck while two colleagues entered the church cellar. A few minutes later, four crates of guns and ammunition were loaded into the truck behind a dozen drums of milk. As the priest wound up his sermon, the Happy Cow Dairy truck made its way out of Erin Cove.

"And so, my brothers and sisters in Christ, let us honor the words set forth in St. Paul's letter to the Philippians. We must never lose sight of the requirement that we love one another as God loves us all, friend or enemy, no matter which side of the border we call home, no matter which political party we support, and, yes, no matter which church we visit to worship Christ, Jesus." Father Mulligan stepped from the pulpit and walked back to the altar.

Following Mass, the priest thanked his altar boys by making the sign of the cross over them while uttering a prayer on their behalf. Then, as always, two coins magically appeared in the tips of his fingers, lighting the boys' freckled faces. The ten-year-olds raced through the open door of the sacristy and down the side aisle. Their minds on the candy case at Rooney's grocery, they paid no notice to the young woman kneeling in the first pew, head resting in cupped hands.

Satisfied that only she and the priest remained in the church, Annie left the pew and silently appeared at the sacristy door. Her uncle was standing at a window, his back to the door. His view was of the small parish cemetery, enclosed with black iron fencing. He leaned against a narrow table that held chalices, communion plates and finger bowls. Smoke drifted up from a cigarette wedged between his fingers. Sensing Annie's presence, without turning he asked, "My dear Annie, any news I might find of interest?"

"Yes, Uncle, there is." Annie moved into the small room. "I talked with Aidan last night. He thinks he may be on to something that could put a lot of money in our treasury. He expects to have solid information in a week or so. Something to do with an American named Logan, the owner of the famous racehorse, Irish Eagle. If he puts it together, he'll be needing to talk to the higher-ups. Maybe from the command staff."

"That's good news, Annie. Your uncles and little Timmy, as they are at rest right here in our little cemetery, will be pleased."

"It's high time Aidan contributed. He's been a reluctant supporter, at best."

Father Mulligan turned to his niece. "That's true. When I spoke with him in this very room after your mother's funeral mass, he expressed his feelings. He wondered why his ma had to be burdened with grief for two brothers lost in this war, and then worry about what might happen next, having five sons. In Aidan's eyes, it just wasn't worth whatever might be gained. Don't be too harsh on your brother. For some, being a part of our effort takes enormous rationalization."

"Uncle, my brother has justification to lay siege to the city of London. It's about time he volunteered. Better late than never, I guess."

"Well, maybe something has awakened in him. In any event, ask if he'll do an old priest a favor and move on his scheme as quickly as he's able. I'll be in Dublin with the West Parish Council come May. The trip will give me the opportunity to talk face-to-face with Commander Donnelly. I'd like to give him some decent news before I die of old age, or one of our parishioners finally puts the barrel of a gun to my head after listening to this drivel I spout from the pulpit each Sunday." The priest crushed his cigarette butt into a finger bowl.

Easter Monday

The garden in front of the McGuire cottage overflowed with flowers, evidence of the arrival of spring. Inside, a narrow slat of sunlight captured curling smoke. Annie stood at the range stirring a bubbling pot of lamb stew. Reaching to answer the wall phone, she cast a bittersweet look at her father in the adjoining room, half asleep in a stuffed armchair.

"Hello?"

"Hello, Annie."

"Ah, it's you, Aidan. I'm always afraid it could be an Erin Cove bachelor. There's not one in the village over the age of fifteen that's worth speaking to." Annie licked the spoon clean, placed it on the counter and sat at the table.

"C'mon, now. You're always singing the same song," Aidan said.

"They have only one thing on their minds, Brother, and that's only after they've had their fill of Guinness."

Annie had just turned twenty-eight. She knew she was still attractive, but realized that asset was fleeting. Now, when she should be in Dublin or London establishing a career or a family, she was at home caring for an eighty-year-old widower flirting with dementia. She loved her father. But she hated the unfairness of it all.

Thank God Aidan had returned to County Cork. He wasn't exactly back home in Erin Cove, but near enough that she didn't feel abandoned. He had been able to secure her a part-time office job at the Empire farm. Not much, and for a British company. But it gave her the opportunity to ride horses, a holdover pleasure from years ago, and a small salary which, when combined with Da's pension, put food on the table.

And thank God for Dot McCarthy. Without the neighborhood spinster's availability to watch over Da, Annie would be even more trapped in the caretaker role.

But she still had the Cause. Often of late, Annie felt her involvement - doing whatever was asked - sustained her. She never doubted the morality of her participation. The Cause wasn't only a means of retribution, it was also a legitimate war. There was an identifiable enemy - an invader. A people had a right to fight for the return of their homeland.

"I can't solve your social problems, Annie," Aidan said, "but can you be at the Goose around eight? It's about what we talked about last week. There have been interesting developments from the American owner of Irish Eagle."

"I'll ring Dot to watch Da. Keep him from burning the house to the ground with his nasty pipe. I hope you've something worthwhile for Uncle. He's been very anxious of late."

"I think he'll be pleased. Say hello to Da."

"You woke him with the phone, but he's gone back to sleep. I'll tell him you rang. He'll be wanting to know when you'll be calling again."

"Tell him soon, Annie, soon."

Aidan hung the phone up in the tack room of Empire Breeders newly renovated west barn. It had been equipped with state-of-the-art security, a prudent investment considering the British roots of the horse farm. The new system seemed all the more important now that the world's premier three-year-old racehorse was in residence.

A copy of the *International Herald-Tribune* lay on a desktop. It was folded open to a column on page five. Aidan reflected on what he had just read. The column was about the never-ending problem of Northern Ireland. The heading of the piece by the American journalist, William Upton, asked and answered a simple question: *Blame? Plenty to Go Around.*

Dot McCarthy arrived about seven-thirty, just as Annie finished skimming the fat from the stew. With her father under the neighbor's watchful eye, Annie left the cottage, soon rounding the corner onto Dock Road. Starting down a slight grade, she experienced the exhilaration that accompanied each departure from her custodial responsibilities. After a few blocks, the cottages on both sides of the road were replaced by a tight row of store fronts, most dark, as the day's business had concluded. It was a ten-minute walk to the Purple Goose for Annie when not accompanied by Da, double the time when he had a thirst, and then a nightmare to return home. The evening was clear and crisp, the sun beginning to drop into the Atlantic. Profiled against the waning light, the chimneys of Erin Cove's cottages spewed streams of smoke.

Annie quickened her pace when she caught sight of the scratched red door of Pierce's Pool Hall. Its proprietor had a way of glaring that set him apart from the rest, and had always made Annie uneasy. She cursed her apprehension as she crossed the road with a quick step to the pub's purple door. As she approached the Goose she could hear voices raised in the closing verse of the ballad, "The Foggy Dew".

From behind the pool hall's large storefront window, Piery Pierce watched Annie make her way across the road. He leaned on a pool cue and let out a slow whistle. "You know, Rilo," the lumpish forty-year-old muttered between labored breaths, "that McGuire broad's a bit of fluff, ain't she now. Hear she lives all alone except for her daffy old da. Do ya think she might like some company now and then?"

Rilo, a scruffy eighteen-year-old, chalked his cue stick and smiled in response to the proprietor's suggestive comment, showing a row of yellow teeth. "Yeah, Piery, yeah."

The ordinary week-day crowd at the Goose was swollen by Easter Monday celebrants. One of the regulars, Franny Coughlin, was in his usual perch by the front window. He watched Annie cross the street and turned on his barstool to greet her as she made her way into the pub. A cloud of tobacco smoke rushed for the open door, swirling around and past Annie.

"Annie, so nice of you to drop in to say hello to us village sots. You're lookin' prettier than ever. How's your pa?" Franny said.

"He's as healthy as that horse," said Annie, gesturing at a poster behind the bar. *Irish Eagle, Pride of Erin* was boldly proclaimed beneath a color print of the colt as he lunged across the finish line at Salisbury Race Course. "But not quite as fast. You've seen my brother hereabouts?"

"He's 'round the bend, talking with Georgie O'Malley," Franny jerked a thumb in the direction of a side room.

Without warning, Mortimer Sullivan, two stools away, began to tumble. Awakened by the sudden sensation of his freefall, Morty reached for any possible anchor, sweeping his pint of Guinness from the bar. The dark liquid played the role sought for years by the male regulars at the Goose, as it covered Annie from her neck to her knees.

"Good God! I'm safer in the slums of Belfast. Get me a bloody bar rag!" Annie shouted to no one in particular.

The barman rushed over from the far end of the bar, rag in hand.

"This is terrible, terrible. Morty, you're a drunken eegit!" Franny exclaimed as he grabbed the rag from the barman and started towards Annie, prepared to wipe her down.

"Franny, give me the damn cloth!" Annie insisted. "What the hell do you think I am? A bloody hound?"

Before Morty had time to right himself from his fall, the barman had him by the collar and was shoving him in the direction of the door.

Annie wiped the Guinness from her sweater and jeans and pushed her way to the end of the bar, through the half dozen or so customers gathered to witness the production. She was greeted there by Aidan who came in from the adjoining area to see what was causing the commotion. "Good God, Annie. You sure know how to make an entrance."

Aidan grabbed Annie's arm and directed her away from the crowded bar, to a corner table in the dining area. "Georgie, Annie and I have some family business to go over. Could we have a moment?" he said, effectively shooing his assistant from the table. Georgie nodded a greeting at Annie and walked into the bar to join in a melodic tribute to the Rising, "Kevin Barry."

"Aidan, these people are in a time warp. Exactly the same thing happened to me last year. Same drunk, same barstool. Doesn't anything ever change around here?" Annie tossed the towel onto the table and sat across from her brother. The only others in the back room were in front of the fire, engrossed in a game of hearts and out of earshot.

"It could be worse. Da won't live forever. Then you'll be free to roam the world and discover problems you never knew existed."

"Ah, the words roll off your sophisticated tongue so easily. It must be a joy to have the luxury of being so philosophical between trips to New York and Paris, or wherever the hell else your precious Empire Breeders send you. Meanwhile, I can look forward to Da's funeral for liberation. Life's so magnificently fair."

"Hopefully, Annie, my position with Empire will pay dividends, and soon."

"All right, I apologize. Pay no heed to my bitching. What's the news for Uncle?"

"Mister Logan has entered Irish Eagle in the Travers Stakes in America. It was always in the cards, and the horse winning so easily in his last out sealed it. The race will be run in mid-August in northern New York State, at a racecourse known as Saratoga."

"So? A rich American playboy gets richer. Why should that concern anyone?"

"If you'll quiet down for a minute, I'll tell you."

Annie reached across the table, dragged her brother's mug of Guinness over and took a long swallow. She set the mug back on the table. "Might as well wear it inside, too. Okay, Brother, fire away."

"Irish Eagle is easily the best racehorse in the world. He's entered seven races in his career, three of them Grade I stakes, and won all of them, without being the least bit extended. He's set three track records. Logan, give him credit, was a genius when he put the American and Irish bloodlines together."

"Hooray for him," Annie interjected.

Aidan ignored the interruption and continued to speak, excitement in his voice. "We'll enter the colt in the Epsom Derby in June and the Irish Derby at the Curragh in mid-July. I'm absolutely confident we'll win both. Then we ship him to the States in August. The competition at the Travers Stakes will be non-existent. Irish Eagle already destroyed it in the Breeders' Cup Juvenile last fall. He'll go off at odds of no better than one to five. There is, quite simply, no way the colt can lose the Travers Stakes." Aidan paused, then continued, "That is, unless I decide that the horse has an off day."

After a moment of quiet, Annie asked, "Am I correct to think there will be a lot of money to be made for the Cause when the great Irish Eagle disappoints the punters?"

"Indeed. The few that have put their money on the competition will gather in enormous payoffs. If we put the pieces of this scheme together, a small fortune will come the Army's way by betting against Irish Eagle in the Travers."

"But, how can this be possible, Aidan? You won't be riding the damn horse. How can you control how it runs its race? Are you going to poison it or something? And even if you could make it lose, how do we know the winner? How does the Army know which horse to bet its money on?"

"If we can get the Army to okay my plan, Annie, I'm hoping with its connections in the States, and its money, we can pull this off. Also, keep in mind that I decide who the jockey will be. But you're right to ask. Nothing's guaranteed, but I think we can do it. I know it's worth a try."

Annie broke into a wide grin. "Aidan, I'm so proud of you. I'm sorry for not believing in you. I should never have doubted your commitment."

"We have to get word of this plan to the Army command. If this scheme is going to work, it has to be put in play as soon as possible. We'll need cooperation from friends in the States, and we'll need money. A lot of money. The more we have available, the more we'll bring back home."

Annie picked up the mug of Guinness and raised it toward her brother. "To Easter Monday. It's been eighty years, Aidan. Maybe our time is 'round the bend. Brits out, Brother. Brits out."

The next morning Annie posted a letter to Dublin. It included seven one-pound notes to pay for an announcement in the *Irish Times*. There was no return address.

6

COUNTY CORK - 2 WEEKS LATER

Steady rain fell on Erin Cove for the fourth day in a row.

"C'mon, Father, the Irish Rail won't wait for the pope, let alone a lowly parish priest, and this weather will slow us down," hollered Freddy O'Boyle from beside his 1970 Morris Minor. The retired coal miner had returned to Erin Cove from the Birmingham mines three years past and quickly assumed the role of parish gopher for Father Mulligan. Freddy had been recruited the previous night to drive the priest and his niece to the rail depot at Cork city, a trip of 30 miles. "It's already half eight. The train leaves in an hour. It's your rear end the bishop will be kickin', not mine."

The lanky priest and his niece were at the rectory door, overnight bags in hand. "Hold your damn horses, Freddy," Annie shouted.

Walking down the path to the tiny car that seemed incapable of fitting him, the priest leaned into Annie and the protection of her umbrella. "I'm thinking this is my swan song, Annie. My nerves can't handle this James Bond stuff much longer."

Annie placed the worn bags and folded umbrella in the Morris boot and opened the door for her uncle who ducked into the back seat. She climbed in beside him and instructed the driver. "Get this old can rolling Freddy. We don't want to miss the train, now, do we?"

Having forgotten his flask, Freddy O'Boyle cursed his inability to patronize the train station pub because of the early hour. Now he would have to make the phone call with a tremble in his dialing finger, as well as in his voice. Watching the tail end of the Dublin train being pulled out of the terminal, he unrolled a piece of paper, carefully dialed twelve numbers on the public phone and awaited the connection.

"Yes?"

"O'Boyle here."

"Yes?"

"I have a report."

There was a brief delay, then: "What have you got?"

Now the delay was on Freddy's end. A nervous cough. Then the tout spoke quietly, his body and face tight into the phone nook. "Father Mulligan's on the 9:30 Dubliner from Cork, along with his niece, Annie. She called just last night, late, to arrange for me to drive them to the station. I had no way to call from Erin Cove without being noticed."

"Annie who?"

"McGuire."

"All right, go on."

"I couldn't hear everything because Father always likes me to have the car radio playin', but they talked something about a horse race. Father mentioned Annie's brother, Aidan." O'Boyle paused again, then spoke with a new confidence, warming to his task. "He's a famous horse trainer, you know. No other names mentioned, but Father's meeting with someone at St. Mary's Cathedral between noon and one o'clock today. Annie reminded him a few times, saying something about his likely to be wandering around the area and missing his meeting."

"Any information about what the person he's meeting will look like, be wearing?"

"Nope, none. That was all I heard, I swear." The connection was broken on the other end. O'Boyle replaced the receiver and breathed heavily. Walking in the rain from the terminal to the car park, he defended his duplicity by remembering that each month his British Miners Pension Trust payment was artificially inflated by seventy-five quid.

Father Mulligan sat alone in a private passenger cabin. He drew his muffler tight around his neck and shoulders as protection from the cold air that rushed in from the open half-window as the train rolled through Munster Province's lush farm country and over its salmon-choked rivers. Suddenly the door to the cabin slid open. Annie entered the small space, uttered a short expression of disgust, quickly stepped over to the window and gave it a shove upward to close. The elderly priest, guilt written across his face, squashed the burning cigarette under his boot. A well-thumbed book of daily prayers fell from his lap. Annie sat across from her uncle.

"You must be anxious to join your brothers, Uncle. An old dog like yourself is probably more susceptible to pneumonia than lung cancer. Good Lord, I go to have a pee and you go through a few fags. Did you really think that by freezing half to death you'd clear out the evidence, and I'd think you've been saying your office instead of feeding that filthy habit?" Annie held her hand out and her uncle dropped a half-filled package of cigarettes into it.

"Find a little charity for your uncle, Annie. A few drags will calm me down a mite. Run me through my secret responsibilities once again, if you'd be so kind."

Father Mulligan was to meet in Dublin this Monday afternoon with the IRA Director of Operations, Liam Donnelly. Commander Donnelly would acknowledge the priest in the last pew of St Mary's Cathedral between noon and one o'clock. Over the clacking of the wheels, Annie prepared her uncle for his meeting. She instructed him about Aidan's proposal to fix the Travers Stakes, emphasizing both her brother's absolute control of the Irish horse, and the necessary cooperation from IRA contacts in the States to make arrangements for which horse would actually win the prestigious race. Also, the scheme would require a substantial amount of money be made available.

When Annie finished speaking, her uncle rolled his eyes and exhaled into a slow whistle. He was quiet for a few moments, then said, "I think we can count on the Americans, Annie. You know, they're as smart and capable as can be. I sometimes think they can do anything they desire. Sense of humor, too. I was chosen to travel with the Holy Father's entourage to the city of Miami some seven or eight years ago. He was only the second pope to ever travel to the States. You'd have thought they'd be praying to the high heavens twenty-four hours a day. But at least some of them were in their little factories making souvenirs. If you can believe it, one of the souvenirs was a water sprinkler. It was a miniature statue of His Holiness, white robes flowing and arms extended. It turned 'round and 'round, spitting water from his blessed fingertips onto the lawns of America. Can you guess what they called it, this little statue?"

"Not in a guessing mood, Uncle."

"*Let Us Spray*. That's what they called it, Annie - *Let Us Spray*." The priest and his niece chuckled as the train rolled on through the countryside, toward the Irish capital.

Dublin

A week old issue of the *Irish Times*, folded to the *In Memoriam* section, lay on the kitchen table next to the soiled dishes from the previous night's meal. There was a single entry circled in red ink. It read:

I see you sit beside me there:

Next time I look the seat is bare.

(for Frances, 6-27-63, love S.C.)

The memorial couplet contained a code used by Annie to arrange meetings with the Army higher-ups. This was a simple one that established the date and participant. The time of day and location were pre-arranged.

The glow from a bedside lamp highlighted the red hair of Maggie Halloran. The reclining woman watched from the bed as Liam Donnelly looked into a battered bureau mirror. He struggled to button down a white collar on top of his black shirt. "Damn, these things are surely the most bothersome decoration known to man. No wonder priests seem pissed so often."

"It's not their bloody collars, Liam. It's because the pope won't let them have a go at the likes of me that's got them riled."

Still struggling with the collar, Donnelly said, "Maybe, my sweet, maybe. It's hard to believe the papistry still insists on virtual castration for the good priests that do their bidding. The church takes a man's humanity away. No kiddos - can kiss the bloodline goodbye. God knows, some of these priests are exactly who we'd want fathering our kids, rather than polluting paper hand towels."

Maggie reached over to the night table and flicked the ash of her cigarette into an empty tumbler. She returned her head to the pillow and stared across the room at the shortish middle-aged man who had finally conquered the Roman collar. "At least you're not burdened with goin' around trussed up like the good sisters, wimples and all."

"True. But they choose to be so burdened as tribute to the Almighty. I must suffer through this costume for the love of Liam Donnelly's skin."

The 55-year-old staff officer of the Irish Republican Army placed a snub-nosed revolver into his shoulder holster, then completed his priestly impersonation by pulling on a black raincoat and matching flat cap.

Maggie pursed her lips together in a pouting gesture, her eyes beckoning Donnelly. He responded by stepping over to the bedside and fondling a bare breast as Maggie lifted her body from the coverings. She reached for him. He stepped back. "Not now, my sweet. I can't be late. I'm off to the cathedral to meet a good priest from county Cork."

"Say one for me."

Donnelly was quickly down the staircase and out of the tenement, happy to be breathing air not infected with the aroma of boiled food and peeling paint. The cocky IRA officer, who usually chose to toil at his trade without the benefit of a bodyguard, changed addresses on a regular basis. For the past four weeks he had been residing in a run-down section of Dublin. The squalid tenements housed a substantial portion of the city's poor. On this raw Monday, most had opted to stay indoors. The streets were virtually deserted, a circumstance which pleased Donnelly. 'Father' wasn't interested in being summoned to arbitrate a tenement imbroglio, not an unusual occurrence in the crowded housing project.

The counterfeit priest commenced his cross-town foot journey at a brisk pace, unhindered by the light mist on his face. The Angelus chimed from the steeple of a nearby church, marking noontime. In a few minutes, Donnelly was crossing the arched Halfpenny Bridge over the River Liffey, enjoying the elevated view of the waterway. His wariness increased as he reached the capital city's commercial area. The terrorist leader, his neck sunk into the collar of his black raincoat, scurried past the statue of Daniel O'Connell on the north side of the bridge, continuing on to St. Mary's Cathedral.

As she had on other occasions since returning home from Dublin, Annie readily accepted her uncle's suggestion that she accompany him to the capital city, delighted with even a brief respite from her Da-sitting duty. Once again, Father Mulligan explained he was welcome at a hospitable Dublin rectory, but only under strict rules, which he started to recite, only to be interrupted by his niece.

"I know Uncle, you can't let me know exactly which parish you'll be at, and no phone number, even for emergencies - the pastor doesn't want to encourage a horde of country priests descending on his limited space and raiding the larder. Not to worry, I'll meet you back at the rail station for the four o'clock tomorrow."

For the first time in this circumstance, the priest thought that he may have noticed a knowing smile and lifting of eyebrows from his niece, but decided not to comment, preferring to let Annie play her guessing game. As usual, he did not inquire about her social plans, fearing the question might lead to an untruth. Perhaps she was extending a like courtesy. In all his years as a seminary student and priest, a significant mystery to Joseph Ignatius Mulligan was why sexual activity, particularly for those in the secular realm, was sinful. Good food, an enjoyable smoke, music, humor - none of these God-given pleasures were against His law. Why sex? In any event, it seemed his pretty niece should be entitled to a wee bit of romance in the capital. Lord knows, there was little, if any, opportunity in Erin Cove.

The pastor parted company with Annie after a cup of coffee and sweet roll at Heuston Station. A taxi delivered him and his worn leather satchel to the 12th century cathedral just before noon, in time for his meeting with Liam Donnelly, known to the priest as an important player in the IRA hierarchy. Wearied from the trip and the pressure of his clandestine activity, the cleric settled into the last row of pews in the church's main section. He was comfortable and content amidst the familiar smells - incense lingering from the earlier Benediction, burning candles and wood polish, as well as the muted, hushed sounds of the cathedral. He promptly nodded off.

Whack! Whack! Whack! accompanied by "No! No! No!"

Father Mulligan awoke with a start as Brother Theodore, the St Mary's choir director, corrected his charges, his wood ruler slamming against his music stand. The cathedral was the home of the highly regarded

Palestrina choir, and the youthful voices responded admirably to their leader's direction. Awakened, and now listening with appreciation, the priest mused that perhaps one of the young voices anxiously straining for the elusive high C was another tenor of the quality of John McCormack in the making. He listened to a stirring rendition of "Amazing Grace", a spiritual barn burner that he understood to have been imported from America's South. While Father Mulligan was remembering some of the wretches he had known over the years, Liam Donnelly slid into the pew.

"Wonderful music they have these days, don't you think now Father, even if the words to the tune came from an English seaman."

Not recognizing Donnelly at first, whom he had met only on rare occasions, all of which had been accompanied by a degree of darkness, Father Mulligan responded as if to a colleague. "Most certainly it is, Father. We've traveled quite a distance from the Gregorian chant now, haven't we."

"What say we walk the Stations of the Cross, Father Mulligan, and you can let me know why you've bothered to leave the beautiful Cork countryside and travel to Dublin in this miserable weather."

Surprised to hear his name from a stranger, Father Mulligan turned to his right and took a closer look at his new companion. He suddenly realized it was Donnelly. "In the name of all the saints, it is you, and you've been ordained, yet."

"I am somewhat notorious, Father, and I do have a fear of discovery. I tend to think that most don't look beyond the priests' uniform. After all, there are so many in Dublin."

"Well, you'll certainly not seem out of place in the house of God."

"Indeed. The cathedral welcomes all kinds. I was attracted to the portrayal of *The Last Supper* at the entrance. Judas is most prominent."

"Now why would you go and pay attention to the one bad apple?"

"In my line of work, Father, Judas seems to be everywhere. Touting is far from a lost art in our country. Unfortunately, the Brits don't seem so loose-lipped. We've never had a good source from the belly of the beast. It would surely be a tremendous advantage." Donnelly stood from the pew. "Come, Father, let us pray those stations."

The Celtic, priestly version of Mutt and Jeff left the pew and started down the left aisle of the cathedral. Halfway to the first Station, Donnelly noticed a middle-aged woman kneeling by herself at the center of a pew a few rows ahead. A white handkerchief secured by hairpins covered the top of her head. She had her face raised at an angle, apparently staring at the crucifix hanging over the main altar. As the two men drew nearer, Donnelly could hear her mumbling in a furious fashion. Then, she started making the sign of the cross, over and over, all the while continuing her mumble. Donnelly head-gestured in the direction of the woman and observed, "Dedicated."

"Oh, that's Catherine Connors," the priest said. "She's well known in Dublin churches. Prays from dawn to dusk for the souls in purgatory. Seven days a week."

"I guess the sisters had their way with her head at school."

"Poor soul. She's known to the city pastors as Cathy Constant. Only stops praying for lunch and the loo."

"Hmm, maybe, Father," Donnelly said, "if Cathy ate her sandwich while she's on the bog, she'd save some time and could also work on freeing those unbaptized babies stuck in limbo."

The priest stopped at the first Station of the Cross. "I don't think that would do much good. As far as I've learned, babies sent to limbo are there forever."

"Oh, my," Donnelly said.

Both men made the sign of the cross and genuflected. The wall sculpture depicted Jesus standing in front of Pontius Pilate. On a plaster ribbon beneath the artwork, the script read: *Jesus is Condemned to Death*. Donnelly stared up at the Roman tribunal. "Our comrades are also condemned to death, Father. But we shan't be quite so docile as Jesus. We always need more guns and bullets. I'm led to believe you may have some information regarding a potential fund-raising effort?"

"This scheme has just been outlined to me by my companion on the train into Dublin. Basically, it seems we raise as much money as we can beg, borrow or steal; bet it on a horse that shouldn't win an American race, but will; and then we cash in our tickets to collect a fortune."

"Interesting timing, Father. We've a little caper planned soon in Britain. If all goes well, it will result in some ready American dollars, a very substantial amount."

"We adore You, O Christ, and we bless You," prayed Father Mulligan as a trio of elderly nuns in black habits approached.

"Because of your Holy Cross, You have redeemed the world,"

responded Donnelly, hearkening back to his youth at St Brigid's in Galway. He followed the priest to the next Station.

Again, both men made the sign of the cross and genuflected. However, they did not linger at this Station, but continued on halfway up the lengthy aisle, distancing themselves from the three nuns at their heels. "If we were Japanese golfers, we could ask the sisters if they would like to pray through." Father Mulligan smiled at his little phonetic joke.

"That's funny, Father," Donnelly said with a smile. "Now, let me know more of this equine scheme of yours."

"Oh, it's not mine. I'm just the messenger."

"Fine, Father, fine. Could I please have the message?"

"You've no doubt heard of the racehorse, Irish Eagle. Apparently, this horse is, or will surely be, one of the greatest racehorses of modern times. Although Irish Eagle is owned by an American, the horse is under the exclusive control of my nephew, Aidan McGuire, a young man sympathetic to the Cause."

"Yes, yes. I know of Aidan, and his position with a Brit breeding firm. I'm also aware that he's your late sister's son. Please go on."

"I'm told that the American who owns the horse will enter him in an important race in the United States this August. The race is known as the Travers Stakes, and Irish Eagle is sure to be a huge favorite to win. However, I'm also told that Aidan will make arrangements to be sure that the horse loses. Apparently he can do this because he is responsible for the horse's training and also chooses who will be Irish Eagle's jockey."

The priest and Donnelly halted their conversation and waited as a half dozen members of the boys choir hurried down the center aisle, school bags swinging, the joy of choir practice having ended evident in their clamorous departure. Donnelly took the priest by the arm and started up the aisle.

"This story is quite interesting, Father. Let's take a seat by the votive candles. I may wish to light one or two."

Father Mulligan genuflected and followed Donnelly into a pew. With a degree of wonder in his tone, the IRA leader said, "Father, are you telling me that the unbeatable Irish Eagle is going to come a cropper?"

"As I understand it, that, sir, is up to you," the priest said. "Also, Aidan would like to meet with you in person, if that could be arranged."

"You've whet my appetite sufficiently. Probably best to set up a meeting in London. It's easier to get lost in the crowd."

The two men continued to talk for a few minutes, then left the pew and walked toward the main doors, stopping while Father Mulligan retrieved his overnight bag from the back bench. They continued outside, into the rain. Pulling at his collar with one hand as he shook a cigarette from a pack with the other, Donnelly asked, "Father, would you by any chance have an extra collar in that carryall? One that's larger than a size 15?"

"Perhaps I could accommodate you. By any chance, would you have a few extra fags in that pack?"

"Indeed, I surely do." As the two men exchanged goods, Donnelly continued, "Let me leave you with some good news, Father. Rumour in our city has it your archbishop has become a father again, by way of his American Doris. Baby girl, I hear."

"At least he's no poof, our good bishop," the priest said, shaking his head. Suddenly, with agility that surprised and impressed Donnelly, Father Mulligan booted back an errant soccer ball to a group of youngsters splashing through the puddles in front of St Mary's.

Earlier, when the two men of different shapes in similar priestly garb made their way to the first Station of the Cross, a gray-haired woman in the back of the cathedral moved with a quickness inconsistent with her apparent years. In just moments she was out of the church, down the front steps and hurrying into the grocery across the road. In exchange for a previously surrendered five-pound note, she had the use of a phone in a small office in the rear of the store. Within seconds, her call was connected.

"Yes?"

"Wilson here."

"Yes?"

"Mulligan's meeting with Liam Donnelly. Donnelly's in a priest's getup, but it's him, for sure. They're still in the cathedral. What should I do?"

"Hold on." In just seconds, the voice returned. "Do nothing. Repeat the order."

"Do nothing."

"A person is not old until regrets take the place of dreams," Kathleen O'Toole read from the tag before she squeezed the tea bag on the other end of the string and dropped it into the kitchen sink. "I wonder who dreams up the sayings on these tags, Annie. That's a nifty way to make a living."

"I don't know who came up with that one, but, if it's true, I'm getting damned old." It was Tuesday noontime. Annie McGuire sat in Kathleen's kitchen, stirring her tea.

After seeing her uncle into a taxi at Heuston station the previous day, Annie walked to Kathleen's flat on Doubleday Street. When she arrived, she retrieved the key from its usual spot and entered the empty apartment. Annie dropped her bag in the spare bedroom, freshened up and dialed the phone. It was Peter Cooney, now a resident in the radiology department at St James Hospital, who answered her call. As on previous occasions since the then students had gone their separate ways, when Annie had told him of her plans to be in Dublin, Cooney, without hesitating, agreed to a rendezvous. She still enjoyed being with Peter, but held out no possibility that the friendship would ever rise to its prior level. The doctor was still great company and, until he was hooked by someone far less independent than she, Annie could count on Peter for an evening of drinks, dinner and reminiscing. Also, if she were so inclined, as she was last night, a room at the Gresham could always be arranged. This morning, after her romantic interlude, Annie returned to Kathleen's flat.

Kathleen, home for lunch from her O'Connell Street boutique, sat across from her old college classmate and spooned sugar into her cup. "I know how you hated leaving Dublin when your ma died, Annie, but have faith. Your da won't last forever. He may seem to be strong as an ox, but the good Lord will take him when the time is right for him, and you."

"I envy your blind faith, Kathleen. It must be such a relief to think everything is pre-ordained, that all we have to do is stand around and wait to be tapped on the shoulder by the Holy Ghost, then led down the corridor to the next room of our lives. It seems..."

Annie's sardonic words were interrupted by the ring of the telephone. Without getting up from the table, Kathleen reached to the countertop for the receiver, listened a moment and handed the phone to Annie.

"Someone asking for Annie McGuire. Very serious."

Annie placed her hand over the mouthpiece. "I left your number with Dot McCarthy and with Millie, my uncle's housekeeper, for emergencies. I wonder what it could be?" She answered, speaking quickly, "Hello, this is Annie McGuire."

Annie's complexion turned pale as she stood from her chair. She listened for about a half minute without responding, then said, "Yes. I'll be on the next train. Thank you for calling." Blindly, Annie stepped to the counter and placed the phone in its cradle. "I guess the time was right for Da, but it wasn't the good Lord who took him."

Kathleen gasped, her hand went to her mouth. Words raced through her fingers, "My God, Annie, what do you mean?"

Annie was still, her eyes fixed on a yellow potholder hanging from a wall hook. She started to shake. "He was murdered in his chair. And they raped and killed poor old Dot. I guess they had a little party afterwards. They left an empty gin bottle."

"Oh, my God." Kathleen stood and reached over to wrap her arms around her friend. "Did they say who, why?"

"No, but I'd put nothing beyond the British bastards. I think I'm going to be sick."

7

SURREY, ENGLAND - SPRING

"Mister Logan, the BBC has it on impeccable authority that Sheik Abdul bin Qasim has extended an offer of 20 million pounds for Irish Eagle. The Sheik, we understand, would immediately retire the horse and have him stand here at Cheveley Park Stud. Is there any way you could possibly refuse this offer?"

The tall, silver-haired horse owner stood behind a bank of microphones in the press tent at the Newmarket racecourses, northeast of London. Logan was flanked on his right by the trainer of Irish Eagle, Aidan McGuire. On a table a few feet to his left, glittering under the television lights, sat the silver bowl that had been presented to the American five minutes earlier. Irish Eagle, Logan's chestnut colt, had just triumphed in the 2000 Guineas, the closest also-ran nine lengths back at the finish line. In the process, the Irish-bred colt had established a track record over the lush green turf course, easily shattering the prior mark. He responded to the question from the BBC reporter.

"Irish Eagle is not for sale to Sheik Abracadabra, or anyone else."

Sir Wadsworth Dangerfield, the press conference chair, looked over the gaggle of standing reporters. For the next question, he recognized a *London Times* reporter at the front of the pack. Pushing five feet tall, freckle-faced and with cropped red hair, learned behavior had her on her tiptoes as she asked her question.

"Mister Logan, where will Irish Eagle stand? Can we assume it will be in the States, or do we have a chance of keeping our European bloodstock on this side of the Atlantic?"

Shouts of "Here! Here!" and "That a girl, Marilyn. Nail the Yank down!" followed the question.

"When I was in the Navy," Logan said, "that's the U.S. Navy, I learned never to assume anything. I would suggest, young lady, that you take that advice to heart. Truth of the matter is that the question is premature anyway. Irish Eagle's racing career isn't over quite yet. Also, last I checked, it's my bloodstock, not yours."

A spattering of negative utterances from the large group of mostly British media greeted Logan's comment. It was painfully clear that American ownership and control of this thoroughbred was considered nothing less than criminal encroachment upon European turf.

A tall, skinny bespectacled reporter didn't bother waiting to be recognized by Sir Wadsworth. He shouted the next question. "Jack, we're all dying to get a close-up look at your horse in the States again, especially as a three-year-old. You blew off our Kentucky Derby. Will you enter the colt in the Preakness or the Belmont, or any other important race in the States?"

Logan recognized Charlie Leonard, chief turf writer and handicapper for the *Baltimore Sun*. "You bet your ass you'll see my horse in the States. Third Saturday in August, big to-do at the Spa, Saratoga. It's called the Travers Stakes. Be there, Charlie Boy!"

Dublin

The usual crowd of academicians, unemployed literary types and Dublin yuppies that frequented the Poet's Corner Pub had been augmented by a throng of strangers. It wasn't that the Guinness tasted any better at the Poet's, nor did it cost less than most anywhere else. What made the Poet's desirable on this Saturday afternoon were large television sets elevated at each end of the long bar and, against the back bar, a giant TV screen that dominated the wall. Without a doubt, the best location in the Irish capital to watch the 2000 Guineas from Newmarket Race Course was the Poet's.

Over the sound of a guitar and bass being strummed in a corner of the room, the voice of R. Jack Logan sounded clearly from the TV speakers. The happy customer on the third stool from the far end of the bar listened to the horseman's ending comment: "Be there, Charlie Boy!" Casually dressed Liam Donnelly polished off his mug of Guinness and wiped his mouth with a napkin snatched from a pile on the pock-marked bar, being careful not to alter his artificial mustache. He turned to his massive, barrel-chested companion who guzzled ale straight from the pitcher, feet firmly planted on the sawdust-covered floor.

"Don't know about Charlie Boy, but we'll surely be there, at least in spirit, now, won't we, Patrick? I must say, Mister R. Jack Logan is most impressive. Rich, handsome, self-assured and owner of the fastest racehorse in the world. No doubt he expects his champion will win that American race, the Travers."

"Sure and he will, sir. He has a racin' heart, that one does. No horse will even be close to our Irish Eagle at a finish line, ever!"

"Your national pride is commendable, Patrick."

"It's our own Aidan McGuire that's the reason the horse don't lose. He's the best trainer anywhere."

"I'll accept that, Patrick," Donnelly responded to his enthusiastic bodyguard. He reached into his pocket as he rose from the stool. "Let's get ourselves out of here or we'll be the night, and we've important things to accomplish." Donnelly placed a ten-pound note on the bar and led Patrick through the rear door and into the humid evening air. Strains of "The Hills of Connemara" followed them down the cobbled alley.

The two men rounded the corner onto O'Connell Street and Donnelly raised his arm to hail a taxi parked a block away. The driver of the taxi neither greeted his passengers nor engaged the trip meter. Donnelly mentioned a destination as he slid into the rear seat ahead of his bodyguard.

An inch of cigarette ash somehow remained intact as the driver whipped the taxi into a U-turn and sped off. Within ten minutes, he pulled up to a row of tenements, just avoiding a scraggly dog chasing a Frisbee rolling on its edge. The two men climbed out of the back seat without paying the driver.

At seven o'clock Donnelly and his bodyguard entered through an unlocked door into a squalid, two-story building that served as an apartment and transient rooming house. Walking to a battered staircase, Patrick stumbled over a Big Wheels tricycle tucked in close to the stairway. He caught himself on the wobbly railing. "Shit!" he exclaimed, and his left foot propelled the toy the length of the corridor, causing it to slam against a door identified as No. 3 with the scribble of a marking pen.

"In the name of Christ, Patrick, why the hell don't you just use a bullhorn to announce our arrival?" Donnelly complained.

The door to flat No. 3 opened suddenly, revealing a scrawny red-headed eight-year-old wearing only a pair of ragged jeans. The youngster glanced down at his toy. He quickly swept the tricycle into the apartment with the back of his leg and scowled at the two men standing at the end of the hallway.

"When it's your fookin' Big Wheels, ya do whatever you fookin' jolly like, but leave me fookin' stuff alone." He slammed the door.

"I can see that little prick's got a future. C'mon," instructed Donnelly. "Lucifer is waiting upstairs to take our order."

At the top of the staircase the two men were met by a huge dark-skinned man who emitted a rank odor.

"Ouzou," Donnelly said, uttering a password as he smiled at the landing guard. "We meet again, Pluto."

The grim-faced giant moved back on the landing, permitting the visitors space to move off the stairway. As Donnelly stepped toward the door next to a wooden chair, the guard quickly stepped in front of Patrick.

"Uh, Uh! No!" he grunted through his plump-lipped mouth. "Not this one."

Patrick, massive as he was, knew he was clearly outmatched. He made no attempt to follow the man he had sworn to protect. Donnelly rescued his bodyguard's pride. "Don't bother about me, Patrick. You can wait out here with my old friend."

Donnelly took the final steps to the door, glancing at half-filled bags of potato chips and corn twirls on the floor. Added to the debris were a few empty two-liter Pepsi bottles. "Been snacking, Pluto?" Donnelly asked, as he rolled his hand into a fist and knocked on the door. "Be a decent host and share some of your provisions with Patrick while he waits for me."

Seconds later Donnelly heard what he assumed was a command being barked from inside the room. The door was pulled open by an unseen person who disappeared behind it. The IRA Commander stepped into a large room furnished with a large bed next to a round table. A variety of bottles and two small bowls, both half filled with white powder, littered the table.

Zlatan Terzik, a British-educated native of the Balkans and second-tier arms dealer, wallowed in the bed, his head propped up on a pair of pillows. Under the bedcovers with him were a boy and a girl, neither beyond their early teenage years, both oriental. The children were looking up at Donnelly with glazed-over brown eyes as they lay to Terzik's left. The bed coverings were down to their waists, exposing bare arms and chests.

Terzik's cream-colored body rose from the covers, a sea of soft hairless tissue broken by a thick gold choker mostly hidden in the folds of his neck. A miniature gold spoon dangled from the choker. Without acknowledging Donnelly's arrival, he casually reached to the bedside table and grasped a glass half-filled with cognac. Emptying the glass with a single swallow, he placed it back on the table and picked up a loose cigarette. From somewhere beneath the bed covers he produced a lighter and touched a flame to the tobacco.

With a brush of his hand, Terzik dismissed the children from his bed. Each naked, they lazily got to their feet, the girl casting a wary glance at the stranger who stood just inside the door. The children's lithe, olive-colored bodies flowed from the bed to a door that opened into an adjoining room. They were followed closely by a small woman with straight black hair who appeared from Donnelly's left, her red kimono creating a blur in his eyes as she crossed the room, breezing between him and the bed.

Donnelly closed the door, took a deep breath and walked to the window beside the table. He looked down on an alleyway cluttered with a few old cars stripped of usable parts. His prior meetings with Terzik had taken place in a variety of settings, ranging from a jellied eel stand in Brighton to Terzik's yacht anchored off the Cote d'Azur. But, my God, thought Donnelly, this is beyond the pale. Although the gunrunner's sexual predilection was no secret, actually being at the scene turned Donnelly's stomach.

"The Shelbourne all full up, Zlatan?" Donnelly asked, continuing to look out the window.

"Unfortunately, the finer Dublin inns shun entourages such as mine. So much for reputed Irish hospitality. But this particular lodging house is owned by a cousin. He's most reasonable."

Donnelly repressed his contempt for Terzik. He knew he needed him. He kept himself from remarking on what he had just witnessed. Nonetheless, when he finally turned from the window, his expression said it all. Terzik responded quickly. "Come, come, my friend. My transgressions pale when contrasted with the sins of you and your allies. How many children never even reached an age when they would be of interest to me because of a bomb placed by one of your minions? How many more fathers and sons will feel a hollow-nosed bullet tear through their rib cages after being fired from your rebels' rifles? There are a number of Irish widows, no?"

Terzik dragged on his cigarette, then continued. "My habits, my business, are well known. So, as they say, get over it. By the way, you did arrange to meet me to discuss business, no? To discuss the procurement of arms to destroy your fellow man? I find your hypocritical attitude to be quite rude."

The obese arms dealer reached his hand over to the bedside table once again, this time fitting his half-smoked cigarette into the neck of a bottle of Martins VO cognac. The marriage of burning tobacco to costly liquor caused a fizzing sound and a miniature plume of smoke. "Oh, God, I must be more careful. So, so wasteful. Speaking of waste, let's not fritter away your time, nor mine."

Donnelly got to the point of his visit. "What is the price and availability of American Stinger missiles?"

"Quite expensive. I would think rather dear for your bunch. Available this coming autumn. As the saying goes, do you expect your ship to come in by then?"

"No, not our ship. But, God willing, our horse."

Erin Cove

"The usual two spoons, Uncle?" Annie asked, reaching for the sugar bowl on the low table. Without waiting for an answer, she continued, "All the men of Erin Cove being so certain of my sweetness, perhaps my stirring the tea with a finger will suffice."

The sitting room of the St Columbkille's rectory was dimly lit by fading sunlight. Across the table, Father Mulligan leaned back on the sofa. "There are times I'm not so sure of your sweetness, Annie. You've wearied us with your complaints of being stuck at home, and then, when the Lord wields his mighty saber and cuts your da from his earthly habitat, and you from Erin Cove, you continue to grumble away." The priest reached his long arm over to the table and plucked a chocolate biscuit from a plateful. "My downfall," he held the biscuit up and smiled, "and cigs."

"Sugar in your tea today?" Annie repeated the question, conceding to herself that her uncle had a point about her whining.

"No sugar at all, thank you," the priest said between chews. "Doc Griffin has restricted my intake of all that's worthwhile. My diabetes. He threatens that any day now my limbs will start to drop off. I'd rather cheat with the biscuits. Anyhow, Annie, what are you doing here on a Wednesday? We usually share a cuppa on Thursdays." He sat up on the couch. "Is there some new information on the murderers?"

"No, at least nothing that they're wanting to share with me and Aidan. They figure it was just the pool hall scum all hopped up on drugs and booze. But I'll go to my grave believing the Brits put them up to it, to send a message to the McGuire family. Scare us into retirement."

"If so, they've surely misjudged you, Annie."

Annie handed a steaming cup to her uncle and sat back in her chair. "What we've been waiting for has been finalized. I bumped into Georgie O'Malley, Aidan's assistant at the farm. He told me that he'd tried to reach Aidan - he's in Hong Kong - to tell him that Mister Logan has confirmed that his Irish Eagle is definitely entered in the race in the States, the Travers Stakes. The horse will be shipped to New York mid-August. It looks like our plans will actually be put into action."

"Does this mean another trip to Dublin? The parishioners will be sure I've a Jezebel hidden away in the city."

"No, Uncle. If you're so inclined, you can stay eternally celibate here in Erin Cove. Perhaps we've the germ of a club. Anyhow, this time it's just a phone call to report that things are in place at this end. I'll handle that. Then it'll be up to the kingpins to make the arrangements, here, and in America."

"You know, Annie, the more I think of it, the more I wonder if we're in over our heads on this one."

"No, Uncle. Not with Aidan involved. He can do most anything he sets his mind to."

"I suppose that's true, Annie. I suppose it is indeed. By the way, why in the Lord's name is Aidan off to, where did you say, Hong Kong?"

"Racing horses of course. For a Cambodian drug lord or some other pillar of the Far East community. Whoever it is pays Empire a king's ransom. Aidan's the best, don't you know. He just doesn't wear it on his sleeve."

"That's the truth, Annie. Your brother's not one to advertise his qualities, and plenty of them he has. How old is he now?"

"Aidan's thirty-one, Uncle. You ask the same question about this time each year. Next, ask about his finding a nice girl and settling down to raise a family." Annie watched her uncle brush crumbs off his sweater and onto the coffee table. "Well, how about that possibility?"

"I doubt it will ever happen. Aidan's mostly interested in his horses. You'll not be surprised to learn he's happy for a bit of skirt when it suits him, but his heart is locked away, I'm afraid, forever."

"It's said a parent is never over the death of a child, and that's what little Timmy was to Aidan, his little boy. He might have been Bridget's son, but he only knew his Uncle Aidan as a parent. I'll never forget the look of pride on Aidan's face the day I baptized Timmy, he being the Godfather. Oh, what a pair they made, Annie."

"Indeed, Uncle. For five years. They were like bacon and cabbage."

"I recall going along with the two of them to a race meeting at Killarney. It was shortly before Timmy went back with his mother. The little guy was so excited. He loved those horses as Aidan did. On the way back home, Aidan promised him that someday they'd have the finest racehorse in all of Ireland, a horse that would never lose. Timmy believed every word." Father Mulligan set his head back and smiled. "The little guy was never away from Aidan. Usually draped around his neck for a ride, he was. That's how I remember him."

"Timmy's still draped around his neck, Uncle. When is the last time you heard an honest laugh from Aidan? Saw a real smile? Aidan's sense of humor, optimism, all gone, buried along with Timmy. All these years since Timmy's murder, Aidan's never mentioned his name, not once." Annie was quiet a moment. "You know, Uncle, I never really had anyone but Aidan. Bridget and the older brothers had no time for me, were out of the house before I had the opportunity to drive them crazy - every little sister's right. But Aidan loved me to pieces. He was my happiness. He made me laugh and, whenever I thought I'd disappointed him, cry. He was the perfect big brother to me. We wrote to each other twice a week when he was away at school. That is, until that British bullet tore through Timmy's chest. Aidan's never come back from that night. Never again enjoyed his life.

"For sure, he goes through the motions. Lives comfortably enough, but he's not the same person. As far as I'm concerned, that bullet took Aidan along with Timmy. And it took a giant part of me as well, Uncle. On that rotten February night in Derry we all lost Timmy, but I also lost the brother I adored."

Father Mulligan leaned across the coffee table and took Annie's hands in his. "Some day, Annie. Some day the real Aidan will come home."

"Ever the optimist, Uncle."

The priest stood from the couch. "The Lord works in strange ways. Aidan's suffering here on earth, as well as your own, can be offered up to benefit the souls of those who have passed on."

"Oh, please, Uncle. If that's the case, the celestial guards can fling open the gates of purgatory. I guarantee you Aidan and I have worked off the sentence of every single inmate."

The priest looked down the front of his sweater. Coiling an index finger, he flicked away a crumb that had escaped the prior purge.

Annie shook her head. "Look at that mess on the table and floor. It's a wonder poor old Millie's only half batty, picking up after you."

8

SUFFOLK COUNTY, ENGLAND

Spring rain hovered in banks of gray-black clouds, as if waiting for a chain to be pulled so it could drop and soak the fields of Britain's mid-section. Slicing through rich farmland below Newmarket, the northerly lanes of the A-11 motorway were clear of traffic as far ahead as Patty O'Reilly could see. The cocky IRA soldier had stolen the Miata he was driving from a garage in Piccadilly last night. He peered at the rear-view mirror and was pleased with the view. An armored van was close behind. Patty could see the pissed expression on the driver's face. For the last few minutes, the Miata had slowed to an agonizing speed in the passing lane. A fag stuck to his lower lip, the uniformed van driver jabbered away at the guard who sat beside him, and leaned on the horn, to no avail. Patty held to a slow, steady pace. A tanker lorry heading in the opposite direction thundered past, shaking the tiny sports car.

Twenty minutes earlier, the Royal Assurance van had followed the Miata onto the dual highway at the outskirts of Chesterford. Patty's assignment was to keep the armored van immediately to his rear while driving at a slow speed to distance himself and the van from any traffic ahead of them on the motorway. A distance behind of the van, a pair of pokey sedans, also stolen, effectively isolated the armored vehicle from following motorway traffic.

With miles of empty motorway ahead of and behind them, the Miata and the close-following van passed a rusted caravan beginning an effort to return to the road from the breakdown lane. Looking into his door mirror, the van's driver was thankful for the timing as he watched the sputtering mobile home succeed only in straddling both northerly lanes. "At least we're in front of that piece of shit caravan," he said to the guard. "But I've still got to contend with this little shit ahead of me." He leaned back on the horn.

With a lengthy section of the motorway to themselves, the Miata and the armored van passed a billboard urging the purchase of Nestle Crunch bars. Patty floored the gas pedal. The Miata lurched forward and began to put substantial daylight between it and the trailing van. Thirty seconds later, the sports car came up and out of a dip in the road and sped past a long cattle-carrier parked in the breakdown lane. Patty waved at the three men huddled in the carrier's cab. Directly across the northerly lanes from the carrier, from behind a hedgerow on the middle island, three more men watched the Miata speed by. All the waiting men wore balaclavas.

As soon as Patty had sped past, the empty cattle-carrier was stretched across the roadway. Six burning flares were placed as if to warn oncoming traffic of a jack-knifed trailer. If things went according to plan, the van driver would have no choice but to stop as he came upon the breakdown. In just seconds, the waiting men would imprison the driver and guard in the cab and blow the van's rear doors off with well-placed plastique. Like opening a can of tuna for these experts.

With a sense of freedom following the disappearance of the Miata, the armored van was traveling through the farmland at high speed when it popped up from the road depression and found itself directly upon the cattle-carrier. A fiery crash splayed splintered pieces of the carrier's wooden slats around the roadway. Somehow, the van stayed upright, screeching and scraping to a halt along the inner guard rail. Although not as planned, the results were usable.

The van driver and guard, neither seat-belted, died instantly when their heads cracked the bullet-proof windscreen. Thinking they no longer needed masks, the armed robbers ripped them off. Uzis in hand, they rushed out of their roadside concealment. Two of their number handled the explosives. In fifteen seconds the van's rear doors were blown away. A bloodied guard fell from the back of the van out onto the roadway. He looked up from the ground with a thankful smile for the Good Samaritans that would lend him aid. He heard, but did not understand, the words spoken in his direction - "Too bad you spied our handsome faces." The guard noticed the automatic weapons only when they flashed. His wide-eyed face rolled over onto a burning flare.

Minutes later, amongst black smoke, splintered wood and gnarled metal, bags of money were being flung into the boot of the getaway car. The investigative report issued by Scotland Yard would not include any witness statements. Even so, there would be no trouble in assessing blame in the robbery of the RAF Lakenheath U.S. Air Force payroll. The explosives used, brutal slaying of the defenseless guard, and information from well-placed touts all shouted IRA.

The take was just over three million American dollars in U.S. currency. Empty money bags from the heist would be discovered in August. They'd be stumbled upon at a farm supply warehouse near the Ringaskiddy Ferry Terminal, about nine miles outside of Cork City in Southwest Ireland.

Scotland - One Week Later

An evening breeze carried the scent of pine down the eastern slope of the Grampian mountain range and throughout the village of Arnott. Nestled along the River Dee in the shadow of the Scottish Highlands, Arnott lay about twenty miles inland from the North Sea port of Aberdeen. At just about six o'clock a green Ford Escort rolled to a stop in front of a two-story granite cottage. Walled in by forests on three sides, the small home had few neighbors, a condition eagerly sought by the purchaser some seven years earlier. McKinnon was carved into the wood sign attached to the top of the door frame.

Ernest McKinnon decided on the small homestead just before Helen gave birth to the couple's first son, Harley. The remote location was not Helen Munson's first choice. For Harley's sake, she would have preferred to remain in the London area. The former mathematics teacher, somewhat fearfully, voiced her opinion to Ernest - better schools, not so isolated from playmates. But the quiet, almost secretive Ernest had insisted on Scotland.

He told Helen it was convenient for his employment, which required regular travel to Northern European cities. Maintenance Supply Ltd. salesmen traveled four to six days each week. The village was an easy distance to Aberdeen Airport, and without the hassle of London traffic and congestion. Also, Ernest had said, it was difficult living out of a suitcase and he wanted to be in the beautiful Grampians during his free time. The change in geography would make it easier to relax, not bring his work concerns home, but rather leave the job at the company's London office, which Helen had never seen.

Marriage was not an option, Ernest told Helen. He had no religious inclinations, and what good did it do? He was hurt badly as a child when social services took him from his married, drug-addicted parents. He went from one foster home to another, finally landing with a decent couple named McKinnon. He still struggled to get over their death in an auto accident on his sixteenth birthday.

Ernest explained the only paperwork that followed him was a school register where he was enrolled while living with the McKinnons. With no readily verifiable background, Ernest suggested, and Helen agreed, that any children would carry her surname. Their second son, Paul, arrived eleven months after Harley. Ernest loved the boys and provided handsomely for the family. Substantial education accounts were already in place. Helen was very impressed with the living one could earn from selling industrial soaps and paper towels.

It was dusk and to the west only the tip of the sun was visible over the mountain top. The remaining daylight barely illuminated the path that led from the road to the cottage's front door. A middle-aged, stocky man stepped out of the Ford Escort and sauntered up the flagstone walk. Helen was standing at the kitchen sink when the doorbell chimed. She wondered who could possibly be calling. When Ernest was home, her friends were warned off, her husband not being one to mix too readily. Ernest looked quizzically into the kitchen from his front room easy chair. His wife shrugged her shoulders. "Can't be the boys," she said, looking through the kitchen window. "They're out back with their football."

"I'll see to the door." Ernest stood his five-foot, two-inch frame up from his chair and, avoiding the sleeping cat, walked over and turned off the television set. Evenings were cool this time of year. Not being one to overheat the house, he wore a cardigan sweater. His hand automatically went to check his toupee. He smoothed the front of his sweater, walked over and pulled the door open. The caller, wearing an open collared shirt and tan trousers, stood with both hands planted in front pockets and a grin on his face. He was silent.

"Is there something I can be helping you with?" Ernest asked, casting a wary glance beyond the man to the Escort parked at the end of the walk.

Liam Donnelly continued to grin beneath a thick, red brush mustache, but expressed surprise in his eyes. "Good evening," he said, looking up at the name over the door. "McKinnon, is it now? I'm wondering if you'd have a moment to join my friend," Donnelly half turned toward the road, "and me for a short chat."

"And why should I be doin' that, now?"

"Because you wouldn't want to disappoint your most important employer, Mister Aidan McGuire, would you?"

The small man's complexion suddenly turned to chalk. He coughed nervously and called back to Helen, "Ah, it's a customer needin' some special attention. I'll be just a minute."

McKinnon felt light-headed as he followed the caller the short distance to the road. When they reached the Escort, Donnelly opened the rear door of the sedan and gestured to McKinnon to get in. He then slid into the front seat beside Aidan, who had turned to look at the little man in the back seat. Aidan's expression remained stern as he spoke.

"It's beautiful here in the Grampians, Eddie, or should I be calling you Ernie. A wonderful place, Scotland. Not my cup of tea, mind you, but you've chosen well for your Scottish family. Then again, Maureen and the children seem well cared for in Cambridge, another of God's chosen places. At least you've been even-handed to all involved."

Eddie McCauley, alias Ernest McKinnon, was silent for a few seconds. He knew his dual world had been tethered by the thinnest of string, which had finally snapped. "How long have you known?"

"Three, maybe four years. It's not important Eddie. We couldn't care less about your personal life."

Donnelly turned, looking over his shoulder at Eddie. "I must admit, this is all quite intriguing. I know many men that would gleefully part with their fortunes to rid themselves of their only wife."

The little man in the rear seat ignored the comment and directed an angry question at Aidan, a tremble in his voice, "Who exactly is 'we', and why are you here?"

"You have no need to know who we speak for," Aidan answered. "In fact, you are best served by ignorance on that score. Why we are here is another story. You're in a position to do something we need. It may seem somewhat repulsive to you at first, considering your splendid reputation in the irons. But your secret family life, or, I should say, lives, can stay just that, secret, and your ability to ride the best racehorses in the world and earn a small fortune can continue."

The sunlight was on the verge of disappearing. Helen could be heard calling Harley and Paul into the house. Long ago the jockey realized he was creating a monster with the two families, but he dearly loved both. He would lie in bed at night, fearing discovery. But what he'd done wasn't so terrible. After all, he accepted responsibility for two wonderful families, and money was no problem. But no one, particularly, of course, his wives and children, would ever, ever understand. He'd do anything to keep them, to not hurt them. He looked directly into Aidan's eyes. "Obviously, I have no choice. What do I have to do?"

"Irish Eagle is about to be entered in the Travers stakes in America. As usual, he's your mount." Aidan paused a few seconds. "The horse cannot finish in the money."

The jockey gasped. Aidan McGuire, one of the most respected horsemen in Europe, was telling him to stiff the greatest racehorse in the world. "But, my God, Aidan ..."

"No buts, you little shit!" The order spit from the mouth of Donnelly. "McCauley, or McKinnon, or whoever the fuck you are today, listen up, real good. You take your orders from Mister Aidan McGuire. This gentleman sitting beside me. Nobody else! If you choose not to do exactly as directed, you will wish you were never born into this brutal world. It is as simple as that. Now, get the fuck out of this car. Go inside your little Scottish cottage and bounce your little bastards on your knees. And remember how much they mean to you."

The jockey stood at the shoulder of the road, staring at the Escort's fading tail lights. He walked slowly up the path and into the house. Harley and Paul were lying on the floor in front of the hearth, turning pages of comic books that featured super soccer players. Helen dusted the dust-free fireplace mantle, her mind racing, wondering who could possibly have called. Things like this just never happened, but she had no intention of asking.

For a small man, Ernest sat heavily in his easy chair. "Boys, to your room." Obediently, the youngsters scooted up the staircase. Their mother's concern heightened. Ernest spoke softly to his wife.

"Helen, are you content with the life I've provided for you and the boys?"

Helen, of equal stature as her husband, abandoned the dust rag on the mantle and sat on the arm of Ernest's chair. Instinctively, she put an arm around his neck and squeezed his shoulder. Unusually, he permitted the show of affection. "What is it Ernest? Who were those men?"

"Answer my question. Are you happy here in Scotland? Are you happy with me? With the life we have together?"

Helen continued to stare ahead, into the hearth. "At first, no. I wished to raise our family in London. But I've grown to love our home. Now, with the boys growing up so fast and their school going so well, the answer is yes, without a doubt, yes. Of course, I would like you home more, but I accept the demands made by your employment. The boys and I are very, very happy, Ernest." She turned to her partner. With her free hand she twisted a gold cross hanging from her neck chain. "What is it Ernest? Why are you asking these questions, and right after those men left?"

The little man stood from the chair and walked to the fireplace. He wrung his hands, made powerful by years of reining mighty thoroughbred horses. "What the visitors wanted is my business, Helen. I just want to be sure, absolutely certain, that I'm important to you and the boys. I know it's not easy, my not being around like the fathers of the boys' chums." He turned from the hearth, stepped over to Helen and grasped her shoulders tightly, so much that she flinched. "I love you and the boys!" he insisted.

"And we love you!" A tear slid down Helen's cheek.

With Aidan at the wheel, the Escort turned onto the M1 motorway, heading back to Aberdeen Airport. Headlamps streamed by as Liam Donnelly peeled back his mustache and winced. "Ouch! Never get used to these buggers. Speaking of phony hair, our favorite jock looks years younger with his hairpiece attached. I absolutely did not recognize him when he came to the door, even though I knew what to expect."

"It plays real well with his dual life," Aidan said. "Awfully well known as a jockey. If he goes into the village without his head of phony hair, some punter would spot him for sure. This way, he's just another villager who travels often. I suppose he keeps pretty much to home and mostly stays out of the village center. Clever with the name. Doesn't have to go around changing monograms on shirts and whatever. Funny, isn't it, the secrets some of us have."

"Tell me again, Aidan, how did you get on to the little bigamist?"

"On New Year's Eve, three years past, I was at an airline counter at Heathrow and this fellow almost ran me over in his haste to catch a flight. Saw him for just a second. There was something familiar about him, but I couldn't figure it. The agent gave me the traveler's name, McKinnon, ticketed to Aberdeen. Still meant nothing to me, until the Newmarket spring meeting the following year.

"There had been a lot of pinching in the jocks' quarters. Eddie was on one of my entries and left his billfold with my right hand man, Georgie O'Malley, for safekeeping. Georgie dropped the wallet and a photo driver's license fell out. He thought I'd be interested. When I looked, I recognized Eddie, but with a full head of hair. The name on the license was Ernest McKinnon, and the address was in Scotland. Of course, I remembered the little man in the airport. A little surveillance activity followed, and here we are. Till today, Eddie never knew I was aware of his double life."

"I had my doubts about the jock," Donnelly said, "but after seeing the fear in the little fucker's eyes, I know he'll do what you say."

"I've gotten to know Eddie well over the last few years. Of course, he's never mentioned his family in Scotland, but he often talks of the wife and kids in England. He'll do anything to protect them. He'll be okay. He'll do what I tell him."

"When I considered the message delivered by your uncle at the cathedral in Dublin, I was more than a little doubtful that it made a great deal of sense. So many loose ends. Having to count on so many people we have no control over. But then, after we met in London and you explained exactly what you had in mind, and why you were convinced it was doable, I put my confidence in you and recommended the operation to my chief. And by God, Aidan, I'm starting to think it's brilliant; even though it's more than a little convoluted, I think it will work. And the reward will be beyond calculation. God save us, I think we can do it."

Donnelly lit a cigarette. He took a deep drag and expelled a stream of smoke that rolled off the windscreen, then continued talking. "A long story made short, the Army Council has agreed to fund this operation. We're going to put a lot of our eggs in this basket. If we're to succeed, everything has to be set up beyond suspicion, Aidan, everything. The deception only works if everyone plays his part to the hilt. Each person involved can only be aware of information that will further our goal. That means it's only the two of us that see the whole picture. No one else, including your dear sister.

"I realize you're hesitant to have Annie involved, Aidan. But remember that she has served very successfully as a volunteer to the Cause on a number of occasions. It seems a natural for her to be a part of this operation. I'm not sure exactly what her function will be, but she's bound to be useful. Her being in the States and around the racetrack won't raise any eyebrows because she's an employee of Empire."

"If we need her, sir, I understand."

"You should also know that your veterinarian, Doc Flynn, has been on board with the Army for many years. He'll be told the race will be fixed, and be available to carry out any order, and I mean *any* order, that you give him. He is absolutely dedicated."

"I've known of his sympathies for the Cause," Aidan said, "but I'm surprised to hear he's been active."

Donnelly watched the darkened countryside roll past his window for a few moments, then said. "Recently, Aidan, we had a huge success with a major heist. It was far greater than anything we'd previously accomplished. It resulted in a staggering amount of cash, of American currency. We had these dollars earmarked for various operations and armaments. But your mission, what it will mean to our ability to level the playing field a little with the Brits, has become all-important. We're going to fund your plan with most of that money, Aidan, two million American dollars."

Aidan, surprised and impressed with the amount, blew a short whistle. "That is far more money than I ever thought would be involved, sir. I will do all that is humanly possible to justify your confidence."

"There's another matter that has to be arranged. We have to get the American currency into the States. Any suggestions will be welcome."

Aidan thought for a moment. "I expect I can come up with a method to transport the cash, sir. Give me a few days to work it out."

"Of course. Excellent, Aidan. I know we can count on you."

Aidan slowed the Escort as it approached an intersection. Across the road a small sign pointed the way to Balmoral Castle, noting its purpose - Royal Family Summer Home.

"We'll be needing a code name for this mission, Aidan," Donnelly said. "Seeing as we're investing a royal amount and it's the summer season, how does Balmoral sound?"

"Balmoral sounds just fine, sir."

London - Two Days Later - Evening

The Volkswagen Jetta was reserved in the name of Henry Pushka. When Aidan McGuire presented himself as Henry at the Avis rental agency in the city, as he had been told, he was not asked for identification or payment. He was simply handed the keys.

Thirty minutes later Aidan parked the gray sedan on a poorly-lit residential street in the Berkhamsted section of the city. He locked the car and walked the empty pavement a short distance to the corner, the evening quiet broken only by soft notes from a flute tumbling through an open window. Stopping at a short brick walk leading to a freestanding, unlit house, Aidan noticed a car parked at curbside across and a short distance up the road. There was no other traffic. He sensed the person in the driver's seat was studying him as he turned and walked to the door.

"Come right ahead, sir," a voice beckoned from the dark corridor behind the suddenly opened door. "No obstacles, just straight ahead."

As the greeter closed the front door, another door opened off the corridor. Following directions from a new voice, Aidan walked into a sitting room, lit only by the glow of a street lamp entering a front window. The door was closed behind him by a hefty, dark-suited man who stayed inside the room, standing ramrod straight aside the door. Aidan could make out a plume of smoke rising from a wing chair which, he knew by the sweet aroma, originated from pipe tobacco. The smoker's profile was hidden from his view. The chair's occupant invited Aidan to take a seat on the couch along the near wall. Although his host spoke softly, and Aidan could not see him, he had no problem hearing his words.

"Gerry Appleyard says you'd like to help us out, Mister McGuire."

Aidan unbuttoned his car coat, drawing the attention of the door guard who was at his side in a second. Aidan raised both hands. "Just a little warm."

A quick frisk and the guard returned to his post by the door, silently admonishing himself for not having conducted the search earlier. Aidan sat on the edge of the hard couch. He responded to the question that hung in the darkened room. "Yes, sir, I would like to help."

"Although many, if not most, of your fellow Irish are not sympathetic to the IRA's campaign of terror, considering that you have lost a pair of uncles because of their Army involvement, and I'm aware of at least one other family casualty, a nephew, one might expect your allegiance to be with them, not here with us Brits."

Aidan had expected his sincerity to be questioned. A soft cough preceded his response.

"Some in my family have been taken in by the rhetoric. They believe that change can only travel through the barrel of a gun. Regardless of how worthy they may think their cause, it can never justify indiscriminate killing, especially children. Certainly, there is room for political argument, but at least the British don't conduct bombing missions. Terrorists are cowards first, whatever else a distant second. They work against the interest of my country. I have no sympathy for them. To take guns and bullets from the IRA arsenal is a choice easily made. If I can help to end this horror, I wish to be involved."

"No nationalistic tendencies, McGuire? A united Ireland isn't tucked away in your dreams?"

"No, sir. No dreams. Just reality."

"You realize that if those murdering bastards get even a hint of your efforts on our behalf, you'll rue the moment you left your mother's womb. It will be beyond your worst nightmare."

"Sir, I've no concern for my own well-being when weighed against whatever good I might accomplish."

"Gerry recommends you without reservation. He tells me you have an idea for a scheme that could be of interest. Two or three million IRA dollars involved? I'll be pleased to listen."

"Thank you, sir. It has to do with the racehorse named Irish Eagle, and an important American horse race known as the Travers Stakes."

Principality of Monaco

Zlatan Terzik had reserved his usual table at the Hotel de Paris' Louis XV dining room for ten o'clock. In response to a series of messages from a Father Sweeney, a code name he was familiar with, his chauffeured, tan Rolls Royce rolled silently to the foot of the hotel's marble steps thirty minutes ahead of his dinner reservation. A white-gloved hand opened the rear door for a slender fifteen-year-old boy, best described as pretty, flaxen hair falling onto the shoulders of his blue cord suit. As he stepped out of the luxury auto, the teenager turned to take the hand of his younger, but more mature-appearing sister as she followed him out of the Rolls. The attendant admired the sophisticated-looking girl, beginning at her ankles and slowly continuing his gaze up the slender frame barely covered by a short, black sequined dress. A provocative slit in the side of the dress rose to a tanned hip, sufficient evidence that the teenager wore little, if anything, beneath. Then, with an effort accompanied by a loud grunt, the arms merchant eased himself out of the front passenger seat and hooked his arms through those of his young companions, leading them up to the hotel's bronze doors.

Inside the opulent lobby, the light from a chandelier bounced off Terzik's pate, carefully denuded of its remaining strands of hair. He deposited the brother and sister with the concierge, who led them to the maître d' at the hotel's three-star restaurant. The corpulent arms merchant intended to entertain his juvenile toys with a visit to the baccarat table at Casino de Monte-Carlo after he rejoined the children and dinner had been enjoyed. The trio would then be whisked by launch across the harbor to the luxury yacht, Gunrunner, Terzik's response to those who found the source of his wealth less than honorable.

He turned to his left, walked down a gleaming corridor and entered the hotel bar. Le Bar Américain overlooked the harbor and was fit out in rich leather and polished woods. Liam Donnelly sat alone at a small table toward the end of the bar. He wore a deep blue suit and sky blue shirt accented by a white linen tie. The IRA commander spotted Terzik, turning slowly as he looked about the elegant room, wondering which guise Donnelly had chosen. The view of the arms merchant, standing in his white suit amongst heavy wisps of cigar and cigarette smoke, had Donnelly picturing a squat island lighthouse in an early morning fog. He raised his glass of whiskey to beckon him. Terzik, with a waddling gait, made his way to the table.

"Ah, so interesting to see a man of the cloth in the most expensive hotel bar on the Cote d'Azur. It is no wonder you're out of uniform, Father Sweeney." Terzik took a seat opposite Donnelly and summoned a waiter with a flick of his wrist. The white-coated server was immediately at the table taking an order for a wet vodka Gibson and another Irish whiskey, both neat.

"You wouldn't expect me to play the role of a soldier of the Holy See when living the moment as a libertine," Donnelly said. "But let's skip the small talk. I am pleased to tell you that in late August we will be in a financial position to take delivery of the Stinger missiles discussed when we met in Dublin. This will be the first of many orders if the goods are acceptable. The briefcase that has just been delivered to your chauffeur contains two hundred thousand United States dollars in one-hundred dollar bills. Call it good faith money. The balance is guaranteed."

"You know, my friend, when I place an order of this sort, I assume full responsibility to pay the bill." Terzik stopped talking as the waiter arrived and placed the drinks on cocktail napkins. "Convince me that a motley band of sots could guarantee anything other than the safe transit of the Guinness lorry to a local pub."

Donnelly poured the remaining whiskey from his glass into the newly delivered drink, raised it to his mouth and eliminated the contents in one swallow. Slowly placing the heavy crystal back on the table, he glowered at Terzik. "You putrid piece of shite. My associates and I have absolutely no use for pedophiles who cannot deliver armaments. Actually, I sometimes think even the guns aren't worth tolerating your existence. At the present time, you are just slightly behind the Brits on our list of things to attend to. The funds will be available at the end of August. If the goods are not, I would recommend conversion and Extreme Unction. You can also assume that non-anesthetized castration is not pleasant. I cannot, for the life of me, think of a more appropriate candidate for the gelder's blade."

Terzik strained to hide his concern. He sipped his drink and set it back in the center of the pink napkin. "Just a little ethnic humor, my friend. Nothing to get all lathered up about. Do not worry, my supply lines are excellent and I've no doubt of your credit-worthiness." The fat man stood, reached into his pocket and placed two 100 franc notes on the table. "Let me take care of this, Father. No need to dip into the collection plate. It has been a pleasure doing business with you tonight, but I really must go on to the dining room. It has been far too long between servings of chef's Mediterranean fish soup." With the meeting concluded, Terzik's confidence made a slight comeback. "And I have some tasty little dessert snacks awaiting me."

The arms dealer turned from the table and started walking to the door, taking quick short steps. Donnelly watched Terzik's hind quarters shake like gelatin as they exited the bar. He wondered to whom he would assign the duty of eradicating this few hundred pounds of excrement after this mission was completed. Then again, he always felt gratified to personally pull the trigger on a traitorous tout. Perhaps similar contentment was available from dispatching a pedophile.

9

BOSTON, MASSACHUSETTS - LATE SPRING

Holding a felt-tipped pen, Waldo Legrande, head usher at the Boston Garden (and 'the man' for hard to come by tickets to Garden games and events) sat at his pockmarked wooden desk. On the desktop, a clear plastic overlay had been thumbtacked over a large seating chart of the city's venerable sports arena. The plastic had been marked with names and numbers. Waldo looked up as his young assistant arrived at the open office door.

"Everything looks good on the upper level, 'cept for a busted trash barrel. I stopped by maintenance to let them know," Harry Meadows said. "What's next, Boss?"

"Today's off to a good start. Got to love it when the Celts and Bruins both make the playoffs. Just got a call from Mister Sparta's office. He needs four down front, bench side, for tonight's Celts - Lakers." Waldo counted out four white and green tickets from a small stack, slid them into a green envelope and handed it to Harry. "Get these over to Hanover Street. Give them to Carmine. You know him, right?"

"Yep. Been there, done that."

Waldo grabbed a tissue from the box on the edge of his desk and loudly blew his nose. "You going by the drugstore for breakfast?"

"Yeah, and I've got to pick up the racing newspaper."

"Pick me up some Contac, okay? This damn cold's got my nose dribblin' like crazy. It'd put D.J. to shame."

"D.J.?"

Waldo looked up at Harry, "You never heard of Dennis Johnson?"

"I'm only twenty, Waldo. Maybe the name's, ah, kind of familiar."

"I'll give you a Celtics history lesson later, Harry. And, what the hell you buying the racing sheet for? Don't tell me you're into the horses."

"It's for school. A course in statistics given by Professor Samuel Smith, also known as Cypher Sam. He's developed a can't-miss system for the racetrack. A hundred kids pack his lectures twice a week."

"Amazing what they're teaching you college boys nowadays."

"College girls, too, Waldo. You ought to catch some of the talent taking the Cypher's course."

"I wonder where Professor Handicap'll be teaching next year."

"If his system works, he won't have to teach next year, or ever."

"If his system works, Harry, Harvard will sign him to a multi-year contract. Boston College can kiss his ass good-bye."

At nine o'clock Harry crossed the North Station concourse and walked into an old-fashioned drugstore. He headed to the newspaper rack, picked up the *Daily Racing Form* and then stepped over to the marble lunch counter. Hopping on to a chrome pedestal stool, he greeted the short, slight and bespectacled pharmacy owner. Saul Silver was wiping down his already spotless marble counter.

"Yo, Sauly, let me have one of your famous dogs and a vanilla Coke."

"Harry, not too often do I give advice that hits me in the wallet. But, like I've told you before, hot dogs will probably kill you. At least give you colon cancer."

"C'mon, Sauly. You know I can't live without your dogs."

"Okay, okay. It's your health. At least they're kosher, but what a breakfast." Sauly pumped syrup into a Coke glass as he spoke. "How come you've been coming in the last few mornings. No classes anymore?"

"Only a field trip this afternoon, a final statistics class Friday, and the semester's over. Then it's just the last week of baseball. Final game's at Tufts next Wednesday. Then I wait for the Red Sox to call."

"You have your final examination on Friday?"

"Nope, just my last statistics class. The Cypher, that's the professor, doesn't believe in examinations. Says life's the final exam. When you die, you find out if you passed or flunked."

"He's right about that, Harry. You working for Waldo today?"

"I'm helping out with some seat shuffling for the Celtic playoffs, running errands and stuff."

Sauly turned to the back counter and opened the glass door on a red tin oven that had WEINEROASTER stamped on its side. With a steel hook in place of the hand he left on Normandy Beach as a teenage GI, he slid a frankfurter off a silver tine and onto a bun rescued from the bottom of the cooker. "Try onions on your hot dog some time, Harry. Onions are very good for you."

While working on the hot dog, Harry's eyes focused on a front page article in the *Daily Racing Form*.

IRISH EAGLE ROMPS IN EPSOM DERBY - LOGAN LOOKING FOR DUAL CROWN

American horseman R. Jack Logan has made a premature claim to the top honors thoroughbred racing has to offer this year - on both sides of the Atlantic. Earlier this year, his undefeated Irish Eagle easily won his first test as a three-year-old, the Greenham Stakes at Newbury in England. Last month, in the first of England's "Triple Crown" events, it was a one horse showcase for the Irish-bred colt as he galloped home in front in the 2,000 Guineas at Newmarket, crossing the finish line in record time. Then, this past Saturday, the handsome Bold Ruler colt strolled to an easy win in the Epsom Derby at a mile and one-half. The betting public at this second jewel in the British crown had made Irish Eagle a one-to-five favorite. Europe's most prominent jockey, Eddie McCauley, was in the irons. Logan credited highly regarded trainer Aidan McGuire for having his colt "fit as an Appalachian fiddle." Irish Eagle needs a win at the St. Leger Stakes in September to complete his sweep of the British racing jewels. In any event, Logan's colt is a shoe-in for European Horse of the Year honors.

The American Horse of the Year award is also on Logan's radar. Even though Irish Eagle did not run in the Kentucky Derby or the Preakness, and will not enter the Belmont Stakes, Logan feels his horse has a shot at the American honor. He has entered Irish Eagle in the Travers Stakes at Saratoga in August and, in his usual brash style, has challenged one and all to show up at the 'Spa' to take on his colt. "We

*decided not to run the Eagle in the States this spring because we had
him pointed for the British derbies. Anyhow, last November he toyed
with the best the States has to offer in the Breeders' Cup Juvenile. We'll
see them again in August, and anybody else who dares to show up in
Saratoga for the Travers."* *(cont. on page 3)*

"Sauly, hit me again." Harry pushed his empty Coke glass towards
the pharmacist. "What's a spa?"

"That's a place where people go to take baths in the mud or in water
that's filled with little bubbles. They claim the minerals in the water
make them feel better. They eat a lot of fancy food and have a bunch of
servants dressed in white uniforms kiss their rear ends."

"Like Saratoga?"

"Yes, like Saratoga. People are better off with vitamins they can
buy right here at Terminal Drug."

Harry turned to page three.

*If successful in the Travers, most likely Irish Eagle will ship back
to Europe for the St. Leger, and then return to the States in November
for the Breeders Cup Classic. For a mere mortal horse, this schedule
would appear to be overwhelming. But the bullish Logan is confident
his horse can handle anything. The colt will ship from the comfort of
his barn in County Cork, Ireland, to Saratoga in mid-August. The son of
Bold Ruler, out of the renowned Irish mare, Wanderlust, could be up to
his owner's high expectations. The ease with which he won the Breeder's
Cup Juvenile at Santa Anita last year is still the talk of the backstretch.
Logan's description was right on - he toyed with them. An Irish Eagle
victory in the Travers Stakes, a/k/a the Mid-Summer Derby, would be
a giant step towards American Horse of the Year honors.* (Reuters)

Harry placed his usual two dollars on the counter. "Here you go, Sauly.
By the way, do you ever think of changing the name of the pharmacy?"

"Change the name? It's been Terminal Drug since I opened fifty years
ago, right after the war. That's because it's in the train station, a terminal.
Why do you ask a question like that, Harry?"

"Dunno. Just wondering." The pink neon tube wrapped around the
wall clock winked, reminding Harry of the time. "See you later, Sauly."

Harry left the drugstore by the Causeway Street exit. Ten minutes
later he crossed Hanover Street and skirted an orange pickup with a

few yards of loam in its bed. The Massachusetts Department of Public Works truck was parked in a handicap space in front of number 68, Harry's destination.

Sparta Enterprises, 2nd Floor was lettered on the upper-glass panel of a door that opened onto a steep stairwell. Harry pulled the ticket envelope from his back pocket. His Nikes took the steps two at a time.

The windows in the second floor room at 68 Hanover Street were covered by dark curtains. Six men of mixed ages sat around a battered and scratched oval Formica table centered under a fluorescent ceiling fixture. The "red dog" pot stood at fifty-five hundred dollars, the biggest since 5 a.m. Angelo, thickset, black-haired, with a slippery cigar hanging out of his mouth, occupied the seat nearest the door to the stairwell. Stuck halfway into his rear pocket was a .38 caliber handgun. He stared at the dealer, fingered his cards for a few moments and spat out his decision. "Match." There was dead silence. All eyes were on the deck of cards in the dealer's hands.

The free-swinging door off the staircase landing wasn't seated into the jam. Harry's knock sent it flying, sweeping in a semi-circle, smashing into the wall and dislodging a framed print of the Roman Coliseum. Angelo reacted immediately. He kicked his way out of his chair, knocking it over as he swung toward the doorway. The pistol came out of his rear pocket. He pointed it at Harry's heart and screamed, "Carmine! What the fuck?"

Harry's hands shot to the ceiling, one of them holding the green ticket envelope.

"It's okay! It's okay!" Carmine Zappella bellowed as he jumped up from his chair. "It's only the kid from the Garden. It's okay, Angelo. Put the fuckin' piece away!"

Slowly, Angelo slid the gun back into his pocket. Still staring at Harry, he sat back down. The card players' attention quickly returned to the table. Angelo slowly turned up the right corner of each of his cards, as if suspecting they may have changed during the brief diversion. He looked across the table. The dealer turned over the jack of spades. Angelo grinned, his teeth cutting into his cigar as he turned over the queen of the same suit.

Shaken, but now trusting that he wasn't about to be shot, Harry finally dropped his arms. He watched the grinning hoodlum reach into the center of the table and gather in the pile of bills, accompanied by groans and expletives from the rest of the players. In a pitch higher than he intended, Harry said, "Hi, Carmine, I brought Mister Sparta's Celtics tickets."

Carmine looked over at the door and noticed the shaft of light filling the staircase behind Harry. "Holy shit, what fucking time is it?"

"About quarter of ten," Harry answered.

Carmine tossed his cards into the center of the table. "You assholes clean up this dump when you're done. I gotta go to the fuckin' garage." He pulled a comb from the back pocket of his black slacks and ran it through his hair. "C'mon, kid. I'll give you a lift back to the Garden."

Harry followed Carmine down the staircase. When they reached the sidewalk, Carmine slid into the driver's seat of the DPW pickup. Harry hustled around to the passenger door, pulled the *Daily Racing Form* from his back pocket and joined Carmine in the cab.

Noticing the racing sheet, Carmine asked, "You into the ponies, kid?"

"Kind of. I'm taking a course at school on how to win at the track."

"Yeah? Where the fuck you go to school? Fuckin' Suffolk Downs?"

"Boston College. The class has a field trip going up to Rockingham this afternoon." Harry reached into his pocket. "Almost forgot. Here are the Celtics tickets for Mister Sparta."

Carmine stuffed the envelope into his shirt pocket while he ignored a stop sign at the corner of Hanover and Cross Streets. "So, you're goin' up to the Rock today. Do yourself a favor, kid. Random Rogue in the fourth race. Kind of payback for you almost gettin' your balls shot off up at the office. Okay?"

Harry was about to ask why Random Rogue when Carmine slammed on the brakes. The truck slid to a stop a few feet in front of an obviously pregnant woman in the middle of a crosswalk. The startled mother-to-be turned abruptly, a look of horror on her face, groceries falling from a brown paper bag.

Leaning out the driver's window, Carmine roared, "You can get knocked down, too, lady!"

As the truck began to resume its journey, Harry watched the shaken woman in the passenger side mirror. She stooped over and began to pick up cans and greens off the street while casting a disbelieving glance in the direction of the truck. An embarrassed Harry looked straight ahead and slithered further into the seat.

"Fuckin' Boston and its fuckin' jaywalkers," Carmine complained, speeding down the street. "Cause more fuckin' accidents."

"Why Random Rogue?" Harry asked, happy to change the subject.

"Cause Carmine says Random Rogue. He's shippin' in from Jersey for this claimer. Hasn't shown a fuckin' thing, but trust me, it's a lock, and he'll pay a nice piece of change." Carmine grinned in Harry's direction. "By the way, kid, do you think you can help me out with a couple of ticks for the Bruins-Canadians game on Sunday? Hot date. Like to make an impression. That can pay off fuckin' big time." Carmine raised a fist and pumped it back and forth. "Know what I mean?"

"Yeah, sure, Carmine. I'll ask Waldo about it when I get back. I'll see what I can do. That reminds me, I've got to pick up some medicine for him. Drop me at the drugstore, okay?"

The pickup turned up a street that snaked under the central artery, the elevated roadway that effectively severed downtown Boston from its North End and harbor. Carmine leaned on the horn, insisting that a semi-trailer run a red light. "C'mon, you wimpy son of a bitch. I've got a time clock to punch and I'm fuckin' late."

Harry asked, "What time do you have to be at the garage?"

"I pull a ten to seven shift."

"You've still got about ten minutes."

"No, kid, no. You don't fuckin' understand," explained Carmine, whipping the steering wheel to his left. The pickup careened around the corner and screeched to a halt in front of the Terminal Drug Store. "I work the graveyard shift. Ten at night to seven in the morning. I'm three fuckin' hours late to punch out 'cause I got caught up in that fuckin' card game. Maybe I can screw 'em out of some OT. Beat it, kid."

As he stood on the sidewalk and watched the DPW truck speed away, Harry was beginning to understand why the Commonwealth was always teetering on the edge of bankruptcy ... fuckin' bankruptcy.

10

BOSTON COLLEGE

Sited in the upscale suburb of Chestnut Hill, a wet spring had blessed the Boston College campus with deep green lawns to surround its Gothic style buildings. At ten o'clock on Friday morning, the Gasson Hall amphitheater quieted the instant Professor Samuel Smith scurried onto the teaching platform. The tweedy scholar marched to the middle of his stage, carrying a folded copy of the *Daily Racing Form*. For the final time, one hundred budding statisticians were on the receiving end of a lecture from the professor known as 'Cypher Sam, the Numbers Man.'

"It is my opinion that this class has produced the most able handicappers since my tenure commenced on this campus twenty-two years ago. You know your way around the *Daily Racing Form*, a publication that puts any and all statistical texts to shame. Our two sojourns to Rockingham Park were, in thirty-seven syllables, absolutely, positively the most successful field trips this course has ever visited upon the unwary and uninformed betting public."

A heavy-set sophomore sitting on the lower right side of the semi-circular classroom started scribbling into his notebook. He whispered to a black-haired, diminutive classmate on his left, "I gotta write that sentence down. I gotta count those syllables."

"Do not trouble yourself," responded the Cambodian classmate, "like always, the Cypher is correct."

"You already know he's right? Wow."

From an upper row of desks, an attractive twenty-year-old student looked down and across the room. She laughed quietly.

"What's so funny, Steph?" Harry Meadows asked from the next seat.

"The Asian kid said Cypher's right about the number of syllables."

"How do you know he said that?" Harry looked over at the student with the floppy black hair and thick glasses. "He's over on the other side of the room."

"I can read lips."

"Really?"

"Yup. My brother Pudgie's deaf. I helped teach him to lip-read."

After a sip of grapefruit juice from a flask taken from the pocket of his corduroy jacket, the Cypher continued. "If we had actually played out our collective gaming wisdom at the pari mutuel windows, it would have meant early retirement for all of us. It was classic handicapping - the best analysis and application of numbers to actual track conditions. Of course," the professor paused, "there was one notable exception.

"I am making reference to the fourth race on Tuesday's trip to the Rockingham oval. We all surely recall the uncanny ability of our school's third baseman, Mister Meadows, to choose a winner, a winner by five lengths, in spite of every scintilla of data pointing to a contrary result. Indeed, the gelded nag, Random Rogue, was at twenty-to-one in the morning line.

"In case you've forgotten, the morning line is the prophecy of the track handicapper. Before the first dollar of the day is wagered, the resident expert gives his or her opinion of what odds are likely to be set by the public when they've finished parting with their money at the betting windows. The morning line is printed in the official track program and is how things are supposed to be, but, as we all know, in this life things aren't always as they appear. Things don't always work out the way we think they're supposed to.

"Simply put, that fourth race was fixed. The wise guys owned it. Unfortunately, at least for those without inside information, this type of happening occurs on occasion. It can be accomplished by using any of a variety of methods - jockeys holding back the favorite, injections of stimulants, letting a horse run true-to-form after being held in prior races. If you end up with good inside information, and happen to have a few dollars to bet, you're luckier than most.

"Although I do not know how Mister Meadows came upon his information, I do appreciate his letting us in on his tip. It displays one of the variables that must be taken into consideration if one is to undertake a career as an inveterate gambler. It also suggests a truism in the world of the racetrack, and elsewhere: there is no such thing as a sure thing. All of which brings me to the conclusion of this lecture," the professor paused, "and my career at Boston College." An audible gasp filled the room. "It seems that the administration has taken issue with my view of the educational value of contrasting the racing abilities of the bobtail nag and the bay. This, combined with a series of rather nasty letters authored by the ex-Mrs. Smith regarding the extortion known as alimony, has resulted in a formal request that I depart this revered campus and ply my trade elsewhere."

The professor took another swallow of grapefruit juice. "I wish you all an abundance of common sense. If sought, I may be reached at the clubhouses at Belmont Park, Gulfstream Park or similar environs. Of course, as Muslims are under an obligation to journey to Mecca, we who are responsible for improving the breed must journey to the Spa. Therefore, during August, I shall be resting between races under the spreading limbs of the ancient elms ringing the paddock at the Saratoga Race Course."

Professor Smith strode off his stage. The students sat in silence. Finally, they rose from their desks and walked from the classroom.

At the less leafy end of Boston, a block up from Carson Beach, a half-dozen or so members of the South Boston Shamrock Society stood around the pool table in the club's bar. A cloud of bluish smoke had settled the space around a pair of ceiling lamps, stealing a portion of the light intended for the green felt surface below. On the table, the white cue ball was positioned behind the ten ball, denied a clear path to the eight.

A sixty-year-old with buzz-cut gray hair rested his cue stick on the bridge created with his thumb and forefinger. With a delicate stroke, he banked the cue ball off a bumper. It rolled slowly back toward the side pocket, avoiding the ten by the width of a hair and kissing the eight.

Gently nudged, the black ball moved three revolutions and fell off the surface into the crocheted pocket. Mumbled expressions of disbelief from the mid-morning group of onlookers filled the room. A wide grin on his face, Buzzy Flaherty rolled the cue onto the felt surface and grabbed three twenty-dollar bills that had suddenly appeared next to the pool stick. He addressed the group. "When are you morons gonna learn not to fuck with the champ, eh?"

There were two telephone lines at the Shamrock's bar. One was listed with Northeast Telephone Company under the name of the club and was tapped by the Federal Bureau of Investigation. The affidavit filed in support of the wiretap warrant dealt primarily with bookmaking, loan sharking and gun trafficking. The other line was an extension of a private phone with an unpublished number. It was billed to Margaret O'Shea, who resided in a studio apartment on the building's top floor. Thanks to an obstetrician with a serious hangover, Margaret was cursed with deafness from birth. She had never used a telephone. It was Margaret's phone that the bartender held aloft.

"Buzzy, phone. Says it's long distance."

The most notorious hoodlum outside of the city's North End let his cigarette fall from his lips to the worn wooden floor, snuffed it beneath a Converse All Star sneaker and sauntered to the bar. He took the phone from the outstretched hand and sat on a barstool. "Yeah? Who's calling?" A light crackle on the line preceded the response.

"Good morning to you, Buzzy. So nice to hear your voice. How is everything in western-most Ireland?"

Flaherty recognized the voice of Liam Donnelly. His attitude changed immediately. "Just fine, sir. How goes the battle? Things are good, I pray."

"Yes, Buzzy, everything is going quite well, thank you. I've called to make reservations for a day at the races. It is certain that the party will be held in August, as we recently discussed."

"That's good news, real good news. We've already started to make the arrangements on this end. I talked to the judge, and he'll cooperate. Now, we'll finish gettin' things set up."

"Thank you, Buzzy. I hope the sun is shining on Boston today. The Dublin sky, not unusually, is the color of dull pewter. Good day."

Buzzy handed the phone back to the bartender. "Call Brendan.

Message is to set up the meeting with the judge and his former clients. Wednesday, any time after noon will be okay."

The slightly built hoodlum tipped a gallon-size glass jug on the bar, unscrewed the lid and plucked out a hard-boiled egg. "Put me down for a chicken dinner," he instructed the bartender, and turned back to the pool table. Between nibbles on the shiny white spheroid, he issued an invitation. "Any of you pigeons got the balls to challenge?"

The following Wednesday afternoon, in the heart of Boston's financial district, three men entered a paneled elevator. As the car rose silently to the 26th floor and the law firm of Jones & Riddle, smoke drifted to the ceiling.

"Hey, look, Mister S," the tallish man with a torpedo-shaped neck and head said as he raised his hand and pointed at a no-smoking sign on the elevator wall, "smoke's so thick you can hardly see the fuckin' no smokin' sign."

In response, 65-year-old Franco Sparta crushed his cigar out beneath his shoe and waived a copy of the *Boston Herald* tabloid in front of his face, chasing away the smoke. "We don't want these fancy Yankee bastards to think we're just a bunch of peasants, Toesy. No smoking means no smoking."

Fifteen minutes earlier, the three men started their walk from the office of Sparta Enterprises in the North End to the downtown glass-encased office building in the city's business district. The trio was made up of Sparta, his bodyguard, Antonio 'No Toes' DeLicata (so-named because he had arrived in the United States thirty-one years ago as a teenager without either big toe), and short, muscular Carmine Zappella, one of Sparta's lieutenants. The use of a conference room at the prestigious law firm had been arranged three days earlier by Massachusetts Superior Court Judge John Devlin, a former partner in the firm.

The elevator doors opened directly onto the firm's reception area. No Toes let out a soft whistle, followed by, "Smells like money, Mister S."

"Danish Modern," Carmine said, drawing a quizzical stare from Franco. "What?" Carmine said, in response to the look.

The slim receptionist wore a charcoal gray suit with a frilly white blouse. She sat at a teakwood desk behind a nameplate that read *Millicent*

Feinstein. Her brown hair tied back into a plump bun, Millicent reached into her well of professionalism and stifled reaction to the odd-looking trio standing at the elevator. The three were of dark complexion, dark hair, and dressed similarly in dark suits and dark shirts, without neckties. They seemed to line up in front of the elevator door by height. What is it they call those things? Millicent wondered. Oh, yes, of course - Russian nesting dolls.

Franco and Carmine walked to the desk. No Toes stayed in the background, moving to the window wall overlooking the city and Boston Harbor. Millicent put on a plastic smile and spoke with a nasal tone. "Good afternoon, gentlemen. For whom are you calling?"

"Judge Jackie Devlin. Tell him Franco Sparta's here," Carmine said.

The staid receptionist typed the names Devlin and Sparta into a computer tucked beneath the desktop, then looked up at a wall clock. "Judge Devlin will see you in the Lodge conference room, directly down the end of the hallway to your right. May I get you gentlemen anything ... coffee, tea?"

"Yeah. Some yogurt, okay?" Franco said. "Raspberry if you got it. Nothing for Carmine or Toes. They had cannolis walking over. Loaded with fat." Franco turned and started down the hallway. "C'mon, Toes, don't want to keep the little judge waiting."

No Toes walked over from the large window and joined Franco and Carmine. He looked back at the reception desk, turned back and whispered with enthusiasm, "That's my kind of broad. Classy. Did you hear her? 'For whom are you callin.' Ain't that great? Like, I was kind of gettin' hard. Glad I stayed over by the window."

Franco shot an incredulous glance at his bodyguard. "Are you shitting us, Toes?"

"No, you know I wouldn't shit you about anything, Mister S. I might ask her if she'll go out with me on a date, maybe for a drink to start with."

"Yeah, do that, Toes. That will make her fuckin' day," Carmine said, as the men continued walking to the end of the hall.

Next to a set of French doors an embossed plate read *In Loving Memory of Ambassador Henry Cabot Lodge*. Carmine led the way into a large room with pale yellow walls. At the northern end, floor-to-ceiling glass provided an expansive view of Boston Harbor with Logan Airport in the distance. By design, the view was as distracting to visitors as it was intriguing. The level to which the curtains were drawn depended on the desired level of the visitor's concentration.

Judge John 'Jackie' Devlin, wearing a pinstriped navy suit, was alone in the room. He sat facing the door at a cherry wood conference table that accommodated up to twelve, the number of partners in his former firm. He was tightening the Windsor knot in his striped tie when the three North Enders arrived.

Franco spoke first, "Jackie, old buddy, nice to see you. What's going down, anyhow? The message didn't say much. Kind of left me in the dark. You know, if it wasn't from you, no way I'd of showed."

"Nice to see you, also, Franco, and Carmine. You too, Toes." The judge stood his five-foot, six-inch frame up from his chair. He reached across the table and shook Franco's hand.

"Like old times, eh, Jackie?" Franco said.

"Yeah, like old times. Sorry I couldn't give you more information in the message. I've arranged this meeting at the request of some other former clients. They asked that I attend, for introductions." The grandfather clock in the corner rang four chimes. The judge shot a nervous look in its direction. "Any minute now, I expect Buzzy Flaherty to arrive. He's very interested in discussing something with you."

"Jackie, you know fucking better!" Franco blurted, slamming his fist on the table. "Maybe you had both the Southie boys and us as clients. That's okay. That was your business. But we never had business with those Irish bastards. We finally got our territories straightened out. But there was a lot of blood spilled in the meantime. We keep our fucking distance now. It's best that way. I think maybe we'll leave, right now."

No Toes turned from the window and started to the French doors. "Ready, Mister S?"

The judge stood. "Franco, wait, please. From what I know it will be in your interest to talk. Something about a horse race, and a lot of money to be made. They just want the opportunity to talk. Make a proposal. That's all. If you're not interested, you walk."

Franco heard "horse race" and recalled a rumor about the Irish mob horning in on that territory, which he considered the exclusive business of Boston's North End and its Florida associates. Still looking at the judge, he spoke to his bodyguard. "Not yet, Toes. Maybe we'll stay awhile." Franco sat at the table.

A soft knock on the door was followed by the appearance of a young woman. She preceded two light-complexioned men wearing windbreakers and khaki trousers. The older and shorter of the two carried a Red Sox baseball cap in his hand. Franco stood up from the conference table. No Toes quickly stepped between him and the two men. "It's okay, Toes." Franco looked at the man with the baseball cap. "Buzzy, how've you been? Long time."

"Just fine, Franco. Just fine. And yourself and family?" Buzzy's smile framed rows of small, even teeth.

"*Bene*, good, thank-you."

"Judge," said Buzzy, nodding his head to acknowledge Devlin who was still standing. He turned back to Franco and Carmine and gestured in the direction of his colleague. "Gentlemen, this is Brendan Sullivan. He has a proposition that I'm sure will interest you. What do you say we all sit for a little Irish yarn."

The young lady who had escorted the men from South Boston, sensing that her presence was no longer necessary and anxious to depart, set a container of vanilla yogurt and a plastic spoon in front of Franco Sparta. "I'm sorry, sir. It's all we could find in the employees' fridge. It's Millicent's, but she said she'd be happy to let you have it and, if you don't want this flavor, she said you could let one of your friends have it."

From his perch by the window, No Toes heard Millicent's name and smiled.

As the group sat, Brendan Sullivan spoke with a light brogue. "Tell me, Mister Sparta, have you ever heard of the great racehorse known as Irish Eagle?"

"Yeah. Sure. What the hell do you think I am, brain dead? He's the greatest horse in Europe. Maybe the world. I hear he's shipping in for the Travers. He can't lose." Franco ripped the cellophane wrapper from a large cigar and No Toes started toward the conference table, a Bic lighter in hand.

"Don't bet on it, Mister Sparta," Sullivan responded. "Irish Eagle will not win at Saratoga. He will not even finish in the money."

Carmine groaned at the far end of the table. "*Marone*! You're gonna tell me you got the greatest colt since Secretariat in the bag?" He looked at his boss. "Mister S, we're wastin' our fuckin' time. These guys are dreaming. Believe me. Fuckin' dreaming."

Buzzy smiled and glanced down the length of the table. "Carmine, let me tell you something maybe even you can understand in that thick guinea skull."

The judge quickly stood and glared at Flaherty. "Watch your damn mouth, Buzzy. It's in everybody's interest to hear this out. Okay?"

Following a few moments of silent cooling, Buzzy spoke again, looking at Franco. "So we can finish this discussion, let's assume we can keep Irish Eagle out of the money in the Travers. If we deal, we leave it to your organization to handle the rest of the field. Who wins, who don't. You have the know-how to control that shit. With Irish Eagle off the board, there'll be huge payoffs. Fortunes for everyone."

"Why the fuck should we trust you to hold the Irish horse? And in the Travers? C'mon," Franco said.

"We figured you'd ask that," Sullivan said. "The answer's easy. We let you control our money. You get it down for us."

Sparta spoke slowly. "You're gonna let us bet your money?" He laughed quietly. "How fucking much?"

Buzzy spoke softly, in a cadenced manner. "An even two million dollars."

Carmine released a soft whistle.

"That's right, Franco, two fuckin' million," Buzzy continued, "and we guarantee Irish Eagle stays out of the money in the Travers. Now the big question. Can your organization guarantee what horses will finish in the money? Win and place will do, but win, place and show is even better, 'cause of all the fancy ways of betting they got now."

Carmine fielded the question. "In an ordinary race, no problem. The Travers? We need a little time. Check out our resources. Maybe a week. We can borrow some talent out of Miami. But there's no sense in even fuckin' askin' about it unless we know we got the Irish horse stiffed. Who'd you get to?"

"There are certain questions I won't answer, can't answer," Buzzy said. "I will tell you that we're dealing with very powerful, dangerous people. They see an opportunity to make a serious score. They need your help. If you choose to come along, you'll make a lot of money. If you choose to sit out," Buzzy shrugged, "who knows what happens?"

Franco brought his cigar to his mouth and took a deep drag, blowing the thick smoke across the table. He pointed at Flaherty and spoke in a calm voice.

"Fuck you Irish pricks. You couldn't fix the last race on the card at the Marshfield Fair, and you won't even get close to touching the Travers, because," Franco raised his voice, "we are not 'coming along'. Don't you ever fucking threaten me. Ever!"

No Toes started over from the window and Brendan Sullivan stood quickly, his chair propelled backwards across the dark wood floor. Suddenly, the diminutive Judge Devlin seemed most imposing of all as he stood, pounding his fist on the table while shouting, "Enough! You've had your meeting. Buzzy and Brendan, go. I will talk to you, Franco, alone."

Later in the day, at about 5:30, Margaret O'Shea's telephone line rang at the Shamrock Club's bar. The bartender handed the phone to Buzzy Flaherty. "Yeah?"

"Buzzy?"

"Yes, it's me, Judge. I've been wondering when you'd call."

"Just listen closely. Sparta will go along, but he has two conditions. First, the two million has to be delivered at least two weeks before the race. Second, Franco has to know how they plan to stiff Irish Eagle, and who's involved."

"I'll talk to Dublin and get back to you."

11

LONDON - ONE WEEK LATER

The kitchen at Mario's in South Kensington was hot and the air was saturated with the aroma of garlic and tomatoes. As usual, on this summer day the kitchen crew and waitstaff shouted to be heard over the sounds of glasses and flatware clinking and clunking, and heavy pans and pots being pitched onto steel tables. On the other side of the swinging kitchen doors, Aidan McGuire sat by himself in the back booth of the private dining area, facing its entrance from the main dining room. He peeled the label off a bottle of ale, dropping the scraps onto the red-checked tablecloth. He was anxious, an unusual condition for him.

"**Sixteen quid?** Shit, what the hell is a quid? Anyway, I don't have any of your English money. How much in dollars?" Carmine Zappella stood beside a taxi in front of Mario's, a roll of American bills in his hand.

"A twenty and a fiver will handle it," the driver responded, having decided against mentioning that the Irishman who hired him at the airport had prepaid the fare, with a generous tip.

Carmine's flight from Boston landed at Heathrow at eight o'clock, London time. After a minor mix-up at Customs, an Irishman hailed him, directed him to the loo, and then to a waiting taxi. The purpose of the trip was clear. He would receive information from two men that would satisfy Franco Sparta that the Irish mob from Southie could actually stiff the great racehorse, Irish Eagle. Sparta's demands were clear. Two people, in person, had to have the right answers to Carmine's questions. If they did, the boys from the North End were in. If not, no deal. Carmine was told that his name for this part of his trip was Peter Antonio. He was to ask for the manager's booth at a restaurant called Mario's, where he would be taken by the taxi.

Drawing a smile and tip of the cap from the taxi driver with two twenties, Carmine stepped across the sidewalk and into a loud and busy Mario's. He barely avoided a white-coated waiter toting a full tray when he followed the pointed finger of the maître d' to the private dining area. Entering through an open archway at the rear of the main room, the Boston mobster spotted the only other person in the room sitting at the back booth. Carmine, a little star-struck by the presence of the handsome face he had often seen in the *Daily Racing Form,* and once or twice interviewed on TV, hesitated, then walked over to the table.

Aidan stood as Carmine approached him. "Hello, Mister Antonio. Welcome to London. A comfortable trip?"

Carmine was silent for a second or two, failing to recognize his cover name provided by the Irishman at Heathrow. Catching on, he said, "Hi, ah, it's you, the trainer, McGuire."

"I think you're right about that. Have a seat. You must be tired after your long flight."

Carmine slid into the bench across the table from Aidan. "Yeah, yeah, but it was a good trip. A little flap at Customs, but it's all right, I think. They're just holding my passport to straighten somethin' out. Any chance for a cold Budweiser?"

"Mister Antonio, I don't mean to be discourteous, but I'm sure you can understand my desire to hurry this meeting along. Although I don't seek to be known to the public, I do have a certain amount of celebrity in Britain. Therefore, this meeting should be as discreet, and as brief, as possible."

"Yeah, sure Mister..." Aidan raised his hand in protest of the use of his name. "Yeah, sure," Carmine continued. "Can we talk here?"

Aidan smiled. "Of course. That's why we're meeting here."

In a low voice, almost a whisper, Carmine asked, "Well, for starters, is this for real? I mean, is the wonder horse in the bag?"

"Yes, it's for real. I can assure you that Irish Eagle will be an also-ran in the Travers. All of the arrangements have been made. There is no possibility that we will fail."

Suddenly, coinciding with the opening of the swinging doors, a tray of antipasto crashed to the kitchen floor. Carmine was startled. Reacting instinctively, his right hand reached under his left armpit, causing him a moment of panic with the realization that there was no holster. When the noise abated, he realized it was only a kitchen mishap. He shook his head, "Sorry, kind of a gut reaction." Carmine returned to the conversation. "I just have to be sure we're all whistlin' the same tune. Know what I mean?"

"Of course, and now, please don't you take offense at my question, Mister Antonio. Can we be sure that your organization will be able to provide the win and place horses?"

"We're ninety-nine percent sure, but we won't be a hundred percent 'til a few days before the race. When there are so many damned people involved, it takes time, but I'm not worried. We'll deliver, maybe even the top three finishers."

"Excellent. That's what I was hoping to hear. One other thing, if I may?" Aidan said.

"Yeah?"

"We won't be in a position to deliver our wagering money until early the week of the race. It's a problem of transporting the cash. I am assuring you, Mister Antonio, the cash is in hand and will be in New York State for your people to receive, and verify the amount, at least three days before the Travers. I hope this is not a problem."

Geez, Carmine thought, as he stared across the table and played with candle wax melted onto the neck of a Chianti bottle, this guy's got all the goods. Looks like a movie star, smooth as silk, nice guy, great with the ponies. He snapped back to the conversation. "Oh, yeah. I mean no. No problem. No problem."

"Excellent, Mister Antonio. Our business is concluded for the time being?"

"Yep, it's concluded. All over. Yep."

Aidan stood and stepped out of the booth. "Will you have time to see London? There are a number of interesting spots."

"Nope. I'm just makin' a U-turn. Headed back to Boston. Midnight flight."

"Well, I hope you have time to try Mario's lasagna. House specialty."

"I'll do that. Got to kill a little time. Nice red sauce?"

"Top-drawer," Aidan assured.

Carmine half stood and accepted the trainer's outstretched hand. To his surprise, Aidan turned to the right and pushed through a swinging door, disappearing into the kitchen. The visitor from Boston's North End sat back down in the booth. Imagine the broads, he thought.

Aidan walked quickly, leaving the restaurant as he had entered - through Mario's kitchen's back door. He stopped to speak a few moments with a man not dressed for restaurant duty, then continued down a hallway crowded with hampers overflowing with soiled restaurant linen, arriving at an open overhead door. Without stopping, Aidan lowered his head and stepped into the rear of a Bright White Linen van backed up to the loading dock. As Aidan pulled down the van's rear door, the young IRA soldier at the wheel spoke to him.

"You can sit on top of one of the hampers. I've covered the dirty stuff with clean tablecloths."

"Thanks." Aidan settled himself onto a soft cloth mound.

"How come so secret?" the teenage driver asked.

"Just the way things are done sometimes," Aidan answered, thinking what a disaster a photo in the *Sun* with an American hoodlum would be. He figured Carmine's passport snafu at Heathrow was orchestrated, along with a cooperative British Air, to be sure there would be no paper or electronic trail of the American gangster's visit to Britain. If "Mr. Antonio" ever had reason to claim he had a meeting in London with Aidan, it would be a hard sell.

Without warning, the van shot out onto Exhibition Road. Aidan tumbled backwards, falling off the hamper. Hearing him thump against the rear door, the driver quickly glanced over his shoulder. "You all right?"

"Yes, at least I think so." Aidan rubbed an elbow that had slammed into the door.

"Sorry. Not used to driving in the city."

Aidan looked up from the metal floor. "Really?"

As Aidan was climbing back onto the hamper, Carmine was being served a bottle of ice cold Budweiser ("reserved for our American guests") and a plate of Mario's famous lasagna. Fifteen minutes later, he wiped the last of the marinara sauce off his plate with a slice of hard-

crusted bread. Criminal if served in Boston's North End, but he graded the red gravy a passable C+. Hard to flunk a meal on the house, which was a pleasant surprise. He glanced at his watch, which read 4:44. Rather than adjust in his head for transatlantic time zones, he hailed a passing waiter carrying a tray loaded with steaming entrees headed for the main dining room. The upset, but polite, food server stopped, put the tray down to access his watch and reported that it was 9:45 in London. Carmine quickly stood from the booth's padded bench and left Mario's.

Carmine waited at the same spot on the sidewalk, now lit by streetlamps, where he had been dropped an hour earlier. As he paid rapt attention to a trio of short-skirted teenagers, part of his thought process picked up someone calling a name that was kind of familiar. Then, shit, that's me, he thought, and turned in the direction of the curbside greeting. "Yeah, I'm Mr. Antonio," Carmine said to the middle-aged man in priestly garb standing next to an open rear door of a taxi.

"I understand you were told you would be hailed by a Mr. Bratton. Actually, it's Father Bratton," Liam Donnelly said in a pleasant voice. "If you'd just come along, Mr. Antonio, you can meet with Mr. McCauley, and we can get you back out to Heathrow in plenty of time for your flight back to Boston."

As the two men settled in the unlit back seat of the taxi, the driver opened the small sliding window in the plexiglass partitioning the front and back seats. His few words sounded like grunts to Carmine. Father Bratton responded with short directions to a nearby address and the taxi left the curbside. Carmine felt strange for some reason in the darkened rear seat. Then it occurred to him - dark, the sliding window, a priest - it was like he was in a rolling confessional booth. He chuckled to himself, then said, "Any chance for a quick confession, Father?"

Donnelly hearkened to the cue. "If your soul is heavy, my son, I will close the little window for privacy and hear your confession. I always have my sacred stole with me, and there is always time for God."

Shit, Carmine thought, he thinks I mean it. The mobster hadn't seen the inside of a confessional box since he graduated from Don Bosco Catholic High School, and he wasn't about to break that string in a goddamn English taxi. "Ah, no thanks, Father. Just kidding. Went just last Saturday at, ah, Arch Street Shrine, and I've been okay, you know, sin-wise, since then. No mortals, anyhow. Planning for the trip and traveling and all."

Donnelly was enjoying his role. He wasn't about to let go so easily. "I noticed your fascination with those teenage girls back on the sidewalk. No impure thoughts to worry about? You know, a single thought of a naked woman can bring eternal damnation to the fires of hell. Remember, you have a long flight ahead. I always make my peace with the Almighty before I fly."

"Ah, thanks, but no thanks," Carmine responded. Then a face-saving thought occurred to him. "Anyhow, I'd have to wait. I just ate supper," he said, confusing his sacraments.

"Your soul, your call," Donnelly said, and moved up to the opening in the plexiglass. "Patrick, next right, then halfway down the block, pull over on the left."

The gangster and the faux priest climbed out of the taxi. With Donnelly leading the way, they walked back along the street a short distance, stopping at a fish and chips shop. The plate glass window read FRIED, ETC. and framed a small counter. The duo walked past a few customers waiting for take-away, turned to their right and skirted a hand-scrawled cardboard sign at the front of a small dining area that read *Table Area Closed*. Sitting by himself at a square, Formica-topped table by the back wall, Eddie McCauley's small muscular torso was barely contained by a white polo shirt. A flat cap was pulled low over his forehead. With a grimace, the jockey looked up as Donnelly took the chair across from him and pointed to a chair for Carmine.

"Nice to see you again, Eddie. Thank you for coming," Donnelly said.

Eddie's hands played with a chrome napkin holder. "Like I had a choice...Father?"

"Let's relax, Eddie. This meeting will only take a few minutes. Mr. Antonio, here, has a few quick questions for you, and then we'll be on our way. Fire away, Mr. Antonio."

Eddie's attitude had affected Carmine. He was ill at ease and stumbled a bit as he started to speak. "I - I'm sorry I got to be here, but, you know, I - I got orders."

"Just get on with it," Donnelly said, then, "Wait a minute." A customer from the take-away area walked past the table, headed for the loo. "Hope he's only going for a slash," Donnelly added.

The men sat is silence a minute or so until the customer walked back past the table and out of the room. Donnelly, concerned at being in a small, dead-ended room, nodded at Carmine. "Okay, now, before someone brings the goddamn *Sun* in with him to take a dump. Let's get this done."

Carmine pulled a piece of folded paper from his pants pocket and placed it on the table. His anxiety had passed. He looked at Eddie. "You look like you're who you're supposed to be, but I gotta be sure. I hear golfers remember every shot they ever hit. I figure jockeys must be like golfers." Donnelly gave Carmine a quizzical look, which hastened him to the point. "You know, they remember every race, at least the big ones." He unfolded the paper, looked at it, then up at Eddie. "Who was your mount in the Railway Stakes at Perth in 1985?"

Without hesitation, Eddie said, "Onatuffet."

"Auckland Cup, 1988?"

"I'm Motivated."

"Any other mounts that day?"

"Rich Widow, in the fifth."

"Ever had a mount in the Golden Slipper Stakes?"

"More than once."

"Where is it run?"

"Rosehill Gardens, Sydney."

"When?"

"The Saturday before Good Friday."

Carmine looked a little puzzled, paused, then said, "Okay, I guess. Your mount this year?"

"License to Kill."

Carmine then asked, "Who are you on in the Travers?"

"Irish Eagle."

"Will he win?"

A brief pause, then, "No."

"How can you say that? He won the Epsom Derby by a dozen lengths."

The jockey cast a sideways glower at Donnelly. "I'm under fucking instructions to lose."

"Will Irish Eagle make the board?"

"He'll finish no better than fourth."

Carmine refolded his paper and slid it back into his pocket. "I'm okay."

Donnelly rose from the table. "Take away a carton of jellied eels, Eddie. Shopkeeper knows his stuff."

Carmine grimaced as he stood. "Eeeyuck! You shittin' me?"

TRAVERS WEEK

12

TUESDAY - OVER THE ATLANTIC

Doc Flynn turned in from the aisle and stepped in front of a cushioned seat. The veterinarian ran a hand through his horseshoe of white hair and reached down to shake Georgie O'Malley's shoulder. "Rise and shine, O'Malley."

Georgie stirred in his chair. The assistant manager of Empire's County Cork farm opened his eyes and saw a row of horse stalls running perpendicular to the front of the aisle. He smelled hay, in both its original and processed stages.

The previous day a ferry transported Irish Eagle from Cork's Ringaskiddy Terminal to the French port of Le Havre. A horse van completed the connection across northern France to Orly Airport. This morning, a flight carrying the Empire Breeders Farm contingent departed French airspace and joined the morning sun in its journey across the Atlantic. The Horse America charter was fitted to carry a dozen head, but the aircraft's stalls carried only Irish Eagle, and his stablemate, a polled Old Irish goat called Charlie, named by Georgie after the Prince of Wales. Georgie had been told that nothing likely to make Irish Eagle comfortable was to be denied. He knew that this was the horse race his boss, Aidan McGuire, wanted more than any other, as though it were some sort of sacred mission. As soon as the silver plane with white trim poked its nose over the Atlantic, the incessant drone of the jet engines had lulled Georgie into a deep slumber. Suddenly, he realized where he was. "Is everything okay with the Eagle?"

Doc sat in the chair across the aisle from Georgie. "I just looked in on him, and he's tip-top. I thought you might like to wake up before we hit landfall. You've been sleeping close to five hours."

Georgie bounded from the chair and up the aisle toward the stalls. He shouted back over his shoulder, "Not that I don't trust you, Doc, but I think I'll take a look myself." Ten minutes later, satisfied that the flight agreed with Irish Eagle, Georgie returned to his seat in the compact passenger area.

"A little breakfast," announced Flynn, a smile on his pudgy face. He held a Jameson's whisky bottle, its neck adorned by a stack of plastic cups. "Sorry about the glassware. All I could manage up here." Doc set the bottle and the cups onto his drop-down tray. "I'll pour," he said, tilting the bottle into one of the cups as the pilot's voice sounded on the speaker.

"Good morning, gentlemen. Welcome to the U.S. of A. We've just passed over the Canadian border and are presently flying over northern New York State. We bucked much less wind than we anticipated and have changed our ETA at Newburgh to 8:15. If you look out the left hand side of the aircraft you'll be able to have a gander at Lake George, a major resort area here in New York."

"The bloke goes on like he had a few hundred passengers sitting back here in the bowels of this flyin' barn, instead of Ike, Mike and their pets," Doc said.

The pilot's voice returned. "We'll be setting this baby down in about fifteen minutes. By the way, you gents may be interested in looking out the right side of the aircraft. Just beyond the city of Saratoga Springs you'll be able to make out its famous racetrack. One of the oldest in America. Y'all have a good day, hear?"

Georgie peered through the small window. He could see the grandstand steeples, the red and white striped awnings, and the dirt oval wrapped around the infield. From the rear of the plane he heard Irish Eagle stirring, whinnying. "The Eagle's awake, Doc," he said, raising his cup toward Flynn. "I think he smells a finish line."

New Windsor, New York

Soon after the 747 was cleared by U.S. Customs at Stewart Airport, a red, white and blue van labeled *Horse America* passed through Stewart's main gate on its way to the New York State Thruway, and the quarantine barn at Saratoga Race Course. The van carried Irish Eagle and his stablemate, Charlie, along with Georgie O'Malley and a Pinkerton guard. Once settled onto the grounds at Saratoga, heavy, 'round the clock security would be in evidence.

Five minutes earlier, Doc Flynn had stepped into a taxi at the airfield terminal. As instructed, he told the driver to take him to the nearby Rip Van Winkle Motor Inn. He had no idea what awaited him.

Back at the Horse America jet, an employee of the U.S. Department of Agriculture strode down the sloped ramp that led from the belly of the plane to the tarmac. In his outstretched hand he held a large, corked glass vial. "Got it," the young man named Danny shouted in the direction of a USDA van parked behind the plane. "Our vet left it in the stall."

When he reached the bottom of the metal ramp, Danny's loafer caught on an elevated hinge connecting the ramp to its metal lip. "Whoa!" he exclaimed and tumbled forward, his right hand flying upward and releasing the vial.

Danny's supervisor, wearing a USDA T-shirt and Bermuda shorts, stood beside the van, glancing with concern at her wristwatch. When she heard his scream, she looked up quickly and watched Danny tumble to the ground. An instant later she saw the vial falling from the sky. It shattered on the cement at her feet, splattering its deep red contents on her bare legs.

"I, I'm sorry, ma'am." Danny limped in the direction of his boss. He whipped a handkerchief from his pocket and bent toward her shins.

"Oh, don't worry about me." She turned in a circle, looking around the field. "Just find the Horse America van. We have to draw another sample from Irish Eagle. But, hurry, we're already late and we have to get the damn blood to LaGuardia for the Fedex flight."

"Horse America's van left with Irish Eagle a while ago, ma'am. Maybe we can catch them on the state highway. They're headed up to Saratoga. Gotta be starting out on Route 9."

The supervisor looked down at the spilled blood, the August sun already baking it into the cement, then at her watch. "Oh, hell. We don't have time to chase them down. They're headed in the opposite direction." She paused, then continued, "Danny, you forget what we're about to do and I'll forget how clumsy you are. There's a pair of Peruvian Pasos shipped in for a show at Madison Square Garden that are still in quarantine here at Stewart. We can take another sample from one of them. Those fancy horses aren't going to have any blood diseases, and Irish Eagle's is certain to be okay. Take one of their blood vials from the van's fridge and remove the old label, then put a label on for Irish Eagle. They'll never know the difference at the lab in Iowa."

Saratoga Springs, New York

Following a two-hour drive up the Mass Pike, Harry Meadows picked up his Boston College classmate at the Albany bus terminal. Their following journey up to Saratoga Springs on the Northway battled a heavy rain, occasionally a downpour, but the weather outside his old yellow Jeep didn't quell Harry's enthusiasm. Five days at the Spa with the gorgeous Stephie was a great way to end the summer and a ready-made launch pad for a senior year romance.

Harry took Exit 14 - Saratoga Race Course. He slowed the Jeep at the bottom of the ramp and turned onto Union Avenue just as the sun returned. Steam rose from the road surface as the Jeep traveled down the broad boulevard, past the racetrack's grandstand and clubhouse on the left and a large complex of white barns and the training track to the right.

"It doesn't look very busy," Stephie observed as she peeled a banana.

"That's because there's no racing on Tuesdays. It's the one day off during the week," Harry said. "It'll give us plenty of time to look around town. Do a little exploring."

Further down Union Avenue, handsome Victorian houses lined the roadway, their windows decked with boxes overflowing with summer flowers.

"Where did you say we're staying?" Stephie asked.

"A bed and breakfast called Cuzins."

"I wonder if the Cypher's in town."

"Must be, Steph. It's August, and this is Saratoga."

New York Northway

"You sure they got a low-fat menu at this Gidjun Putnam place, Carmine?"

"Absolutely, Mister S. I talked to the travel agent guy myself. They get a lot of rich old bastards up here who are health nuts. They come for the waters or some shit like that. You can bet your ass they ain't gonna come all the way here to get healthy and then eat all the shit that's gonna kill 'em. Wouldn't make sense."

"I heard about those bath places. Seeing that I'm on the track's shit list and they'll run me off the grounds if I show my face, maybe while you boys are at the races, I'll take a look-see."

Franco and Carmine were in the back seat of a Lincoln Town Car as it streaked up the wet highway. The Mafia chieftain held a glossy brochure up to his baggy eyes and read slowly. "'Come, visit this serene ambience of old world charm, tasteful accommodations and enough activity to keep you busy in any season.' That's what it says in their handout, Carmine, right here. What's that mean? - serene," Franco struggled with the next word, "...ambiance? It sounds like they have royal fuckin' ambulances or somethin' for the sick people. And," he studied the brochure again, 'activity to keep you busy in any season.' What the fuck's that supposed to mean?"

"Probably means you can get laid any time of year." Carmine watched the passing countryside. "Looks like the rain's lettin' up. Let me see that brochure, Mr. S. Maybe it tells us where to get off this fuckin' highway."

In the front passenger seat, Ricky DePolito, late twenties, bottle-blond and with a Miami tan, spoke without looking up from the *Daily Racing Form*. "I've been up here a thousand times, Carmine. Exit fourteen's for the track. The Put's off thirteen, it's the next exit. It's in the State Park."

"You paying attention, Toes?" Carmine said to the driver. "Next exit. Better get over."

No Toes swung the heavy sedan into the right lane, cutting off a pickup truck and earning a blast of its horn from the woman driver. The bodyguard watched the pickup in the rear view mirror, then noticed the driver. "Pretty woman in that truck."

"I thought you were in love with Millicent, Toesy," Franco teased his bodyguard, trying his luck at a falsetto voice. "You got all excited when you found her number in the phone book. Still don't know how you remembered her fucking name."

"You still callin' every day, Toes?" Carmine asked. "I think they call that stalkin'. Better be careful."

"I think maybe she'd like me," the bodyguard said with childlike sincerity.

"Maybe I should call Millicent - I love that name - and tell her all about you. What do you say, Toesy?" Franco continued his teasing.

No Toes did not respond to the taunt. Carmine noticed his hurt expression in the rear view mirror. "Toesy doesn't think we're funny, Mister S."

Franco shrugged, then said, "I'll tell you what won't be funny, Carmine. It won't be funny if those Irish bastards don't produce the two fucking million. That won't be fucking funny."

No Toes put on the blinker as the Lincoln approached Exit 13 - Saratoga Spa State Park.

13

NEW YORK CITY - TUESDAY EVENING

It was a little after six o'clock. Aidan's view from the window of his corner suite was of Fifth Avenue and the curved entrance into the Plaza Hotel. Beneath the window a row of multi-colored flags hanging from the hotel's portico drooped, motionless in the humid air of the August evening. Summer's attack on the city continued unabated. The megalopolis, imbued with the day's onslaught, began to bleed the heat back into the stifling atmosphere. Across from the hotel, high-wheeled surreys lined up at granite columns marking an entrance to Central Park. The necks of the horses that hauled the carriages through the public preserve were white with lather, their heads bowed. And their day was not over. It was as if they knew the Olsons from Omaha were planning to end their day of touring the Big Apple with a carriage ride.

The speed and relative comfort of the Concorde from Paris to New York was undeniable, but the pressure of the trip that began in Cork, combined with planning for Saturday's Travers Stakes, had taken its toll on Aidan. The interminable cab ride from Kennedy International in a cab with non-functioning air-conditioning was the final ingredient in a recipe for exhaustion.

After a cold shower that partially revived him, he stood naked at the corner windows of the sitting room, a towel draped around his neck. The room was decorated with pale green and white striped wall covering which matched the fabric on the sofa. Two easy chairs and a straight back chair at a writing table completed the furnishings. Aidan sipped from a glass of mineral water. He was feeling a horseman's twinge of sympathy for the hackneys when a muted ring from the portable phone on the writing table interrupted his thoughts.

"McGuire here."

"McGuire here, yourself."

"Hello, Annie. Are you in Boston?" Aidan placed his glass on the coffee table and picked up a package of Marlboros.

"Indeed. I'm at Auntie Clara's. She says to be sure to say hello for her – hello. All right, Aunty? Aidan says hello to you too, and wishes he had time to come to Boston, but his business won't spare him a minute for his own pleasures."

"Did I say all that, now?" Aidan lit a cigarette.

"When did you arrive in New York and how was your trip?"

"About an hour or so ago. The trip was fine, as flights go, but tiring. Can't stretch out in those little tubes. And you?"

"Don't complain to me about the Concorde and your fancy French food and champagne. Try seven hours in coach on a 747. Smelly passengers, a donut and a piece of cheese."

"Sorry I asked. When will you be speaking to our friend about Balmoral?"

"I'm about to go over to a social club for supper. The contact is due in about dinner time."

"Good. I'm planning on a little sleep and then I'll be out for a bit. Should be back by twelve. Call me around then and let me know how it goes."

Aidan placed the phone on the coffee table, picked up the Waterford tumbler, sipped and returned to the window. He watched as a father lifted his son and gingerly placed him in one of the horse-drawn carriages. The man then climbed into the carriage and put his arm around the boy's shoulders. The youngster looked to be about five or six years old. Perhaps his final summer before schooling began. He looked up at his dad. He was excited and happy, loving his tiny space on earth, his little life. A tear ran down Aidan's face.

A sudden crack. Aidan looked at the shattered portion of the Waterford left in his hand. At his feet, shards of sparkling crystal lay in a pool of mineral water, disappearing into the plush carpet.

Boston

"I tell you, Annie, the neighbors won't know what to think. You come visiting, looking pretty as a picture, like a movie star, and us leaving the house all fancy-like in a cab."

"You folks ought to take a taxi every now and then. It can make you feel real special."

Annie, wearing a navy blue pantsuit, sat crunched between Aunt Clara in her Easter outfit and her Boston Red Sox jacket-wearing husband in the back seat of a Yellow Cab. They sped along Gallivan Boulevard in the Dorchester section of the city, headed for the Shamrock Social Club in South Boston. The twenty-minute ride would get the Dooleys and their niece to the club in time for the Tuesday night boiled dinner. A menu standard throughout the city on Thursdays, the Shamrock's manager had guessed, accurately, that the folks he catered to could handle the boiled combination featuring meat and cabbage at least twice a week.

"You know, Annie, we've heard about the Shamrock, but never been there. Isn't that right, Joe?" Clara said to her stoical husband. "It must have quite the reputation if you know about it all the way over in Cork."

"We get a lot of visitors from Boston, Auntie. They all recommend it," Annie lied, having no intention of sharing the real purpose of her visit to the club. "I like to be able to bring you as my guests, for putting me up."

"You're such a sweetheart, Annie. It's a pleasure to have you visiting. It's hard to believe you're still a single woman. What's the matter with those Cork men?"

"Have you a fortnight to listen?"

"Well, you never know," Aunt Clara said, "maybe the right man's right here in Boston."

Giant shamrocks painted on the walls decorated the club's dining room. Men and women, middle-aged to elderly, were seated at an even dozen tables that ran the width of the room, each able to accommodate twelve diners. Annie sat across from Clara and Joe at the end of a table, toward the middle of the crowded room. At six-thirty, she excused herself, saying she needed to use the loo. "If I'm not back, go ahead and start when the meal arrives. I'll catch up."

At the top of a short flight of stairs from the dining room, Annie found the bar. The few middle-aged men nursing their beers and a pair of younger men at a pool table were quick to notice her arrival. All eyes followed her as she walked across the room to the bar.

"You look like you might be a little lost," the short-sleeved bartender suggested and pointed in the direction of the staircase Annie had just climbed. "Dining room's down a flight."

"I think I'm in the right place..."

"Welcome aboard, sweetie," a bar customer interrupted Annie. "What'll you have?"

Shades of the Goose, thought Annie. "You've a member known as Buzzy?" Annie asked the bartender, ignoring the offer of a drink.

"Buzzy? Sure, but he's not here. Haven't seen him since about noon. If he's not in by now, I don't think he'll be back 'till tomorrow."

Annie sat at the end of the bar and dug a few peanuts from a bowl. "I'll wait here. He was due five minutes ago."

"Okay by me, sis. I'm sure the boys won't mind."

Ten minutes later Buzzy arrived at the bar. "Anyone looking for me?" he asked of no one in particular. The bartender nodded toward Annie. Buzzy watched Annie turn in his direction and was momentarily awed by the appearance of the auburn-haired beauty. "I sure hope it's you I'm lookin' for darlin', but my luck's usually not that good."

Without responding, Annie slid off the barstool and walked to a small table. Buzzy smiled at the bartender and followed Annie. He sat across from her.

"Mister Flaherty, I presume."

"Call me Buzzy, okay? Drink?"

"No to both, Mister Flaherty. You've a message for me that I expected fifteen minutes ago. I found it necessary to go back to the dining room and then leave again, telling the people I'm with that I had the trots from your damn water, and would be in the ladies room indefinitely. You have jeopardized this part of the operation. I am not amused. What is the message?"

Ten minutes later Buzzy was back at the bar, palming a double whiskey. He was contemplating the gorgeous woman who had just embedded a fear in him he'd seldom experienced.

"You okay, Buzzy?" the bartender asked. "You're lookin' a little, like, sick, or something."

"Yeah, yeah, sure. I'm fine. Just fine."

New York City

The cab's trip meter read $11.60. Aidan handed a twenty-dollar bill to the driver who snatched it and spoke as he slid the money into his shirt pocket. "It's about half-way down the block, next to the coffee shop. You can see the giant coffee cup and donut hangin' out over the sidewalk. You want any change?"

"Keep it. Thanks." Aidan stepped out of the cab. At seven-thirty on the dot, cream-colored sport coat slung over his shoulder, he walked into the cooled air of the Third Avenue Christian Science Reading Room.

An elderly woman sat at a desk just inside the door. To her right, a variety of chairs and three round tables with reading lamps hosted only one patron, a magazine open on his lap, his eyes closed. When Aidan announced his business, the receptionist smiled knowingly and directed him to a door to the right of her desk. Aidan donned his sport coat and opened the door into a rectangular room.

Bookcases filled with hard-covered volumes lined the four walls surrounding an oval table. On the opposite side of the table from the door, a white-haired man in a black pin-striped suit sat reading a newspaper. He didn't hear Aidan enter the room, as his ears were covered with padded earphones wired to a tape recorder clipped to his belt. The recorder was delivering a Haydn oratorio, "The Seasons." Aidan pulled out a chair and stood behind it, across from William Upton.

Aidan's presence surprised the man, a syndicated columnist who often thought he would have preferred a podium and baton to his typewriter. He looked across the table with a start. "Oh, hello. Sorry, I didn't know you had arrived. I'm William Upton."

Aidan accepted the liver-spotted hand offered by Upton, who remained seated, and introduced himself. "Aidan McGuire, an honor to meet you, Mister Upton."

"What?" the slim Upton asked as he removed his earphones and pushed the newspaper aside.

"I said I'm Aidan McGuire and it's an honor to ..."

Upton raised a hand. "Stop, please. A lot of folks would disagree with you. A few ex-wives for starters. Sit down. Sit down. So, you're over from Ireland for the big race at Saratoga?"

"Yes, sir. I'll be going up to the racetrack in the morning." Aidan looked around the room. "This is an interesting place to meet, Mister Upton. Are you one?"

"One what?"

"A Christian Scientist?"

"Oh, hell no. Give me an aspirin any day. But my sister is - she's the blue-haired gal out front - and their little room here makes for a convenient place for meeting with people who don't want to be seen talking to a newspaper columnist." Upton reached to his midsection and fiddled for a minute, ending the stream of raspy music sounding from the earphones, now draped over his suit coat lapels, then said, "Mr. McGuire, when you called me a while back to ask if my typewriter was available to further the prospect of peace in Northern Ireland, my answer was an easy yes, because it was an easy question. Now, as you requested, I am pleased to sit down and talk to you in person, but you haven't come into this pizza oven of a city just to socialize with an old man. Tell me, why would a famous racehorse trainer want to talk to me in private? You wouldn't have a hot tip for me, by any chance?"

"There'll be no advice along those lines, sir," Aidan said with a smile, put at ease by Upton's informal manner. "My wanting to meet with you has nothing to do with horses."

"I'm all ears."

"I've read your columns in the international press with great interest, Mister Upton, particularly those that deal with what is often referred to in Ireland as the Troubles."

"And it's also the British Troubles," Upton interrupted. "In fact, terrorism is a problem for all freedom-loving people on this earth. Free societies will surely disappear unless we cage that monster. That will only be accomplished through political intercourse. Negotiating from behind the barrel of a gun is a waste of time and effort, and costs too many lives."

"To be sure," Aidan agreed. "Many seem to have the right words to describe the atrocities, but you, sir, can also understand the pain the participants are inflicting on themselves, both in the North and the Republic. I have seen what terrorism has done to my country's soul, to its spirit. It is devastating, Mister Upton, as you have so clearly written."

"It's nice to know that at least someone appreciates an old man's words. Maybe I'll keep typing."

"Mister Upton, over the years my family has lost four immediate members to British bullets, one just five years old. To some in my family, even my dear younger sister, retribution is the obvious answer, and the IRA is the obvious vehicle for that revenge. I'll admit to considering it, but know there must be another answer. This war consumes my family and countless others. It must stop, Mr. Upton."

"All wars must stop. I'm willing to go one at a time. Any suggestions?"

"Yes, and that's why I've asked to meet with you, sir. Within a few months, I hope to be in a position to start providing first-hand information regarding activities and, perhaps more importantly, the real goals of those involved in the conflict. I'm expecting there will be enough verifiable information for a journalist of your standing to use, and that it will help you to put some persuasive pressure on those who can make a difference. Perhaps I'm overly optimistic, but I know I have to do what I can."

"Let me see if I've got this right, Mister McGuire. You work for the Brits, don't you, at this Empire horse farm thing?"

"Yes, sir. Empire Breeders it's called. It's a private enterprise, but British to be sure."

"Does it have you sharing steak and kidney pie with important types in England?"

"Very important types, sir."

"And you have, shall we say, connections to the IRA?"

"Yes."

"How high up?"

"Very high up, sir."

Upton looked at Aidan, eyebrows raised. "You have their trust? You can get into their heads?"

"I think yes, to both questions. If not now, hopefully soon."

"Obviously, Mr. McGuire, you know you're dealing with very volatile and dangerous people, in both camps. I hope you're one hell of a tightrope walker."

Aidan nodded and said, "Understood, Mr. Upton."

"My columns are fueled by human misery. It is difficult to sit at my old Underwood knowing that so many attitudes seem impossible to change, but there is always hope. You have given me a measure of that today. I thank you for it. Perhaps this Anglo-Irish opera will finally find a role for a tenor. There have been far too many basses." The journalist reached into a pocket and withdrew a business card. He pushed it across the table. "My private phone number is scribbled on the back of the card. And, Mister McGuire, please don't dawdle. I won't last forever."

As Aidan stood from the table, Upton pulled a package of Lucky Strikes from his suit coat pocket and shook a cigarette free. He smiled as he held up the smoke. "Don't tell the old blue-hair on the way out. Okay?"

Shortly before eight o'clock, Aidan walked out of the Reading Room into an evening that had finally shed a good measure of the day's heat. He was upbeat, thrilled with the response from the famed journalist to his proposal. He now had a true ally in place.

Establishing a reason to justify his stopover in New York City, Aidan had suggested to Empire Breeders that, as a public relations gesture, he dine with the chief resident of the British Consulate General on his way to Saratoga. Dinner had been shelved in favor of informal drinks and snacks, and scheduled for nine o'clock at the Plaza's Oak Room. He hailed a cab to return to the hotel.

After a brief visit to his suite, Aidan stopped by the front desk, was told there were no messages, and crossed the lobby to the Oak Room. As he walked into the popular bistro, Consul General Noel Colchester spotted and hailed him from a nearby table. Turning in the direction of the greeting, Aidan recognized Noel, whom he'd once met at the HiHo club, but had no inclination who the two women with him at the table were. One, thirtyish, blond and very attractive. The other, the half century vintage of Colchester.

With a boisterous greeting, Colchester met Aidan halfway between the table and Oak Room entrance. Arm around Aidan's shoulder, he led him back to the table. "Aidan McGuire, please say hello to my lovely wife, Judy, and Barbara Sweeney, over from London on a trade mission. When Babs got wind of our meeting the famous horse trainer for drinks, she begged and pleaded. It worked." Colchester smiled at the blond beauty. "We were happy to bring her along. Right, Judes?" he said, turning to his wife, who maintained a fixed smile on her face.

Ninety minutes later the foursome stood in the hotel's marble lobby. "Babs, you can share our cab and then take it the rest of the way to the Marriot. The ride's on the Consulate," Colchester said, then, looking at the blonde's twisted smile, got the hint. "Now that I think of it," he continued, "your hotel's on the other side of town. You just let me know the cost of your cab, and we'll reimburse."

Following goodbyes, the Colchesters turned to walk to the entrance and the line of yellow cabs queuing in front of the hotel. Aidan, left standing alone with the blond, smiled and nodded another goodbye. He started toward the elevator bank when she stopped him cold. "Gerry Appleyard asked me to make contact, Aidan."

"Whoa." Aidan turned back to Barbara. "And you are exactly... who?"

Barbara smiled her row of perfect teeth. "Domestic counter-intelligence. You know, MI5. We come in all shapes and sizes."

Isolated from others by the expanse and bustle of the lobby, Aidan asked, "And, the message?"

"There is solid information that the IRA has placed an order for a very substantial arms purchase."

"That is interesting. Anything else?"

"Just that I'm available for any messages you need to have delivered." Barbara smiled as she handed Aidan her business card. "I'm also available for most any other request - starting tonight."

"Very tempting, Babs, but I have a long week ahead, and really need my time and energy elsewhere." He paused just a second, then returned the smile and held up her business card. "Does this number work in London?"

"Indeed it does."

Just after midnight Aidan answered the phone in the sitting room of his Plaza suite. He heard his sister Annie's voice. "Hello, Aidan."

"Yes. Hi, Annie. What have you learned from our friends in Boston?"

"You're alone, and this phone is secure enough to talk?" Annie asked.

"Yes, to both." Aidan stood and walked to a window.

"We're on," Annie said. "Everything appears to be in place.

What's required on our end is to have Irish Eagle start the race and finish no better than fourth. Of course, we have to deliver the Army's cash to be wagered. Flaherty's Italian associates will handle the betting arrangements. I don't know where you have the money, Aidan, but Flaherty says a limousine will hail you tomorrow morning, about seven, at your hotel. The limo and the driver will be at your disposal. Once you have the money, Flaherty says you just hand it over to the driver. He'll count it in front of you and state the amount and an identification code on a cassette recorder. Then he'll give you the cassette. That's your receipt." Annie stopped and drew a deep breath.

"Sounds simple enough," Aidan said, "well planned. What's Flaherty like?"

"A punk. I told him in no uncertain terms what he could expect if he plays his part anything short of perfect. He's got the fear in him."

"I'll be surprised if he's a problem."

"This is a huge operation, Aidan. They're counting on us big time."

"Don't worry, Annie. We've got this nailed down on our end. The cash came over on the charter flight with Irish Eagle. It's sitting in sacks of Erin Cove oats right now, on the ground at Stewart Air Field, about an hour north of here by auto. We've made arrangements for the money to be taken off Stewart. Now, with the Italian's vehicle and driver arranged, the last piece of the delivery puzzle is in place. There'll be no cock-ups. I'll see you in Saratoga tomorrow, as planned."

"If you won't be needing me, I think I'll stay around Boston until tomorrow night. I can get a flight to Albany that arrives at nine. I'm told there's always a shuttle bus or limousine from there to Saratoga Springs."

"You don't change plans over nothing, Annie. What's up?"

"It's hard to describe. I think it might be known as a date. A fellow I got plunked next to at dinner this evening, actually. He'd like to take me to lunch, show me around Boston tomorrow. I think I'll take him up on it."

"Well, whenever you get to Saratoga, go to the Holiday Inn in the city center. Your room will be waiting for you. Ring me when you arrive. Have fun, Annie, but be careful. The U.S. can be a dangerous country."

14

NEW WINDSOR, NEW YORK - WEDNESDAY, 2:30 A.M.

Outside a one room, shingled cabin housing the U.S. Customs office at Stewart Airfield, a red Dodge pickup, *Dutchess County Farm Supply* stenciled on its doors, sat with its motor running. The hum from the idling truck mingled with an army of trilling crickets infiltrating the surrounding high-grass fields. Hank, the strapping nineteen-year-old behind the wheel, was illuminated by the interior light. He was engrossed in an issue of *Hustler Magazine*, studying the specialties of Far Eastern prostitutes. A San Jose Sharks cap, its peak to the rear, sat atop his straggly head of dirty blonde hair.

Ten feet off the road, separated by a stretch of burnt lawn, a high, chain link fence topped with curly razor wire ran to the left and right of the cabin, into the night. At twenty yard intervals, attached red, white and blue signs read: U.S. CUSTOMS SERVICE - NO ENTRY!

Doc Flynn stood in front of a gray metal desk just inside the cabin's screen door. His usually pinkish face was crimson. He glared at the uniformed customs agent who sat behind the desk. A variety of government forms covered the desktop.

"Look here, now," Flynn addressed the civil servant, "I have direct orders to deliver these oats to the driver of that lorry sitting outside the door. Irish Eagle is at Saratoga Race Course, and his damn food is here! All the papers from your agricultural department are in order to import these oats. We're not dealing with a draught horse here. This is the greatest thoroughbred in the damn world!" The Irish veterinarian leaned into the desk. In concert with the beat of his right fist on the desk edge, he concluded: "This delivery cannot be delayed!"

U.S. Customs Officer David George Jones stared back at the portly intrusion on his graveyard shift. "Listen up good, Quinn..."

"Flynn."

"Flynn, Quinn, whatever. Anyhow, I ain't just fell off no turnip truck. I know your nag's probably the biggest deal to ever ship into Stewart. I'm aimin' to be at the track on Saturday myself. Gonna wheel that Irish sucker in the trifecta. Now, I know everything's supposed to go like clockwork in this world, but fact of the matter is that it don't. I'd sure like to help you out, but those sacks are considered sealed containers, and you want to move them onto U.S. territory. Agriculture's not the only problem. DEA would have my ass if I let them sacks off the grounds before they were opened up or, at least, sniffed by the dog squad, and those boys won't be 'round 'til mornin'. We got this war on drugs goin' on here in the U.S., you know? Real serious business 'round these parts."

"Drug war? DEA? What in God's name are you talking about?"

Jones opened the desk drawer and withdrew a thin tube of beef jerky, slid it from its cellophane wrapper and gnawed off an end. The activity roused the interest of the floppy-eared hound splayed out beneath the nearby window. It raised its head from the floor in hopeful inquiry. Jones ignored the Bassett. Then, emphasizing each word, the customs agent responded to Flynn, "Drug Enforcement Agency."

Flynn was on the verge of panic. His mind raced. Everything was supposedly taken care of with Customs. He'd been told to simply check in at the cabin. Now this moron was running his own extortion game.

"Also," Jones continued as he reached back into the drawer and found a toothpick among the pens and pencils, "I'm more 'n a little curious as to why you and this dude with the pickup show up at two-thirty in the mornin' just for some bags of oats. Seems real strange to me. Got me wonderin' what the fuck's in those sacks."

Flynn's brogue became more pronounced as his ire increased. "Tis 2:30 to you, officer. But it's 6:30 in the morn' by my clock. And let me assure you, the only drugs I'm familiar with get shot into lame horses!"

"Oh, yeah, that's right, time zones. Forgot 'bout that," Jones responded. "Well, I'm real sorry I can't seem to help you out. But regulations are put there for a reason." The skinny customs agent paused for a few seconds, looked straight into Flynn's eyes, then continued, "Usually can't be overlooked, you know."

Jones maintained eye contact with Flynn, who was now wiping perspiration from his forehead with a wrinkled handkerchief. Suddenly, Jones pushed the drawer closed, got up from his chair and walked around the desk. As he fed the remainder of the Slim Jim into his mouth with one hand, his other palmed and jiggled a large ring of keys hanging from a belt loop. "What do you say we get a little air, my Irish friend. Stuffy as all hell in this damn shack." Jones walked around the veterinarian. "Make sure the screen door shuts behind you. Mosquitoes big as bees 'round these parts." He then commanded, "C'mon Moonshine." The Bassett ignored Jones, moving neither an eyelid nor an inch.

Flynn winced at the stench of garlic carried on Jones' breath, then followed him out of the cabin and to the parking area. The agent continued a few yards in the direction of the pickup, then suddenly stopped and turned back in the direction of the cabin. The veterinarian and the Customs agent faced each other, standing just beyond a circle of pallid light thrown by a street lamp. Jones picked at his teeth.

"Don't know 'bout Ireland, but here in the U.S., government personnel aren't exactly overpaid. Makes it real tough, cost of livin' 'n all. Pick up an occasional side job, but it's still a tough go. Just got my property tax bill. 'Bout a thousand dollars."

Flynn stood with his hands in his pockets. As he digested the solicitation, he felt with his left hand for the thick wad of bills he carried. He knew that the outer layer, to at least ten deep, was made up of hundreds. His stubby fingers quickly counted off ten bills which he took from his pocket, along with a coin, which he dropped at his feet. Grunting, the veterinarian stooped over to pick up the coin. While down at his shoe tops, he placed the bills on the ground in front of Jones.

"If only that gate would be unlocked for about thirty minutes," Flynn whispered, "it would be a thousand blessings, to be sure."

Jones glanced at the ground in front of him. In the moonlight, he recognized Ben Franklin on the top bill. He bent over and slapped his lower left leg. "Damn mosquitoes!" Halfway back up to a standing position, bills in hand, he mumbled, "Twenty minutes. That's all, and no lights. I been told you already got a key." Smiling, Jones stood the rest of the way up and put his hands in his pockets. "I sure hope the luck of the Irish holds up on Saturday."

As soon as the customs agent slid the tall silver fence gate across the paved driveway, the red pickup entered the moonlit compound. Doc Flynn directed Hank to a large quonset style warehouse a quarter of a mile down the unlit roadway. With the exception of a single low wattage bulb over the side door, the building was dark. A sign over the door read SEALED AREA - NO ADMITTANCE.

"There's a loading dock on the other side of the building. I'll meet you there. Remember, no lights," Flynn instructed the driver. He grabbed a flashlight from the front seat as he slipped out of the truck. "Two minutes."

Flynn's key stuck when he tried to insert it in the sleeve of the lock securing the side door. He cursed the poorly made duplicate and glanced at the overhead light. Sweat beaded on his forehead. Although there was no one to be seen in the field around the storage building, the veterinarian felt as if he were on stage. Finally, the key slid in and turned. He pushed the metal door open, stepped into the gloom of the building and closed the door.

A small amount of moonlight made its way into the warehouse through a bank of high windows. The wide aisles were clear, various-sized crates lined up on either side. With his flashlight beam leading the way, Flynn traveled silently down and across the building. He reached the loading area and directed the beam of light to the backside of an overhead door. Easing the handle clockwise, he unlocked the door, and then pushed it upwards, pausing with each screech of metal wheels on runners.

When the door was raised, Flynn saw that the pickup was backed up to the loading platform, motor still running. Hank sat on the edge of the cement dock, legs dangling, cigarette in hand.

"Jaysus!" Flynn whispered angrily, "Just what in hell are you doing, you imbecile! Get off the damn platform and kill the motor and fag."

Hank turned toward Doc Flynn, a blank stare on his face. "I'm just doin' what I'm told. You didn't say nothin' 'bout bein' quiet. Just told me to come over here, and here I am. What's this shit 'bout a fag?"

"The damn cigarette!"

Hank dropped from the dock to the ground, flicked the cigarette away and sauntered to the front of the pickup to turn off the motor. In a little over ten minutes, green-stenciled burlap sacks were tucked into the bed of the truck and tied down under a plastic tarpaulin. Twenty minutes after entering the sealed compound, the pickup carrying two men and twenty-five sacks marked ERIN COVE OATS raced through the open gate on its way to state highway 9W.

The pickup returned to a dark Rip Van Winkle Motor Inn at three -thirty in the morning. The single-story motel was separated from the highway by a narrow shoulder of grass and a cracked cement parking area fronting on the sixteen units. Appropriately, the "Rip" spent most of the time snoozing like its namesake nowadays, its heyday rendered obsolete by the high speed Northway.

Hank plunked down on the end of the bed and Flynn approached him with ten fifty-dollar bills in his hand. He held them out to his helper who stared at the bills for a moment, then took them. There was a complacent smile on his narrow face. "Why's it I don't think we've been so damn secret just for a few bags of crummy oats?"

"You're not being paid to think, ah ..." Flynn hesitated. He had meant to address his young helper by name, but realized he had no idea what it was. "In any event, you've been paid handsomely for a few hours effort. Now, be on your way."

"State police barracks just down the highway, 'bout a mile. Passed 'em comin' up here, 'member?" Hank paused, then shook his head knowingly at Flynn. "No way you'd get those sacks outta here yourself. They're heavy suckers, and you're old and fat. I could just call 911. Course, you probably don't give a damn. Just sleepin' with sacks of oats ain't against any law I know 'bout."

Flynn remained silent and attentive, arms folded, leaning against the wall across from the foot of the bed. Hank continued. "Suppose I could tell 'em you made a move on me. Offered to pay me for a little action.

Don't think that ain't happened to me before. Seems bald fatties like you go for guys like me." A toothpick appeared in Hank's hand. He stuck it in his mouth, rolled it with his tongue. "'Gainst the law, you know."

Flynn suspected the driver was bluffing and was tempted to call him on it. But the mention of the state police unnerved him. The complications could be enormous. The veterinarian knew the price he would pay if the IRA's cash was not delivered as ordered. He stared back at the young man, hiding the contempt he felt, wondering what to do with him. To this point, even with a few problems, Flynn was where he was supposed to be, and he had the cash.

Flynn's instructions were to clear customs at Stewart Airfield, report to room 7 at the Rip Van Winkle Motel, and wait for further orders. The motel manager had delivered a sealed Federal Express box in midafternoon. It contained American fifty and one-hundred dollar bills that totaled three thousand dollars, a loaded .44 Smith & Wesson magnum revolver fitted with a silencer, a key taped to a diagram of the interior of the warehouse at Stewart Field, and typed instructions.

A pickup would be at the motel at two in the morning. The driver would return him to the airfield and help collect the green-stenciled sacks of oats that had been moved from the Horse America plane to the sealed warehouse. The agent on duty at the Custom's cabin would leave the main gate to the field unlocked and be busy elsewhere between 2:00 and 4:00 a.m. Doc was to come back to the motel room with the sacks, pay the pickup truck driver $500 and wait until contacted. In the meantime, he was to protect the burlap sacks at any cost.

Two problems had gotten in the way. The customs officer got greedy, and this cretin with yellow hair had also decided to shake him down.

"You know, my friend ..."

"Name's Hank."

"Hank," Flynn continued without missing a beat, "I don't have the vaguest idea what's in these sacks, save some of Ireland's famous oats - best in the world, you know. Something to do with the limestone, I'm told. But you're right, Hank. I don't think we're too anxious to have the state police poking into these sacks. Not any of their business, really. You've done an outstanding job, young man. What would you say to a doubling of your fee for the night's work? We'll make it an even thousand

and forget that you ever mentioned the state police. Sound fair, does it?"

"An extra thou would sound fairer."

Flynn expected that Hank would gladly accept a doubling of the agreed fee and this problem would be resolved. Now, he quickly concluded, he couldn't trust him.

"Ah! You Americans. All born hagglers." Flynn paused, feigning contemplation. "Okay, it's a deal. Fifteen hundred." He looked directly at Hank. A lecherous grin appeared. "But there's one more little favor I'd like. Guess I'm not too different from the other fat old guys. You're a handsome young guy, Hank. It's been a hot day for you, a lot of heavy lifting. A shower would feel real good, wouldn't it? That's all. I just like to watch muscular young men in the shower."

"Goddamn!" Hank slapped his thigh and stood from the bed. "I figured you right." He chuckled. "Kinda grimy anyhow. Okay, an extra thou to take a shower and let you watch. Nothin' else. Right?"

"That's right. But you've got to soap up real good. I like that. Lots of shiny soap."

Hank pulled his T-shirt over his head as he walked around the bed to the bathroom. "Be all set in a minute, pal."

"All right, Hank. I'll get you the extra thou." Flynn went to his suitcase that lay open on a metal rack by the door and reached under his clothing. He turned toward the back of the room. Light through the open bathroom door shone onto the wall. Walking back by the bed, he heard the familiar sound of a stream of urine rushing into a toilet bowl.

Hank, a goofy grin on his face, turned to Flynn who stood a few feet from the doorway. "Want to watch me piss? No extra charge."

Flynn raised his arm. The bullet left the silenced barrel of the revolver five feet away from Hank. It entered his lower forehead on a slight upward path, just above the bridge of his nose. Hank experienced a split second of hot, excruciating pain before everything stopped. Bits of Hank's brain tissue and skull spit against the bathroom wall. Doc Flynn knew the single shot was fatal. As Hank's body fell backwards and into the metal shower stall, his urine splashed across the mirror over the washbasin.

Cursing his pot belly, Flynn reached down and managed to tuck Hank's long legs inside the lip of the rusting shower enclosure. He pulled the stained vinyl curtain across his handiwork, shut off the bathroom light, closed the door, and pushed the revolver into the waistband of his slacks. It had been years since he'd been called upon to kill for the Cause - the last a tout that he stabbed repeatedly with a carpenter's awl and carved up with a switchblade in the loo at a Welsh pub. There were no pangs of conscience then, or now.

The veterinarian left room 7, locking the door behind him. He walked diagonally across the parking area to a poorly lit phone booth. Glancing at his instruction sheet, he dropped coins into the slot and poked a phone number onto the keypad. While waiting for the connection, Flynn looked down the row of parking spaces in front of the units. He was relieved to see that the only room with a car at its door was on the far end and was dark. He was comfortable that the thud of Hank's body falling into the shower stall hadn't been heard by anyone. Even if it had, he figured here in the States it was unlikely that anyone would have inquired.

After a short phone conversation, Flynn fished more coins from his pocket and fed them into the phone box for a brief second call. He then returned to the room. He left the door unlocked, pushed some clothes around in his suitcase and found his bottle of Jameson's and a plastic cup. With the lights off, he opened the frayed drapes and sat in the faux leather arm chair by the window, watching the lights of an occasional truck speed over the highway. Sipping the whiskey, he palmed his smooth head and looked down at his sizable stomach. Nothing I can do about the hair, he thought, but time to watch the calories. The thought of fitting the profile of Hank's standard pervert bothered him.

Doc was on his third tumbler of Jameson's when the Nynex Telephone van pulled up next to Hank's pickup. Two, twenty-something men wearing tight T-shirts and jeans came into the room without knocking. The first carried a gym bag in one hand, a flashlight in the other. The second carried a large canvas bag. Flynn stayed at the window. He chose not to watch the disposal team at work, observing only as the men walked in and out of the room. In under fifteen minutes they were gone into the waning darkness of early morning, one driving the telephone van, the other Hank's red pickup. Not a word had been spoken.

Light coming through the window permitted Flynn to see the results of his visitors' assignment. The space where the oat sacks had been piled was empty. Neatly placed on the bed were five plastic bags, wrapped tightly around their contents. Flynn confidently guessed they contained stacks of American currency. He walked over to the bathroom and snapped on the light. He was stunned by its cleanliness. Hank, his clothes, his brain and his piss had all vanished.

The veterinarian returned to the chair by the front window to wait until someone called or arrived. He was tired. It was five o'clock in the morning. He closed his eyes, but did not sleep, nor did he know what he was waiting for. It started to pour.

By mid-morning the puddles in the motel parking area had evaporated. Tall and skinny Elmo Pratt, the owner of the Rip Van Winkle with the Mrs., turned the office air conditioner knob to the coldest setting. He looked through the upper half of the window, but didn't know what to make of what he saw. Scratching his Adam's apple, Elmo called to his wife of fifty-one years as she stirred lemonade in the adjoining kitchenette.

"Leona, come take a gander at this."

"Wait just a minute or I'll spill the damn lemonade. Not as young as I was yesterday, you know." The waspish old woman had never forgiven Elmo for being ten years her junior. She joined her husband at the window. The motel owners watched intently as a muscular man in a white short-sleeve shirt and black slacks walked back and forth from room seven. He carried packed green trash bags from the motel and placed them in the trunk of a stretch limousine.

"That bald Irishman, or whatever the hell he is, sure has a hankerin' for different types of vehicles. He arrived in a yellow cab, comes back again in a red pickup, and now here's a white stretch job. Wonder what in hell he's up to, anyhow," Elmo said.

The couple stayed glued to the window and watched as the man in the white shirt made his final trip, slammed the trunk closed and climbed in behind the steering wheel. A moment later the Irishman came out of the room carrying a suitcase. A handsome younger man was with him. The Irishman placed his bag on the front passenger seat and joined his younger companion in the rear section of the limo.

"Wonder what in hell ... " Elmo's voice trailed off in uncertainty as he watched the limo drive out of the Rip's parking lot and turn into the northerly lane of the state highway.

"Told ya," Leona smiled in anticipation of a rare burst of humor. "You never should of got new towels. Stole every damn one of 'em, I betcha'."

Aw, shut up, Elmo mused as his wife chortled. They're your towels, too, you old frump.

At eleven o'clock the long Cadillac took the on-ramp to the multi-lane Northway on the easterly border of Catskill Park. Their legs stretched out, feet resting on the facing seat, Aidan and Doc leaned back into the comfort of the soft leather, fighting the inclination to nod off. Doc had not had any restful sleep since leaving Ireland two days before. A stream of cool air being fed into the rear compartment made it easy for the occupants to forget about the heat wave that sucked life from the conifers lining the roadway. Doc assumed the limo driver was a low-grade hoodlum. He spoke in a hushed voice.

"Do you think it's a wise thing to have this big boat of a car drivin' us right up to the hotel, now, Aidan? Seems that it might raise an eyebrow or two."

"I've been to Saratoga in August before, Doc. Limousines don't create a commotion. There'll be plenty of big spenders in town. They don't usually drive around in Hillmans. Besides, it does have a certain degree of comfort to it. I've been told that the car and driver are at our disposal for the day. I see no good reason not to take advantage of our Italian friends' generosity."

"I'll not quarrel with you, Aidan. It's been a long forty-eight hours. I'm happy not to have to climb onto a coach packed with sweaty strangers and squealing kiddos."

Flynn opened his eyes, leaned forward and took a bottle of beer from the fridge tucked under the padded top of the console. He offered the bottle to Aidan, twisting the cap off.

"No thanks, Doc. You go ahead and get some shut-eye when you've finished your brew. I'll keep an eye on our driver."

A minute later, Aidan reconsidered, reaching into the fridge for his own drink. By the time he had his beer opened and raised to his lips, he could hear the veterinarian's steady, deep breathing. Doc's eyes were closed, the beer bottle balanced precariously on his lap.

15

SARATOGA RACE COURSE - EARLY THURSDAY MORNING

The Saratoga backstretch stirred to life before sunrise. Trainers, grooms, exercise riders, hot-walkers, security officers and canteen workers were wide awake and busy by 4:30. Hidden from most racing fans, the efforts of the early risers meant that a hundred or so racehorses would breeze a few furlongs on the main track or training track throughout the early morning. The workouts, scheduled to conclude at about ten each morning, gave horses entered in races later in the week an opportunity to stretch their muscles and acclimate to the track surface.

At nine-thirty on most race day mornings, the grandstand was dotted with a few hundred tourists and some of the more serious gamblers at the Spa. The tourists were attracted by the grandeur of the 'sport of kings' and the track's buffet breakfast. The gamblers, ever hopeful for an edge, came with binoculars and stopwatches, anxious to analyze the workouts of the week's entries. But this Thursday was unusual. The grandstand welcomed thousands, not hundreds. Word had spread quickly throughout the Spa that the wonder horse from Ireland was scheduled to work this morning in anticipation of Saturday's Travers Stakes. This would be an opportunity for a close-up look at Irish Eagle.

Knots of onlookers, many of them trainers, owners and their assorted guests, hugged the track's outer rail, brightened with a fresh coat of white paint for Travers week. The owners were convinced that they finally had the right horse entered in the right race with the right company. Even though some cagey old trainers may have known better, they realized they made their living dealing in hope.

"Yes, sir, he's got the stamina to close on that bunch. We'll rate him for the first half mile, then let him have his legs. Make the move about the top of the stretch. We'll be okay." Then an escape hatch "as long as we get some racing room," or, "if he jumps out of the gate okay, little concerned about that four hole ..."

When race day finally arrived, owners and their entourage would be sure to wear the right outfit. A photograph in the Saratoga Winner's Circle was sure to be displayed on the piano for years to come, obvious at every cocktail party.

"So, tell me, Little Sister, how was your date in Boston? A half-decent bloke?" Aidan leaned against the rail. He and Annie were alone, across the track from the green and white striped eighth pole that marked the start of the final furlong to the finish line.

"He was good company. No obvious warts. Worth another look if I ever get back to Boston, or can convince him to do a little traveling."

"Unless he's blind or dense, he's already packed his bags."

The light thunder of a galloping thoroughbred drew Aidan's attention. With a rolled-up track program he gestured at a chestnut colt starting down the homestretch. "Here comes the competition - Khando. Placed in the Kentucky Derby, won the Preakness easily, and they kept him out of the Belmont in June. Said he had a cold, but word is he can't handle a distance of ground."

"Could he be the likely winner?" Annie asked.

Aidan paused a moment before answering his sister. "I suppose he has a decent chance. It pains me, Annie, to even think of any horse other than Irish Eagle in that winner's circle on Saturday. We could just about loop this field. They're all entered for second money, and for their people to be able to say they've been on the same track with the great Irish Eagle."

Annie brushed an errant strand of hair from her face. "When does the pride of Ireland get his workout on this hallowed racetrack?"

"Georgie and Doc will be leading him out soon. We have to wait until the rest have had their turn. He's still in quarantine. The import regulations say he can't even be on the same track with the local stock until he's cleared by the government officials."

"When will that happen?" Jean-clad Annie brushed hair from her face again, slipped out of her navy blazer and slung it over her shoulder.

"Before Saturday at post time, I would hope," Aidan said with more than a hint of annoyance. "They're still waiting for the blood samples to be analyzed. All imported horses have to be tested here in the States. The results should be back sometime today. In the meantime, he and Charlie have their own private quarantine barn."

Aidan and Annie watched quietly as Khando, his coat slightly lathered, was led up the track by a skinny Hispanic groom with a pointy beard.

"Sired by Seattle Slew," Aidan said. "Maybe he's the best of the rest."

A pair of thoroughbreds - a bay and a roan - breezed down the homestretch side by side, the exercise boys standing in the iron stirrups as they flashed under the finish line wire. There was quiet between Aidan and Annie, accentuated by the rhythmic thump of hoofs on the dirt track as the works drew to a close. Aidan sensed an opportunity. He'd been aching to speak with Annie. To explain that after Timmy's death he had to choose at that fork in the Irish road, the unavoidable dilemma, and why he chose as he had. She meant so much to him, and he lived in guilt for distancing his true feelings from her for so long, for not trying to dissuade her from a life of futile retribution.

There seemed to be no way to approach her, to win her trust. Their relationship teetered on the edge, but if he did nothing it was sure to tumble into the abyss. He knew she'd argue, but he had to air his view, pound home his logic. As he mustered his courage to speak, he heard her voice.

"In all honesty, Aidan, I couldn't care less about these damn horses, except that our treasury will be healthy for a change, our armory more full, thanks to what will happen on this track come Saturday. I hope you're not disappointed, but they've no value to me beyond that." She turned to Aidan, defiance on her face. "There's only one reason I'm here, and it's not to pretend I'm improving the breed, or whatever that stupid saying is. It's to keep reminding the British bastards that we don't turn the other cheek, and never will. It's simple, Aidan. Brits out."

The moment had passed. Aidan turned back to the track.

Shortly after ten o'clock Aidan wondered aloud why Irish Eagle was late for his turn on the track. As he and Annie started walking in the direction of the quarantine barn across Union Avenue, he spotted a slow-moving entourage just inside the entrance to the track grounds. Georgie O'Malley led Irish Eagle by the reins, with Eddie McCauley in the saddle and Doc Flynn alongside. There were a dozen photographers and turf reporters in tow. When the crowd in the west end of the grandstand noticed the slow moving troupe with McCauley on the back of Irish Eagle, it started to cheer. In seconds the enthusiastic welcome spread, and the cheer turned into a welcoming roar for the horse from Ireland.

Saratoga Springs - Thursday Morning

Secretariat stood on a field of grass within the border of the large gold frame. The painting of the great thoroughbred overlooked the tony racing crowd gathered at the National Racing Museum. Until this year, in the opinion of many, if not most, the Triple Crown champion known as "Big Red" was the greatest to have ever thundered down a homestretch. Now, in the Saratoga quarantine barn a mile or so down Union Avenue, a new wonder horse scratched at the straw-covered dirt. The consensus of those who labored or seriously played in the sport was clear - Irish Eagle was very likely to replace Secretariat at the end of a sentence that began with: "The greatest thoroughbred in the history of the sport was..."

In addition to the East Coast horse racing elite assembled in the Museum's Hall of Fame room, it seemed that the rest of the thoroughbred racing world also made it to the Spa this year. The most influential among them found their way into functions such as the Travers Post Position Breakfast. In most years, the event at which post positions were drawn was little more than a stop for the day's initial nourishment, perhaps a Bloody Mary, or the provincial eye-opener, a Saratoga Sunrise. But in this year of Irish Eagle, entry to the breakfast, like every other event associated with the Travers, was highly prized.

Oliver Chipps, secretary of the New York Racing Association, stood at the podium. Slight and balding, Chipps wore a white linen jacket and matching bow tie over a mint green shirt. To his left and right sat the representatives of the dozen thoroughbreds entered in the Saturday's Travers. Throughout the room, tables hosted coffee urns, pitchers of fruit juice and baskets of baked goods, all efficiently replenished by Spring Bubbles Caterers. The presence of the national sports media provided even more electricity to the already enthusiastic gathering.

Chipps gave the microphone a few pokes with his index finger, causing familiar thumps, and asked for quiet. Far from a born toastmaster, he spoke haltingly. He uttered the usual opening remarks, making mention of the great horses, trainers and owners whose likenesses had earned space on the green-painted walls. The secretary looked to his left at Irish Eagle's trainer.

"Will we be adding to our gallery with your Irish-bred champion, Mister McGuire? We have the right color on the walls."

Aidan fiddled with his tie, striped in the silver and green racing colors of Logan Stables. He pulled a microphone over, leaned into it and responded to the hushed crowd.

"If not, I hope you've a working set of gallows in your historic park here in town. I'd rather hang in Saratoga than face my countrymen at the Purple Goose, that's the local pub, back home in Erin Cove."

Annie sat at a table next to Doc Flynn. She smiled in Aidan's direction and whispered to Doc something about Aidan having done his homework on the local history.

After the chuckles following Aidan's comment, a reporter from the *New York Times* stood from one of the front tables and began to ask about Irish Eagle's transatlantic flight. Chipps cut him short. "Hold the questions, please. First, let's get the post positions settled." He placed his hand on the plump section of a football-shaped wire basket. The contraption, suspended between wooden legs, sat on the table in front of the secretary. As Chipps spun the wire basket, the wooden pegs numbered one through twelve leapt like Mexican jumping beans.

Saratoga Race Course - Thursday Noontime

Mustard shot out of the spout screwed onto the gallon jug, past the end of Harry's hot dog, and plopped onto his left Nike. "Damn!" he exclaimed as he shook his foot vigorously trying to evict the watery condiment.

"Wrong dog," Stephie said.

Typically, before the first race of the day at the Saratoga Race Course, an optimistic buzz filled the cavern-like grandstand interior. As in racetracks around the country, this was the location of most of the track's betting windows, the engine that fueled the thoroughbred industry. The racing oval, with its manicured, flower-bedecked infield and tote board was located on the front side of the huge betting parlor. To the rear, a crowd began to surround the open paddock where some of the most talented racehorses in the country would be saddled throughout the day. The ground floor of the grandstand was the guts of the structure. In addition to the betting facilities, food counters offering most everything forbidden by any decent cardiologist filled the space. The bustling area was open to the track side, inviting sunlight and fresh air to battle with the aromas from pizza ovens and beer stands.

At noon the food court began to fill with the wide variety of humanity that gravitates to racetracks. Narrow tables littered with track programs, tout sheets and coffee and beer cups jutted out from whitewashed walls. Squares of wax paper separated the Formica surfaces from the steaming pizza slices, hot dogs and pretzels fueling this mishmash of visitors to the country's second oldest track. Harry and Stephie wore one of the uniforms of the day - shorts and T-shirts. Stephie stared across the table at Harry as he stuffed the end of the hot dog roll into his mouth. "I don't know how you can eat that. Any idea what goes into a hot dog?"

"Jeez, Steph, you sound like my friend, Sauly. No, I don't know, and I don't want to know, thank you very much."

"Well, well. What do we have here? A summer school field trip?" The voice was unmistakable, even if somewhat less assertive than Harry and Stephie recalled. The veil of the mustache and Van Dyke beard was easily pierced, as the Boston College students immediately recognized their former statistics professor.

"Professor Smith! How are you?" Stephie's greeting began with enthusiasm, then became one of concern, for she could sense that the academician was a little out of sorts. "I hope everything's all right."

Cypher Sam, wearing a ragged blue sport coat and khakis, set his cup of beer down on the table. "I must admit, I have been better."

"Oh, that's too bad," Stephie said. "What's the matter?"

"Well, to begin with, the ex-wife has been very agitated about an alleged lack of support for my two kids. She dropped a dime on me to the Massachusetts Department of Revenue." The former teacher appeared mildly embarrassed. "I've been reduced to a grainy photograph in wanted posters hanging on walls of state office buildings. A campaign known as 'Deadbeat Dads.'"

"How much are you in the hole for, Professor?" Harry said.

"Lots. If I quadrupled what's left of the severance package I was able to squeeze out of those niggardly Jesuits, I'd still be in deep shit. Oops, sorry." He smiled an apology to Stephie. "Add a miserable run of luck at the track and you can understand why I'm on the lam, and not looking to be recognized. Like the whiskers?"

Harry, a wrinkle across his brow, looked at his former teacher.

"Where do you live when you're on the lam?"

"I have a roomette off the state highway a little north of here, a town called Corinth. Couldn't afford anything closer to the track."

"Gee," Stephie said quietly.

The professor drained his cup of Coors as the public address announcer informed the crowd that there were five minutes to post time for the first race.

"This too, shall pass," he prophesied, "and, if I don't get to the betting window, so will the daily double, without my contribution. Wheel the eight horse, Poppy B, in the second race. I think my luck's about to change." He started off in the direction of the betting windows.

"You know, Steph," Harry said as he watched the professor walk off, "he's really got to be on the skids. Sauly told me once that you can tell things are tough if you have to put up with anything that ends in 'ette,' like in roomette."

"And that grubby sport coat really could use a trip to the laundry."

"C'mon," Harry said, turning in the direction of the betting windows. "Let's take his advice. At least we know we'll still be alive in the second half of the double. We'll have all nine starters in the first race. Eighteen bucks to wheel the eight horse, my treat."

Fifteen minutes later, "OFFICIAL" flashed on the green tote board dominating the center of the track infield. The number nine horse, Jiggle Me, had finished in front, paying $46.20 for a two-dollar win ticket, and becoming the first half of the daily double. Harry and Stephie, back at the grandstand food court, wondered if the professor would return. Once again, his voice arrived before he did.

"Excellent start, students, a long shot. Just what we wanted. If our eight horse wins the second half of the double, which he's the odds-on favorite to do, I figure we're looking at at least two hundred buckaroos for each deuce wagered. You did get down on the double, didn't you?"

"Yep. Wheeled the eight, Professor, just like you suggested. Now we wait," Harry paused and looked at his program for the entries for the second race, "for Poppy B to gallop home."

"Exactly. He's the class of the race. Early speed in a sprint. Should go wire to wire. Well, now that I have you youngsters pointed in the right direction, I think I'll point myself to the Jim Dandy Bar over in the clubhouse. Like to rub elbows with the rich and famous on occasion. Believe me, they're all up here this week. I'll be glad to see the wonder horse pack up his tack and head back to the land of leprechauns. I've never seen so many amateurs here at the Spa. Trying to get a glimpse of history. Can't blame 'em, but what a pain in the ass."

Professor Smith turned to start to the clubhouse when Stephie reached over and touched his arm. "Professor, we're going to eat at a restaurant called Mangini's tonight. The women who run the B&B we're staying at said it has great Italian food. Will you come with us? Harry's driving." Stephie waited for a response, and then flashed her prettiest smile. "Please?"

"I know the place. Out at Saratoga Lake." The professor smiled at Stephie. "Have to eat occasionally. Sure."

"Great! Where and when should we pick you up?"

"On the edge of the track grounds at Union Avenue there's a place called Siro's. I'll be there with about a thousand of my closest friends after the last race."

16

SARATOGA RACE COURSE - THURSDAY AFTERNOON

Shortly after the first race was declared official, the possible payoffs on the daily double were flashed on the TV monitors located throughout the track. Long shot Jiggle Me's win in the first race insured a generous return to holders of winning double tickets. The start of a day at the track seemed on course for the betting public. At the administration office on the first floor of a two-story, white clapboard building on the track grounds, the phone was ringing, the fax machine was spitting out glossy paper, and the electric typewriter was clacking away as usual. Just inside the office door, pears, apples, tomatoes and pint containers of various berries covered a table, barely leaving enough room for a small sign that read: *Take What You'll Eat*. For the moment, the office was without the usual horsemen bellyaching about one thing or another, some between bites of an apple. It was a typical race day at Saratoga.

Oliver Chipps sat at a wood partners desk and munched on an egg salad sandwich. His administrative assistant during the meet at Saratoga was Jane Weeks, a plain looking, stout-of-build, local resident. Jane sat across the large desktop from her boss, shuffling a few documents between manila folders. Hidden away in an alcove at the back of the room, a husky gray-haired woman scribbled entries into a variety of bound ledgers.

"Where does all that fruit at the door come from?" Chipps asked.

Jane inclined her head toward the alcove. "Cindy."

"She's got a garden?"

"If you call five acres a garden." Jane reached to answer a ringing phone. "Administration…. He's not here, but Mister Chipps is. He's the racing secretary…. Just a minute." Jane covered the mouthpiece and spoke to Chipps who placed his sandwich on a piece of waxed paper. "Asked for the track vet, but I don't know where Frank went."

"All right, I'll take it." Chipps reached across the desk for the phone. "Chipps here." As he listened, he slowly stood from his chair. Then the bow-tied racing secretary asked in an artificially calm voice, "You are absolutely certain of this? … You are." He placed the phone back in its cradle and sat back down in his rubber-wheeled chair.

The door opened and the young track veterinarian, Frank Sampson, entered the office carrying a cup of cherry slurpee. He noticed the silent, ashen-faced Chipps and dropped the frozen drink to the floor.

"God, Mister Chipps! You okay? Jane! Call the track Doc!"

"Don't go calling anyone, Jane. I'm fine. It's the wonder horse that isn't," Chipps said. "I just hung up from the National Vet Lab in Iowa. The pride of Ireland flunked his blood test. They say his sample is positive for glanders. Regulations say he can't be tested again for at least seven days. That means he spends Saturday, Travers Day, in quarantine. Can you believe this? We are going to have to scratch Irish Eagle from the Travers Stakes. Oh, my God. Oh, my God."

Chipps cupped his face in his hands and leaned onto the desk. His left elbow squished squarely into the remainder of the egg salad on whole wheat.

Ten minutes after the call from Iowa, Jane Weeks hung the phone up and looked across the desk at her boss. "Mister McGuire isn't in the quarantine area, Mister Chipps. He hasn't been seen all day. There's some guy, Irish brogue, who said it's just him, a groom and a couple of Pinkerton guards. But I suppose you don't want to talk with any of them, do you?"

"No, no. Of course not. I need McGuire, and pronto."

Jane rifled through a sheaf of documents. "He hasn't answered the public address page, so he's probably not on the grounds. Ah, here we are. Our records have him staying at the Holiday Inn, downtown. Shall I call?"

"No, never mind. Frank and I will head right over. Let's just hope he's there. C'mon, Frank, we've got a miracle on the agenda." Chipps pushed the door open, stopped, grabbed a pear off the table, and turned back to Jane. "And not a word to anyone, Jane. Not a word!"

Followed closely by the track veterinarian, Chipps bolted out the door and down the short staircase. Rushing to the parking lot, the track officials barely avoided trampling a jockey wearing a white silk blouse with a red diamond on its back. Jacinto Vasquez, the racing meet leading rider, was on his way from the paddock to the jocks room after his mount, Poppy B, was announced as a late scratch in the second race.

Downtown Saratoga Springs

The desk clerk at the Holiday Inn hung up the phone. "No answer in Mister McGuire's room, Mister Chipps. Are you sure he's not at the track?"

"Of course I'm sure. I just came from the damn track," the racing secretary declared. "What do I look like, some kind of idiot? I have to find him, and fast. Ring all of the rooms reserved by Empire Breeders. Then every damn room in the inn if you have to. See if anyone has any idea where McGuire is."

While Chipps paced about the lobby, the inn's manager, nattily dressed and with a thin mustache, appeared. He recognized the distressed racing secretary, a source of occasional business for the inn's function department.

"May I help you, Mister Chipps?"

Chipps stopped in mid-stride. "Bet your boots. You can find Aidan McGuire for me. And please, don't ask me if he's at the track."

"Oh, Mister McGuire's not at the track. He's right outside the door at the end of the hall, sitting by our pool. I just brought him a message from London."

Chipps, leading the track veterinarian, walked swiftly down the corridor, out the door and into the blistering mid-day sun. On the far side of the pool Aidan was stretched out on a chaise lounge next to an umbrella-topped table and three resin chairs. He wore a yellow bathing suit and sunglasses.

As the two men skirted the pool, two overweight kids, a ten-year-old and an eleven-year-old, raced across the apron toward the diving board, nearly toppling Frank into the chlorinated water. Neither the behavior of her sons, nor the verbal tirade from the track veterinarian interfered with mother's involvement in the *Readers Digest* condensed book of the month. She was, after all, on vacation. If dad can leave the kids and go off to the track, mom can sure as hell get lost in a book by the pool.

Aidan looked up at the approaching men. Recognizing Chipps from the racing museum breakfast, he stood to greet him, then noticed the men looked grim and out of place. Suddenly, he felt uneasy, wondering about the reason for the visit. With concern in his tone, he said, "How do you do, Mister Chipps? I didn't expect to see you again so soon."

"This is Frank Sampson, Mr. McGuire. Frank is our track veterinarian."

Aidan nodded toward Frank. "Veterinarian?"

"Yes, I'm afraid there is a problem with Irish Eagle," Frank said.

"What problem?" an alarmed Aidan said.

Chipps and Sampson sat at the table, ducking under the shade of the umbrella. Aidan remained standing. "Well?"

"You're familiar with glanders disease?" Sampson asked.

"Of course. I'm a horse trainer. It's a disease of the lymphatic system."

"And," Sampson added, wiping his brow with a napkin he found on the table, "highly contagious."

"Are you suggesting that Irish Eagle is carrying glanders?"

That's what we're told by the National Veterinarian Laboratory. That's what his blood tests showed," Sampson said.

Chipps spoke up. "I received a call from the lab about an hour ago. Tried to find you right off. Nobody else is aware of this development. At least for now."

"This is absurd! We had the horse tested for all the blood diseases before we left Ireland. One hundred per cent healthy. You have to be mistaken."

Chipps shook his head. "They triple checked out in Ames - that's where the blood was sent for testing, in Iowa. No doubt. They say the sample they have is infected with glanders."

"Well, it's obvious, isn't it? They've got the damned blood sample mixed up. Send them another sample, for God's sake." Aidan glared down at the sitting men.

"The problem is," Chipps said, "federal regulations say they can't check the same horse again for seven days. We've got to do something in two days or Saturday's Travers Stakes is going to be just another race."

Aidan sat in the third chair at the table. It occurred to him that he'd be waking from this nightmare at any moment. "This cannot be. It simply cannot be. What do we do now?"

"Perhaps Mister Logan will have a suggestion. Can you reach him right off, Aidan? He must be told in any event. It's his horse. Otherwise, I suggest that this be kept under wraps until we have exhausted all avenues."

Aidan rubbed the back of his head. "I'm sure he's at the track. Hell, he's so wrapped up in winning the Travers, he's sure to blow when he hears this. I'll call your office later in the day, after I've spoken to Logan. You can try to reach me here at the motel if you discover there's been an error at the lab."

"God, I'd love to be able to deliver that message," Chipps said. He looked at his watch and stood. "I'm due to greet the governor at the airport in fifteen minutes. C'mon, Frank, to the airport."

The veterinarian stood and stepped away from the table, just in time to receive a soaking from the splash of a perfectly executed cannonball by the eleven-year-old.

Aidan pulled on his shirt and hurried into the lobby. He hailed the inn's manager who was coming out of the gift shop, placing a Lifesaver into his mouth.

"Excuse me. It's urgent that I contact a Mister R. Jack Logan at the track, right off. Could you have the clerk ring the owners' box area and transfer the call to my room?"

The manager pushed the little round candy into a cheek with his tongue. "Oh, dear. We can't do that. Some silly old blue law prohibits phone calls to track patrons, something to do with bookmaking. Doesn't make much sense anymore when there are a lot of those cell phones around. Say, does Mister Logan have a cell phone?"

"No, he doesn't like them. This is a legitimate emergency. There must be some way to reach him."

The manager pondered the situation for just a second, twisting the foil candy wrapping with his fingers. "It's slow in the kitchen at this hour. For an important guest all the way from Ireland, we can certainly spare a pot washer. I'll have a boy take the van out and find Mister Logan."

"Please hurry. I'll be in my room."

Within the minute, Aidan sat on the edge of his bed, stabbing the zero on his phone. "I need to ring up an overseas number, as quickly as possible, please."

A voice that Aidan did not recognize answered the call. It asked for a four number code, which Aidan provided. Then Aidan gave a brief description of the problem as described by Chipps and waited for a response. Thirty seconds later he was asked a single question: *Has the two million dollars been delivered?* He answered in the affirmative, and the connection was terminated.

A loud knock, more so a thud, on the open door to Aidan's room announced the arrival of R. Jack Logan. The tall Texan stormed into the room without waiting for an invitation.

"I want to know what the hell is going on! Is my horse okay?"

"It has to be a mistake, Mister Logan. It's the blood sample." Aidan took a deep breath and continued. "The U.S. government laboratory says Irish Eagle is infected with glanders."

R. Jack Logan - famous, wealthy, macho - suddenly felt faint. He reached a hand over to the edge of the bed, stunned by what he had just heard, and slowly sat.

"Glanders? You can't be serious. No, no. You can't be serious. If you're right, it means they want to either put him down or ship him right back to Europe. Tell me this is a miserable fucking joke."

"It's no joke, but it is surely a mistake, Mister Logan. Before beginning the trip from Ireland, the colt tested negative for glanders and everything else at the Troytown Vet Hospital. The real problem, according to the racing secretary and the track vet, is one of timing. Apparently, your Agriculture Department won't draw another blood sample for five or six days. I'm tracking down our vet, Doc Flynn, but he won't have any sway with the authorities here in the States. I know my way around the European circuit, Mister Logan, but I have little experience here in America. There must be something a man of your influence in the industry can do." Aidan's voice took on a strident tone. "This horse has to run on Saturday."

"You're telling me?" The Texan was silent for a few moments, then asked, "Where's the goddamn phone?"

Logan's aide, who had held his ground at the doorway, suddenly appeared beside the bed and handed the room telephone to the Texan. Moments later, Logan spoke to the front desk clerk. "Sonny, this here is R. Jack Logan. You call Boston right off and get me a mouthpiece named Jeffrey St. James. He's with a law firm calls itself Bolls and St. James. I expect you'll call me back with St. James on the line before I can finish a goddamn cigarette!"

Fifteen minutes later, Aidan and Annie McGuire sat at a cocktail table in Rascals Lounge, off the Holiday Inn lobby. They were alone except for the bartender whose attention was on a Yankee baseball game on the TV. After a long draw of his draft ale, Aidan spoke. "Logan's meeting with his lawyer tonight. He didn't seem to get a clear answer on the phone of what, if anything, can be done in time for Saturday's race."

"God almighty, Aidan, we're staring at a disaster." Annie sipped from a bottle of Heineken. "The money's gone? All of it?"

"Handed over to some young hoodlum yesterday morning. Every dollar. God knows if it's been wagered yet, or is still in the trunk of a limousine. But, from what I hear of American gangsters, I don't suppose they'll be any refunds."

"They know who they're dealing with. Mafioso bleed like everyone else bleeds. They must know better than to get on the wrong side of the Army. If this cock-up with the horse's blood is their scam, they couldn't possibly think that we'd just pat their backs for being so clever and walk away. No, Aidan. They're not that dense."

"It seems unlikely they are. No, I don't think they're involved. They stood to make their own fortune betting their money on a fixed race. In any event, if Irish Eagle is scratched from the Travers, we have to get that money back, Annie. Donnelly could not have been more clear. His was a phone call I'll never forget. Can you contact Flaherty right off? Let's at least find out what he knows."

Annie stood from the table. "I'll reach the little bugger."

17

SARATOGA LAKE - THURSDAY NIGHT

Harry stood behind Stephie and Professor Smith, both of whom had finally found seats at the bar. "Can you believe we don't have a table yet?" he said, reaching between the two into an oversized brandy snifter to grab a fistful of little crackers. "Thank God for these Goldfish."

"Busy all over town during Travers week. 'Specially out here at the Lake. Believe me, I know," the Cypher slurred. Waving in the direction of the bartender, he ordered, "'Nother beer. Any chance of a glass this time?"

The bartender walked over, shot a look of concern at Harry and asked,"Who's driving?"

"It's okay. I'm driving," Harry said. "I guess I'll have a ginger ale."

The bar at Mangini's was noisy with laughter and loud talk. Hungry men and women who made their living on the speed and endurance of racehorses waited for dinner tables at the popular lakeside restaurant. Also present were a substantial number of track groupies who liked to be where the action was. Most of the babble throughout the smoke-filled room was about the Travers, principally the unlikelihood of any horse being within a half a dozen lengths of Irish Eagle at the finish line. Saturday's race was an easy boast of trackside knowledge, although there were a few detractors whose comments could be heard in snippets throughout the room.

"Remember the great Arazi? Couldn't lose, they all said. Hardly finished in the Derby."... "Can always break down, you know."... "Hate the cliché, but it's true, 'Saratoga, the graveyard of favorites.'"

"What do you think about the big race, Professor?" Stephie turned to find him staring at her.

"You don't have any idea how damn pretty you are, do you?"

Stephie began to blush. "Uh oh, Professor, I think that last beer did it."

A loud exchange of words from the nearby foyer drew attention from some of the bar patrons. A voluptuous brunette in a short white dress stood beside a tall silver-haired man who was the source of the commotion. He was having an animated conversation with a short fellow wearing a bow tie while a third man, younger, stood by quietly.

"Big guy's Irish Eagle's owner," the professor said.

Harry and Stephie watched as the quartet followed the maître d' into the dining room. "Who's he talking to?" Harry asked.

"Ollie Chipps. Racing Association Secretary. I don't know who the young guy is."

"None of them look too happy," Stephie said.

"Hey, college boy, what brings you to Saratoga?" The voice was familiar to Harry as a hand reached past him and into the bowl of orange crackers.

"Hey, how are you, Carmine?" Harry greeted the office manager from Sparta Enterprises. "I came up for the Travers, and to check out the wonder horse. A little vacation before school starts and the Bruins and Celts open up at the Garden. You here for the big race?"

"Yeah, a little business and a little fun," Carmine said, his attention diverted to Stephie, who was staring at him. Noticing Carmine's interest, Harry introduced her as the maître d' appeared.

"Meadows party of three. This way, please."

"Our table's finally ready, Carmine. We better get going. Nice seeing you."

Stephie and the professor stood from their barstools and turned in the direction of the dining room. Carmine reached over and took Harry by the arm. "Let 'em go ahead kid. Tell 'em you'll be right with 'em."

Harry explained that he'd be delayed a minute, then turned back to the bar to see that Carmine had captured one of the emptied barstools.

"What's up, Carmine?"

Carmine gestured to the empty stool. "Sit down for a minute, kid. You treated me real good in the spring during the playoffs. Those Bruins - Canadian games were tough tickets. I don't want you to think Carmine Zappella forgets his friends."

"I'd never think that, Carmine. You remembered me already. That tip on the race at Rockingham."

"Who knows, kid, maybe I'll need a few favors again. Sometimes you can't get a ticket to a game at the Garden with a fuckin' gun. Know what I mean?"

"Yeah, I know. I'll be glad to try and help out." Harry wondered where the conversation was headed.

The bartender appeared. Harry refused a drink offered by Carmine, who ordered himself a Budweiser. As soon as the server departed, Carmine leaned into Harry. "Listen kid, I'm really gonna give you somethin' to take to the bank. It stays with you, okay? This is fuckin' hot and a sure thing. Just listen to me for a minute and remember what I tell you. You don't write nothin' down, and you don't do no braggin'." Carmine kept his voice low. "The wonder horse," Carmine dropped his voice another notch, "Irish Eagle, is not gonna finish in the money in the Travers."

"You're kidding."

"There are some things Carmine doesn't joke about. Now listen up good, and remember these numbers." Carmine spoke three short series of numbers, then repeated them. "Got 'em? Good. Bet 'em in the Travers every way you can - straight, trifecta, whatever - and you're the richest fuckin' college kid in Boston this year. Now go and order something with marinara sauce. The guy who runs this joint's kitchen's from the North End. Knows his fuckin' way around a red gravy. And who's your honey? Nice touch, kid." A cold Bud appeared in front of Carmine as he stood and slapped Harry's back. "Gotta hit the head."

The din in the dining room equaled that in the bar area. Piped in music - *Barry Manilow - The Complete Collection, and Then Some* - was barely audible. By the time the antipasto plates were cleared from the table, Oliver Chipps, struggling to keep his voice down and still be heard by R. Jack Logan, had detailed the usual process involved in getting a horse out of quarantine, and explained why Irish Eagle was still being held in the track lock-up. Then Chipps asked the young man sitting next to him what legal avenues were available.

The junior associate from the Boston law firm of Bolls and St. James looked across the table at Logan. "You're our client, Mr. Logan. Is it alright to speak freely?"

"Yeah, sure."

The lawyer then glanced at the brunette in the short white dress. She was busy surveying the noisy dining room while chewing on a breadstick. The associate thought she seemed annoyed. He looked back at Logan.

"She's obviously not interested in what we're saying," Logan said. "Go ahead, for God's sake."

The young lawyer cleared his throat with a nervous cough and spoke. "Our office met with a representative of the Department of Agriculture for over an hour this afternoon. We absolutely could not change his attitude. He insists that waiving the regulations in this instance would set a precedent, particularly because it's such a high profile import. The only possible way to resolve this is to file a lawsuit. The federal courts have jurisdiction. According to Attorney St. James, because the race is only two days away, we can't take the time to proceed in the lower courts. If we lost, we wouldn't have time to appeal. So we're going directly to the Supreme Court on an emergency petition. It's a little tricky on the procedural end, but Mister St. James was able to schedule a hearing in front of a single justice, that's Justice Zachary Smoot, tomorrow. It's a real gamble, but we don't have any choice. Actually, it's kind of a legal miracle just to get the hearing with Justice Smoot."

Suddenly, the table and its crockery shook and rattled from the slam of Logan's fist. Chipps quickly reached for his quivering glass of red wine.

"What the hell's this real gamble shit, and where the hell is St. James?" Logan demanded.

Her eyes wide, the brunette stopped chewing and stared at Logan, wondering who St. James was. Momentarily startled, the young lawyer was silent for a few seconds, then he realized there was a question hidden in Logan's outburst. He finally responded. "Oh, he's in Boston. Finished up a trial today. But he's guaranteed to be available tomorrow to bring the petition. I spoke to him and filled him in on everything from this end. They're working on the briefs in Boston right now. Will probably be at it all night."

The lawyer concluded his response on a positive note. "Believe me, sir, we'll be ready. We're asking the court for a restraining order against the DOA, prohibiting the enforcement of the quarantine order. We're claiming that the blood from Irish Eagle had to have been mixed up, or the test results were a false positive. This is because the horse's blood tested negative in Ireland, just before he was shipped. We're arguing that those results should be accepted by the DOA." Responding to a blank stare from the brunette, the lawyer said, "That's the Department of Agriculture," then continued. "We'll also argue that if the ban on the horse isn't lifted, there will be what's known in the law as irreparable harm, because the race cannot be run again. You need irreparable harm to get a restraining order."

The young lawyer drew a breath and reached for the sole remaining breadstick, drawing a negative glance from the brunette. Thinking better of his choice, he redirected his hand to an open mini-package of crackers. Chipps set his rescued glass of wine back onto the white table cloth. "This is going to the Supreme Court in Washington?" he asked.

"Yes and no," the young lawyer said, spitting a few cracker crumbs out with his words.

"Look-it, junior, I'm not interested in fuckin' riddles. Just what the hell are you saying?" Logan said.

"We're not going to Washington. The Supreme Court's not in session now, and Justice Smoot spends the summers on Nantucket. So that's where he'll hold the hearing, in the local courthouse on Nantucket Island. Right off the coast of Cape Cod."

"This all happens tomorrow?" Chipps asked.

"Tomorrow, Friday afternoon, sir. I'm flying over to meet Mister St. James on Nantucket. I'll be carrying the affidavit you signed earlier, Mister Chipps, on behalf of the New York Racing Association, stating full support for the horse to run on Saturday. I also have Mr. Logan's affidavit. The records from the Troytown Vet Hospital were faxed over from Ireland and will also be submitted. There won't be any actual witnesses. Just oral argument from Mister St. James. He's the best."

Logan leaned into the table. He spoke slowly and emphatically, not bothering to keep his voice down.

"I don't give a shit what it costs, or who we have to buy. I own the greatest racehorse in the world. He is going to win the Travers Stakes for me on Saturday. Understood?"

Obviously, this Logan character is an important client, the lawyer figured, but he couldn't be called on the carpet for suggesting to this blowhard what had to be at least a minimum ethical standard of the firm. "I certainly understand, Mister Logan. But I have to tell you that they don't teach you how to bribe judges, especially Supreme Court judges, in law school. This case will be decided on its merits. Mister St. James seems to think we have one whale of an argument."

"Maybe you went to the wrong damn law school."

The waiter arrived with four steaming platters emitting a heavy aroma of garlic.

"More breadsticks, please," the brunette said. "And can you turn the music up? He's really good, and I can *hardly* hear him."

Friday Morning

It took some convincing, but when Harry, Steph and the professor arrived in Harry's Jeep from the lakeside restaurant on Thursday night, Harry was able to secure the parlor couch at the Cuzins' B&B for the unsteady body of Professor Smith. Now, the professor's morning was being experienced through a pounding headache. He sat at a wicker table on the wrap-around porch, nursing a cup of coffee. Harry joined him at the table.

"Morning, Professor. Looks like it'll be a nice sunny day."

"That sun will be blazing. I'll do my best to stay under cover."

Harry decided he could trust the professor to keep Carmine's secret and, perhaps, solve the unfrocked academic's pressing money problems. "Professor, can I tell you something in absolute confidence?"

"Of course."

"Do you remember that field trip to Rockingham, when I went against the picks of the rest of the class and ended up with a fifty-eight dollar winner?"

"Indeed I do. My recollection is that a horse that had no chance won in a gallop. Name was Random something or other. The race was fixed. No doubt in my mind about that."

"Remember the guy who I was talking to at the restaurant bar last night, just before we went in for dinner?"

"Honestly? No."

"Well, anyhow, he's the one who gave me the Rockingham tip. Last night he gave me another tip. This one's kind of hard to believe, but he convinced me it's good."

"Really? And what might that be?"

18

NANTUCKET ISLAND - FRIDAY MORNING

On the south side of the island, an angry outburst broke the summer serenity.

"That miserable little bastard! He's at it again!" Slamming the screen door behind her with as much violence as she could muster, a dark-haired thirty-year-old woman stormed out of a cottage and onto an open deck, She slapped the front page of the *Boston Globe* onto the bare stomach of a woman reclining on a chaise lounge who called herself Azalia. "Read this shit, baby." The heading for the lead story beneath the fold read: GAY PARADE PUT ON HOLD – JUSTICE SMOOT HALTS MARCH.

"One of these days that little bastard is gonna be in my crosshairs, and then we're gonna be making it with his cute little widow while they tuck him into a pine box."

"You get too worked up over this shit, Celeste, sweetie," Azalia said. She pushed the paper aside, stood and stretched her taut body toward the sky. She was naked except for a rope necklace, bracelet and anklet. A sheen of perspiration, saturated with the scent of coconut-based tanning oil, covered her from head to toe. She looked out over the tidal pond separating the cottage from sand dunes edging the Atlantic.

"We've got this private little piece of the world, nobody bothers us and we grow our own weed. What the hell do we care if a bunch of limp-wristed faggots can't march in a shitty little parade? Let's go inside. I think I can make you forget about the little judge."

"You know, Azalia, a trip to the fucking bedroom won't solve everything. I'm beginning to think you're shooting up with testosterone." Celeste opened the screen door and reached back for Azalia's hand. "We have to get right to it. I'm flying over to Boston to bail out some sisters. I have to get back to the Wheelhouse for the late Friday crush or Murph will be bullshit."

Friday Afternoon

"We got us a verdict!"

The proclamation carried throughout the second floor of the Nantucket County building on Broad Street, the site of the county courtroom. It was just after the lunch break when the court officer marched into the courtroom and down the center aisle on his way to the judge's chambers. He announced to the four men sitting in the room, "Jury's ready to go chasin' blues off Surfside."

One of the men was a 30-something freelance reporter hanging around the courthouse hoping to get a taste of the real Nantucket. He had taken a seat towards the back of the room. The reporter folded up the *Inquirer and Mirror* and moved down the aisle to the middle of the room.

Attorney Jeffrey St. James and his young associate sat in the front row of the public gallery, along with the bald, portly court stenographer, Oscar Bannion.

"What kind of case did the jury decide, Oscar?" asked St. James.

"Driving under. It'll be a not guilty."

"Why are you so sure of the verdict?"

"The defendant's a school bus driver. Testified he only drinks on weekends. Needs his license. No extra drivers and school starts back up in two weeks."

"But I understand the jury's been out since ten this morning. That's over three hours. Not an automatic not guilty in my book."

"I don't think a Nantucket jury has ever reached a verdict before lunch," explained the perpetually red-faced stenographer. "The county picks up the lunch tab at the Jared Coffin House." Oscar stood and walked the short distance to his stenographic machine, sat and started to thread a roll of paper to record the jury's decision.

Shortly after the Nantucket District Court judge returned to the bench, six good and true residents of Nantucket County marched into the jury box. They remained standing as the court clerk asked if they had reached a decision. The foreman, sporting a three-day growth of beard, twisted his tan baseball cap in both hands while he answered the court clerk's inquiry.

"We sure have. Not guilty."

He and his fellow jurors smiled toward the judge (a juror on furlough from Parris Island also saluted) as they left the courtroom along with the defendant, his lawyer and the assistant district attorney, also sporting grins.

The judge glanced down at the Boston lawyers in three-piece suits. "Island justice. Actually seems to work pretty well, with just a few glitches. Justice Smoot is in chambers going over your petition. I'll tell him you're here. Yo, Oscar."

Ten minutes later short and slight Zachery Smoot, Associate Justice of the Supreme Court of the United States, came into the courtroom, stepped up on a platform, and seemed to get lost in the high-back chair behind the judges bench. Officer Barnes began to announce to the world that court was convening when a sudden wave of the judge's arm cut him short.

Oscar stood smartly by his steno machine, hands clasped behind his back, his rounded stomach straining the middle button of his seersucker suit coat. Attorney Jeffrey St. James and his associate stood behind the counsel table, virtually at attention. At the same time, a man with a smattering of brown hair, wearing a wrinkled tan poplin suit, rushed through the rear door.

"Be seated!" the court officer instructed in a much louder voice than necessary, and he followed his own instruction, dropping heavily into his chair by the window. The stenographer and the reporter sat. The lawyers remained on their feet.

White-haired Justice Smoot wore a green polo shirt and khaki trousers. He was not wearing a judge's robe.

"You gentlemen will excuse my garb for a hearing on an emergency petition, I assume. The uniform is in Washington. Feel free to rearrange your duds in any way that makes you comfortable. I have been properly fortified with a plateful of Nantucket scallops and am ready to listen to your arguments. I recognize you, Mister St. James. If you and all others who plan to speak up or wish to be recognized on the record will identify yourselves and spell your names, I'm sure our court reporter will be most grateful."

Justice Smoot nodded at Oscar whose fingers were traveling quickly over his keyboard, capturing every spoken word with an array of strange symbols.

St. James identified himself. When his nervous junior associate had difficulty remembering his name, St. James came to the rescue and identified the bag-carrying assistant.

The man in the rumpled suit patted his prominent brow with a handkerchief, uttered the name Edward Kirk and further identified himself as being from the U.S. Attorney's Office in Boston, and representing the Department of Agriculture.

"Sorry to be out of breath, Your Honor. Ran up from the dock."

"That's no problem. Things aren't too formal today, Mister Kirk. Kind of on vacation, you know. All right, everyone can sit." The octogenarian judge peered over his bench. "Now, you tell me, Mister St. James, what's so all-fired important about this little horse race in the backwoods of New York. And then, Mister Kirk here, for the government, can tell me why it all amounts to nothing but a steaming pile of manure."

A steaming pile of manure! Thank God Mister R. Jack Logan's not in this courtroom, the young attorney thought. His mind's eye pictured the horse owner dangling the judge out the second floor window.

As St. James stood at the counsel table, Rhonda Smoot, '91 Cornell Law Review, slipped onto a bench at the rear of the courtroom. The judge's young wife enjoyed listening to legal arguments, and knew a little something about racehorses, having spent more than a few afternoons at Suffolk Downs, near her family's home in Revere. But of greater interest to Rhonda was the urbane, handsome St. James. On a few occasions in Washington, she'd heard the lawyer argue at the Supreme Court. Rhonda found St. James's persuasive manner, combined with his sense of presence and confidence, to be the ultimate aphrodisiac. When her husband mentioned today's hearing, Rhonda's spirits soared.

"If the Court please, Mister Justice Smoot," St. James began, "there is no way to avoid irreparable harm if a horse by the name of Irish Eagle is not permitted to run in the Travers Stakes race at Saratoga Race Course in Saratoga Springs, New York, tomorrow afternoon. With the greatest of respect, Your Honor, this is not just a little horse race. The hopes, dreams and, yes, the very lives of some are entwined with this horse whom some refer to as the greatest to ever have set a hoof on a ..."

"Oh, please, Mister St. James," Justice Smoot raised the palm of his right hand at the lawyer, "you are not addressing a jury, just an old judge. Actually, an old judge who usually takes afternoon naps. Please get to the meat of this petition. And by the way, a horse is a which, not a whom."

"Well, Justice Smoot, it's like this...."

The freelance reporter now realized he was in on a major sports story. He began to scribble furiously in his pocket-size spiral notebook, turning the little pages at breakneck speed.

For the next twenty minutes, compact little sounds rose from Oscar's steno machine while it produced symbols rivaling the hieroglyphics of ancient Egypt. Anticipating the cold beer that would shortly be traveling down his parched throat, the rotund stenographer recorded the final official comments of the day. They came from Justice Smoot. When transcribed, they would read:

Thank you, gentlemen. I will have a decision on this petition tomorrow morning, and I will sign one of the proposed orders you have been nice enough to provide our rather lightly equipped and understaffed court here on the Island. No need to be in the courtroom, because there will be no further argument, and no reconsideration. My decision will be faxed to your offices by nine o'clock. Have a good day.

Around three o'clock Oscar Bannion walked into the Wheelhouse bar. Over the clamor of Friday afternoon revelers, he heard the high-pitched voice of Alice, an elderly, occasionally muddled regular at the popular watering hole. An unofficial island mascot, Alice waved the stenographer over to her end of the bar. "Over here, Oscar! This guy's leaving."

The stenographer shouldered his way through the thirsty crowd and set his small suitcase next to the last barstool just as it was vacated. "Weekend's started, Alice. The Huns have arrived." Oscar sat and looked down the length of the bar. The bartender was giving his attention to a detachment of citizen-sailors, their 48-foot Chris Craft tied up at the marina. They came in for lunch at noon and continued to dine on olives and suck on limes.

"I hope Murph looks in this direction."

"You hate crowds, Oscar. How come you didn't go right back to Hyannis, like you usually do on Friday?" Alice asked.

"I am going back. A special job kept me later than usual. Judge Smoot held a single justice session of the Supreme Court here on the Island this afternoon. Thought I'd grab a pizza before I catch the ferry."

"Pretty important stuff for our little courthouse. What's it about?"

"A horse race up at Saratoga, in New York. The government wants to ship a nag called Irish Eagle back to the land of the leprechauns, or maybe kill the poor bastard. Flunked his blood test."

"What's our Smooty gonna do? He won't let 'em kill the poor horse, will he?"

"Got me. I just write it down, don't make the decisions. But the nag has a big shot lawyer in his corner. Jeff St. James flew over from Boston to represent the damned horse. Smoot said he'd have a decision tomorrow morning." Oscar smiled as the bartender approached. "Where's Celeste, Murph?" Oscar asked as a dripping bottle of Bud was plunked in front of him. "She usually helps out behind the bar, doesn't she?"

"Yeah, but I guess certain things are more important to her than making a living. Some of her soul sisters went and got themselves arrested at one of their damn protests. She had to fly to Boston with some cash to bail out a few. Believe me, she's one angry broad."

Murph wiped his hands on a rag and walked a few feet to wait on one of the Island's selectmen who had hooked his cane on the lip of the pockmarked bar.

"What happened to our favorite politician?" Oscar asked.

"You mean that fat ass, Jeffries?" Alice said. "Broke his foot up at the news store. I heard he was drunk, but he's suing poor Herb anyhow. No wonder everyone on the Island hates the bastard."

"How come you guys keep electing him?"

"Owns half the town. That's a lot of jobs."

Ignored by the bar crowd, the TV hung over the bar's back mirror projected the image of Jim McKay of ABC's Wide World of Sports. The sportscaster was reporting from Saratoga Springs. Although McKay's voice was drowned out by the noisy bar, it was clear that he was agitated. A lip reader could have made out that he was reporting about a judge on the island of Nantucket deciding the fate of "the world's greatest racehorse, perhaps of all time - ever!"

19

SARATOGA RACE COURSE - FRIDAY AFTERNOON

The British Broadcasting Corporation placed the report of an arrest in the recent Liverpool bombing in the second slot and led Friday's late newscast with a satellite feed from the paddock at Saratoga Race Course. The signal from northern New York carried the image of Britain's respected racing reporter, Edward Singer. The casual attitude of the track patrons lolling in the background was in sharp contrast to the appearance of the ferret-faced Singer, who wore a blue BBC blazer and striped tie. He was in obvious distress, speaking in a stream of words, seemingly without drawing a breath.

"It is absolutely unbelievable. We are getting no cooperation. Not from the American press, not from any official of the New York Racing Association. What is known at this time - it's about five o'clock here in the States - is that Irish Eagle has been ordered out of the United States by its agriculture ministry because it claims the thoroughbred failed to pass his blood tests. That order is being appealed in the American high court. However, we can get no official to talk to us about the situation. You cannot believe the frustration level here at the racecourse and throughout this resort area. This, and Irish Eagle scheduled to run in the Travers Stakes in just about twenty-four hours! It's, it's just incredible!"

"Edward, can you hear me? This is London. Can you hear me?"

Edward transferred a sheaf of papers from his right hand to his left, along with the microphone, and then managed to drop everything as he fumbled with the transmitter in his right ear.

"Yes, Peter, I've got you," he said, momentarily forgetting that his microphone was on the ground in front of him. Then, "Oh, hell! I may have you, but not the bloody mic!" He bent and picked it up. "Here I am, Peter, finally."

"Is the horse, is Irish Eagle sick? Is he ill? Is there any chance he will be destroyed, put down?"

"We just don't know, Peter. The only information we received came from Cable News. They apparently have a stringer of sorts on the island of Nantucket, located out in the Atlantic Ocean. He reported on a brief of appeal to the high court of the United States. I haven't the foggiest of notions what is really going on. It's all terribly confusing, and no one around here seems the least bit bloody interested in explaining anything!" Edward appeared on the verge of tears.

"This is London again, Edward. Peter in London. What is America's high court doing out in the middle of the Atlantic on some island?"

"Lord knows. But apparently it's been asked to cancel the agricultural ministry's order and let Irish Eagle run tomorrow, just about twenty-four hours from now. I tell you, this is all very difficult to believe, or understand."

"There must be papers or something, briefs, perhaps, on file with the high court. Can't anyone get hold of them?"

A skinny groom, cigarette dangling from his lips, wearing baggy khaki trousers and a Mets baseball cap walked between the camera and the reporter. He led a chestnut colt, Stumblebum, the second choice in the eighth race on Friday's card. Trying to avoid confusing the viewers, the single camera went to a wide angle. Without slowing down, let alone stopping, Stumblebum proceeded to defecate in front of millions of European television viewers. When Edward was visible again, he answered the question, ignoring the short interruption.

"Guess not, Peter. No papers, at least for us in the press. Seems everything's locked up on Nantucket Island, or just not available for some reason or other."

"Do you think they're afraid to let this great European horse run in this race? Establish an American record that may last forever? Do you think that could be it, Edward?"

Edward tapped his earphone again. "Afraid of what?"

"Nothing, Edward, nothing. Just wondering aloud - why are they doing this?"

"Peter, with these Yanks, who knows? Who bloody knows?"

Dublin

Liam Donnelly turned on the TV in the sitting room. He expected to hear of the arrest of one of his explosives geniuses. To his surprise, the broadcast started with the report from the BBC reporter in Saratoga. The IRA chief rose from his chair, dropping his glass of whiskey to the side table where it clunked loudly, wobbled, but stayed upright. He stood in front of the small screen, staring.

In the adjoining kitchen, Maggie Halloran was slicing hard cheddar to serve with crackers. When she heard the TV, she glanced into the adjoining room. She saw the glass drop, a look of disbelief on Donnelly's face. Moments later, over the whistle of the tea kettle, she heard him talking on the phone. He told the operator to connect him with a number in Boston first, and then in a place called Saratoga.

Maggie puttered around the kitchen while Donnelly made his calls. She listened carefully.

Boston

Buzzy Flaherty turned to the fifty-year-old sitting next to him in the bleacher section of Fenway Park. "Gimme some bills, Mikey," he said. A few seconds later, Buzzy slapped a twenty onto a *Herald* tabloid lying on the cement aisle in front of his seat, Andrew Jackson face up. "Ball," he predicted.

A very seriously overweight man known as "The Lard" half-turned from his seat in front of Buzzy and placed his twenty on top of Buzzy's. "Covered."

Seconds later, the crack of a Louisville Slugger meeting a major league baseball resounded throughout Fenway Park. The ball sliced between the first and second basemen and landed a single hop in front of the right fielder. The fat man reached behind his back and had the forty dollars in his shirt pocket before the batter reached first base. The base runner who had been on second crossed home plate with the first run of the game as the crowd for the Friday night Red Sox game let out a collective groan.

"Roman's a first pitch hitter. Won't take unless it's a mile outside, and that ain't gonna happen with McCourt on the mound - control freak."

"You think you're so fuckin' bright, you fat bastard," Flaherty responded, and, not so playfully, whacked the man on the back of the head with the *Herald* he had rolled into a makeshift cudgel. The two men were part of a group of bleacher fans who bet on virtually every pitch of every game at Fenway. It was the top of the first inning and the Boston air was heavy on this humid August evening.

Ignoring the whack, the gambler turned and placed a ten-dollar bill on the aisle. It was his turn to call the bet. He went for a three to-one-shot: "Foul ball."

"You're on," Buzzy said.

The tingle of the silenced pager in his pocket reminded Mikey Canavan of the toaster with the frayed cord in his mother's kitchen. The disabled Boston cop who busied himself as Flaherty's gopher read the caller's name. "It's the judge, boss," he said to Flaherty, who watched a foul ball roll down the safety net behind home plate.

"Here, you lucky son of a bitch!" The hoodlum from South Boston tossed the *Herald* into the aisle, slapped three tens on the cement, stood and bulldozed his way out of the aisle.

Thanks to a high-speed lift from a Boston police cruiser, Flaherty arrived at the South Boston waterfront within twenty minutes. He strode into the Hibernian Yacht Club, ignored greetings from a group at the bar and continued down a corridor to the poker room. The battered room was crowded with chairs pushed into round card tables. There were no players, just Judge Jackie Devlin palming a glass of whiskey, an open bottle on the table.

"Can you fucking believe it?"

Flaherty sensed near panic in the judge's voice. "Believe what, Jackie?"

"The fucking Irish horse. That's what!"

"Sorry, Jackie, but I seem to have missed something. The race is tomorrow, right?"

"I just got an emergency call from Dublin, the very top."

"Yeah? Funny, I got a message earlier to call the McGuire broad in Saratoga. Maybe I should get back to her."

"Yeah, maybe you should." The judge pushed the bottle across the table. "Have a good swallow, Buzzy, and then tell me how the fuck we get the IRA's money back."

20

SARATOGA SPRINGS - FRIDAY NIGHT

What was left of the sun setting behind the Adirondacks illuminated the criss-crossed concrete landing strips at the Saratoga County Airport. From the east, a yellow twin engine charter banked for its final approach.

"Hello Saratoga, this is Gordo 7839er. Yellow Bird charter out of Boston. Anyone home?"

The charter's radio coughed, followed by a grainy voice that filled the plane's cabin. "This is Saratoga, Yellow Bird. 'Bout to button up for the day."

"Glad I caught you," the pilot responded. "I'll be dropping my passengers and heading right out. Like to gas up if you're still pumping."

"Pump's still on, Yellow Bird. You're looking good. No traffic. Straight on in."

"Tell him we're expectin' to be picked up. Ask if there's anyone waitin' for us," Buzzy Flaherty said.

Buzzy's voice startled the pilot. When the charter lifted off from Boston's Logan Airport an hour earlier, he'd asked his two passengers if they were going up to Saratoga for the big race. His inquiry had been met with an inaudible grunt, and neither had said another word until now. He pushed a button on his handset. "You got any ground transportation waiting around for arrivals, Saratoga?"

The airport manager looked through glass doors into the parking area. "Yup. Cab's still here. Fellow came in half an hour ago asking after a Boston group. Brogue thick enough to cut with a knife. That your party?"

Flaherty nodded in response to the question. The pilot answered, "That's us, Saratoga."

Without warning, the plane dropped and angled into a runway. Buzzy Flaherty made the sign of the cross and closed his eyes. Brendan Sullivan continued to sleep.

Following a stop at the men's room, Buzzy sauntered out of the terminal. He stopped at the edge of the sidewalk and looked into the parking lot. A white cab marked with green stripes, its motor running and Brendan Sullivan standing beside the rear door, waited. Thinking he heard "Mister Flaherty," Buzzy turned back towards the terminal. The voice belonged to a casually dressed woman standing against the outside wall. Buzzy's first reaction was that she was a knockout. In an instant, his appreciation was replaced with a feeling of dread, uncertainty. It was that damn Irish broad. He forced a smile.

"So nice to see you again, my dear."

"I'm not your anything, Mister Flaherty, save your worst nightmare if this horse race doesn't turn out as planned." Annie walked slowly towards Flaherty. "We've turned over millions of dollars to hoodlums we don't know and have absolutely no reason to trust. We have done so based on your assurances. We expect you will take care that our money is safe."

"Miss, let me tell you something. If the guinea bastards don't produce, they'll pay the goddamn price."

"Mister Flaherty, if this race does not go as planned, it is you who will pay the price. Believe me, you do not want to know the manner in which it will be exacted."

The daylight was about to disappear when the cab carrying Flaherty and Sullivan arrived at Northway Mobile Estates. The trailer park was carved out of a heavily treed lot three miles west of Saratoga Springs. Light glowed through the windows of the metal box homes set alongside seven dirt roads. The roads, including those named Galway, Roscommon and Waterford, stretched out like vanes of a fan from the green trailer that served as the park office.

Blood red competed with blues and greens for the honor of most favored trailer color. Flying in the face of any suggestion of mobility, the trailers were secured to the ground with cinder block foundations. Overhead, a jumble of wires ran from tilting poles to the trailers, and water pipes ran along the ground, further anchoring the two room rectangles.

"We've all the units on Galway Boulevard, that's the street we're on now," Leo Gaffney, the short, wiry driver told his uninterested passengers as he pulled into a dirt driveway. "When we have new arrivals, we can provide a place to stay a while that's not so dear."

"That's wonderful," Buzzy said.

The cab's headlights reflected off of a long-stemmed metal Claddagh symbol stuck into the dirt next to the office trailer. Doc Flynn stood on a small landing under a lighted rusting overhang. He was dressed for the humid evening in an undershirt and tattered shorts. As the men climbed out of the car, he greeted them. "Whiskey's poured."

Following perfunctory introductions, the cab driver headed for the TV in the rear bedroom. Flaherty, Sullivan and Doc Flynn sat at a narrow table dropped from a flat cabinet in the kitchen/sitting room wall. A spotlight built into the low metal ceiling illuminated the area. In short order, the veterinarian explained why there was no possibility that Irish Eagle was infected with glanders, or any other disease, and that the positive result of the blood test was most likely an amateur's cock-up at the testing facility. He filled the glasses again.

"Do you really think the guineas have nothing to do with this shit about your horse?" Flaherty asked.

"After talking with the New York racing officials, I can't believe that they would have the wherewithal to reach into this level of the sport," Flynn said. "I know the Mafia, mob, or whatever they're called, is a big deal here in the States, but to get into the testing of blood is unlikely. Not only would they have to intercept the original blood sample, they'd also have to come up with a substitute that was infected with the disease.

"From what I understand, there are only two people who had access to the blood that was tested. A supervisor with the agriculture ministry was present and took charge of the blood as soon as it was drawn at Stewart Airfield. I've dealt with the same lady in the past when Empire's shipped to the States. She's no more Mafia than I am. The other is the technician in some godforsaken laboratory out west of here that ran the test. He's hardly likely to be involved."

Flaherty drained his whisky, set the glass back on the table and placed a hand over it to prevent an automatic refill. "I don't trust the oily bastards, never have, especially that Sparta fuck. Rather do business with the devil himself. I warned Dublin about this whole scheme when we had to cut the guineas in. Now they call when the shit hits the fan and want to know where the fuck the two million is."

"When and where do you meet with the Italians?" Doc asked.

Flaherty glanced at his watch. "Forty-five minutes. A joint called Spa City Diner. We both wanted a public place. You been there?"

"Twice, crowded each time." Doc reached behind him, banged his fist on the bedroom door, and shouted. "Leo, time to go."

Flaherty looked at Brendan, who drained his whisky glass and stood up to an unexpected thud as his head smashed into the low ceiling.

"What the fuck!" he exclaimed, rubbing the top of his head.

Flaherty shook his head. "You're a fuckin' eejit, Brendan."

The cab carrying the visitors from Boston sped off in the pitch dark from the trailer park, headed for the Spa City Diner. Flaherty, sitting up front, lit a cigarette and quizzed the driver.

"What can you tell me about Sparta and his friends' summer vacation?"

The driver adjusted his scally cap. "They checked into the Gideon Putnam Hotel in the state park on Tuesday under false names. Expensive, especially in the high season of August. There were four of them in two adjoining suites. Then, on Wednesday morning, a woman arrived and moved into Sparta's suite. His roommate, who apparently is his bodyguard, must use the couch in the sitting room for sleeping."

"How old's the broad?"

"Mid-thirties, I'd think."

"A looker?"

"Yeah, she's a bit of stuff. Sexy. Been around, I'd say."

"How do you know all this shit?" Brendan asked from the rear seat.

"We have green card holders working at the hotels during the season. One of them is a desk clerk at the Put. She's very observant, very thorough. When she calls with something of interest, I go over myself and have a look."

"What else?" Buzzy asked.

"Wednesday, Thursday and today, the two worker bees stayed around the hotel during the morning, then left for the day. Probably went to the track. At night they were back at the hotel. Mister Sparta, his lady friend, and the fourth man, big, quiet, and always close by Sparta, did not leave the hotel grounds at all."

"Can't go to the track," Buzzy said. "Sparta would be spotted and run off."

"Mostly he stays inside the hotel, in his room, at the restaurant or bar, on the porch," the driver continued. "Usually the lady is with him. Occasional they walk about the grounds."

"That's all?"

"One more thing. Mister Sparta made a reservation through the hotel for him and his lady friend for tomorrow afternoon at the Roosevelt Bathhouse. Five o'clock."

"What's that?" Flaherty asked.

"It's an old brick building in the state park, not too far from the hotel. People go there to bathe in the warm spring waters, get rubdowns. It's a very popular thing here in Saratoga."

"La-di-da," Brendan sang from the back seat.

As always during August, the Spa City Diner was busy following the last race on the Saratoga card. The long counter and front booths of the popular eatery were full.

"I swear, August brings in all kinds," Candy, a hefty waitress with honey-colored hair piled into a net, said to Charles, the short-order cook. Through the kitchen service window, she watched the hostess greet two middle-aged men in dark clothing. "Looks like the deuce is mine. May's bringing them down back."

"That's the genuine article," Charles said, wiping the perspiration off his black brow with a soiled white rag. "New York or Detroit, I'd guess."

"All I know is, they ain't Saratoga Springs, not by a long shot." Candy pointed to a smoking piece of meat on the grill as she pushed open a swinging door, "Minute steak's working overtime." The waitress sashayed out of the kitchen and down to the end of the dining room. She was surprised to find her two customers at a table that had been separated from the others, pushed into a corner by the emergency exit.

"Special accommodations?"

"Yeah. How's your Chianti, sweetheart?" Carmine Zappella said.

"Far as I know, it hasn't turned. This is Saratoga, why not gamble?"

"Yeah, why not? Couple of carafes, and a bunch of glasses. We got company comin'."

"I'll keep my eyes open for your friends. Male or female?"

"Males, and ugly. Two of 'em. And bring us somethin' smothered in red sauce, you know, tomato gravy. You pick it. Just be sure there's plenty of garlic."

After Candy arrived with the Chianti and glasses, Carmine lit a cigarette and turned to his colleague from Miami. "Where'd you disappear to today, Ricky? Missed you after the double. You find some afternoon delight?"

"Yeah," Ricky responded with a nervous laugh. "I guess you could call it that - afternoon delight."

Carmine was about to ask for more detail when Buzzy Flaherty and Brendan Sullivan arrived at the table. Without ceremony they sat, just as Candy arrived with an oversized platter of Italian sausages bathed in marinara sauce, four empty dishes and a basket of rolls. She placed the food in the center of the table. "That be all, boys?"

"Yeah. Except for a little privacy." Carmine waved the waitress off and reached over to spear a chunk of sausage with a toothpick he plucked from his mouth.

Buzzy extracted a roll from the plastic basket, ripped off an end, stuffed it into his mouth and chewed. After a few tense moments of small talk, he lit a Marlboro, flicked an imaginary ash onto the floor and spoke.

"Boys," he looked across the table at the pair of Italian hoodlums, "we are very, very concerned about the safety of our money."

Carmine cast a disbelieving glance at Buzzy. "Are you shittin' us, Flaherty? I don't know what the fuck you're up to, but it's your fuckin' horse that's got the fuckin' problem!"

Ricky was seething. The Miami gangster leaned into the table, hands clasped together, both index fingers pointed at Buzzy. "I cashed in every fucking chit I had to set this fix up, then the fuckin' Mick horse shits the bed! And you're asking us what happened? Give me a fucking break!"

Buzzy put the roll down and placed his hands flat on the table. He leaned forward, lifting slightly from his chair. "My people have delivered a fucking fortune to you. Now, you fuckin' tell me - where the fuck is our money?"

Ricky paused, then spoke in a controlled, but determined tone. "In the interest of keeping the fucking peace, I'll tell you where your fucking money is, Mister Flaherty. Every fucking dollar."

It took just a few minutes to relate the general whereabouts of the IRA's two million dollars. It had been laid off with bookmakers in major cities, particularly Detroit, Cleveland, Phoenix and Las Vegas. Ricky held back inside details of where the cash would actually be bet, most of it off-track in order to keep the anticipated payoffs huge. The race-fixer then concluded his comments.

"Of course, these guys taking the action don't all have shit for brains. Some of the money will leak back and get laid off at the track as insurance. Might have some effect on the track odds, but not too much because everyone else at the track will be on the wonder horse." He paused a moment, then stared at Flaherty. "As far as fortunes being involved, for every fucking dollar you've got tied up, we've got two. Hear me? That's four fucking million. Our family's money, and your money, is out of our hands. And if that fucking wonder horse doesn't make the starting gate tomorrow, the whole fucking scam is down the toilet."

The conversation stopped when Candy returned to see if any refills were required. "We're all set." Carmine waved her off again.

"In short," Ricky concluded, "our half of this deal is going down like clockwork." He dipped a piece of bread into the red gravy, chewed a little and then took a deep drink of the rough red wine. Then he sat back, lifted his hands and examined his fingernails.

"Now," Carmine said, "you tell us, what the fuck is goin' on with your horse?"

"I don't know what in hell happened to that horse's blood, but the fuckin' nag don't have glompers..."

"Glanders," Ricky corrected.

"Glompers, glanders, who gives a fat fuck," Flaherty said. The horse ain't sick, and we had nothing to do with the fuck-up. Why the fuck would we want the horse scratched if that would flush the fucking scam down the toilet? This is our idea, remember? I'm not saying we don't think you have your paws all over this fuck-up, but, if you're telling it straight, I guess we just wait and see if the horse's owner can pull the right strings and get the nag to the fucking starting gate tomorrow."

Even to the wary gangster from Boston's North End, the logic in Flaherty's response was inescapable. Why the hell would they want the horse scratched? If that was the case, they never would have dreamed this scheme up in the first place. Carmine stood and said "Wallet." He slowly reached into the inside pocket of his jacket and withdrew his billfold. He took out a hundred-dollar bill and floated it down to the table where it landed between the sausage platter and a carafe of Chianti. "On me. See you at the fuckin' races."

Flaherty stood. He was face-to-face with Carmine. He decided on the final word. "Don't stiff us, Carmine. We know where you're at up here, and what you're doing. We even know all about Franco's imported squeeze. And we're keeping our eyes open. My people don't play fucking games. They're on the news every night, blowing people up."

Carmine stared back at Flaherty. "Just be sure your horse shows up at the fuckin' starting gate, and loses, big time."

Candy and Charles watched from the kitchen as the two Italians walked past the cashier's desk and out the front door. Flaherty and Sullivan followed, pausing while Buzzy pumped quarters into a cigarette machine at the door.

"Detroit," Charles announced his hometown guess as he laid out a strip of bacon on the hot grill.

"No way, Charles. They're definitely Boston. They got no 'R's' in Boston. They were being pretty close about what they were talking about, but I heard one of them say 'hoss'. That means horse in Bostonese. Got a twenty-eight dollar check here. Hope they didn't bolt on me."

21

NANTUCKET ISLAND - FRIDAY NIGHT

Inside the opening in a short hedge, a brick walk crowded by rose bushes led to a porch lit by a ceiling lamp. A replica of the Scales of Justice and the name, Smoot, were carved into a plank hanging on chains from the porch ceiling. The sign had been a gift from a local cabinet maker when Harvard Law School Professor Zachery Smoot bought the weathered shingle cottage from the craftsman fifty-five years earlier.

Justice Smoot sat in a cane-seat rocker looking out across the coastal road at the Atlantic Ocean. He watched the lights on a pair of 50-foot scallopers rounding the island's easterly shore on their way into Nantucket Harbor. A soft evening breeze pushed wind chimes just enough to break the silence. The jurist tapped his fingers on the flat arm of his chair as it gently rocked.

"What do you think, thumbs up or down, Sweetums?" the judge asked. He was engaging in his occasional practice of seeking the opinion of his wife on a pending case. Maybe a little out of the ordinary for such a prestigious justice, but, if ever alleged, the husband-wife privilege would keep this little habit a private matter.

Rhonda stretched out on the hammock a few feet from the rocker. The hem of her sundress had risen to her thighs. She turned to the final page of the defendant's memorandum in the case of Logan Industries versus the United States Department of Agriculture.

"Not bad for a government brief, Honey" she responded. "I think I know which way we should go on it."

The judge, still wearing his green polo shirt and chinos, reached for his Tom Collins on the table next to the rocker. "You're going to have to make one hell of an argument if you think that the Feds should waive their import regulations. This Irish Eagle has no more rights than an ordinary mule as far as I can see." The judge thought back to the afternoon's proceedings. "Boy, that St. James can be a pompous ass."

Rhonda, in silent disagreement with her husband's assessment, tipped herself out of the hammock, stepped over to the rocker and kissed him on the lips. The judge's hand drifted out from his lap to his young wife's thigh. Rhonda was his fifth, and most exciting, wife.

"Not now," Rhonda said. "I've got my legal cap on." She reached down and moved his hand away. "I'll nuke some mac and cheese and we can discuss the case over dinner, then walk over to the Gray Lady for a nightcap."

The judge got up from his rocker and followed Rhonda into the cottage. "Case seems open and shut to me."

While taking a yellow carton from the freezer, Rhonda asked, "How about that State Fair case St. James cited? Dealt with importing hogs from Mexico for a barbecue."

"That case dealt with animals that were doomed within a day of import. This animal's still on the hoof after three days. Nope, the horse hasn't got a prayer. I'm afraid the luck of the Irish has expired. I hope my Hibernian nana will forgive me from on high."

At about ten o'clock, the crowd in the Wheelhouse finally thinned out, leaving a group of tourists at a corner table and a few locals at the bar. Murph loaded glasses in the dishwasher while Celeste, standing a few feet from him, counted bills from an old bronze register.

"I didn't get a chance to ask you about today, Celeste. How'd it go up in Boston?"

"Have you ever had the pleasure of hanging around the Boston Municipal Court, particularly on a hot, humid afternoon?"

"Happily, no."

"It's indescribable, believe me. Dirt, sweat, tempers and chaos, for starters. Then some bottom-feeding district attorney conspires with an asshole judge who thinks exercising the right to free speech is criminal behavior if it's in front of a Cardinal's goddamn mansion."

Celeste stopped counting and placed a roll of bills into a canvas pouch stenciled *Harpoon Bank*. She poured herself a Coke from the metal snake gun as the front door opened. Selectman Jeffries, jabbing his cane in front of him, made his way to the center of the bar.

"I leave my goddamn keys on the bar?" he asked. "Not in my pocket. Just when I need 'em."

"Ah, no. Nothing here, Selectman." Celeste observed Jeffries, obviously drunk, fumbling through his pockets. The Wheelhouse was on notice from the Alcoholic Beverage Control Commission that a customer had been stopped by the State Police for driving under the influence earlier in the week. That was the second incident within a thirty-day period. Once more and it would be an automatic two week license suspension - a disaster, particularly with the Labor Day weekend on the horizon.

"Where you headed, Selectman?"

"Meetin' some of the folks from the yacht club, they were in here earlier, out in 'Sconsett."

Jeez, thought Celeste, the Staties couldn't care less about protecting a town selectman. Murph had the same thoughts. He pulled a steaming rack of glasses from the dishwasher and placed them on the bar. "Mister Jeffries, it's been a pretty long day. You must be beat. How about I call a cab for you? I'm sure I can get one right off."

"I don't need a fuckin' cab," Jeffries responded. "What you need is some goddamn manners. As a matter of fact, I'll have a peppermint schnapps."

Celeste reacted quickly. "Oh, that's just Murph. He's super cautious all the time. Didn't mean anything. Just trying to be helpful." She looked at her business partner with *Apologize, stupid*! emblazoned in her expression.

"Yeah, sorry, Mister Jeffries." Murph began loading the glasses into the slots of an overhead rack.

Triumphantly, the selectman pulled his keys from his back pocket, held them aloft. "How the hell'd they get back there?"

"The problem isn't with you, Selectman," Celeste said. "It's the damn do-gooders, blaming the problems of the world on someone who has a cocktail every now and then. Tell you what, why don't I drive you out to 'Sconset? That way we won't call a cab, and no one will be making up stories about how you needed one." She pushed her breasts against the flimsy fabric of her T-shirt. The selectman mellowed. He seemed to have forgotten about the schnapps.

"Not such a bad idea maybe, darlin', but problem is, I need my car once I get out there, or else how the hell will I get back to town?" Jeffries smiled, "Who knows, I might even get lucky."

Oh, this horse's ass, Celeste thought and tossed the sack of bills on the bar in front of Murph. She walked out from behind the bar. "No problem, Selectman. I'll drive you out in your car and I can catch a ride back, okay?" She didn't wait for an answer. "Car's in the alley, right? Let's go."

"Sounds good to me. Nothin' like a fuckin', oops, sorry, a pretty chauffeur." Jeffries followed Celeste out the door, placing his keys in her outstretched hand. "Here you go. Happy motorin'."

As Celeste and the selectman left the Wheelhouse, the few men nursing their beers at the bar paid no attention to the news from the TV. Maybe because it seemed to be old hat.

"In Belfast, Northern Ireland last night, three off-duty British soldiers were shot to death as they left a popular nightclub. A spokesman for the outlawed IRA said the attack was in retaliation for the unexplained death of one of its leaders in a Belfast jail, where, under British law, he had been held without trial. The British prime minister condemned the availability of illicit weapons, claiming they made such attacks a constant threat."

Celeste turned the key in the big sedan and looked over at Jeffries, slumped in the passenger seat. "Exactly where do you want me to bring you, Selectman?"

"Gray Lady," Jeffries was able to mumble, just before he passed out.

At least, Celeste was thankful, there'd be no attempt at conversation or, worse, groping. At the end of the short alley she turned in the direction of the village of Siasconset. The big Buick's motor hummed softly as it sped along Milestone Road, headed to the exclusive village on the island's eastern shore. Celeste wasn't used to heavy American cars, being the owner of a VW bug. She marveled at the power and easy handling. After the bedlam of the Wheelhouse, she enjoyed the smooth quiet ride.

Traffic was light. Only a few jeep-style vehicles, crammed with college kids heading into town, whooshed past the Buick. The August moon was high and bright, illuminating the wild flowers on both sides of the country road, their buds tucked away for the night. Ten minutes out of town, the outline of seaside cottages registered against the horizon. The tranquil ride was suddenly interrupted by a series of loud, erratic snores from Jeffries. Celeste wondered what she would do to rouse him once she reached the Gray Lady in the village center. God, men are pigs. The Buick slowed as it entered the village. The flagpole in front of the post office and general store was straight ahead. A single street lamp illuminated the small area.

About fifty yards down Main Street, Celeste saw the white arbor that led to the front door of the Gray Lady lounge. Tiny white lights were strung along the entryway and in adjacent trees. Celeste could hear piano music through the open windows of the high-priced bistro. Elton, an eighteen-year-old towhead, sat beside the entranceway on a small wooden stool. Behind him, a piece of whitewashed plywood held keys, hooked onto rows of nails. Tired of reading his paperback, Elton waited patiently for a well-heeled customer to summon his valet parking services.

Celeste looked to her right at the snoring selectman, his head wedged between the seat back and window, eyes closed, mouth agape. *Hell, I might as well slip the parking kid a ten and let him worry about this lump of crap and his fancy wheels. This kid must have dealt with him before. I can use the phone there to call Zalie for a lift.*

"Good night, Your Honor. We thank you and Mrs. Smoot so much for joining us this evening." Brantz, the overly-solicitous maître d', bowed at the waist to Justice Smoot.

"You're welcome, you're welcome. Mrs. Smoot's talking with your wine steward about a tasting party or some such nonsense," the judge said, annoyed with Rhonda's insatiable appetite for flirting. He knew she couldn't tell a fancy French vintage from Ripple - probably prefer the Ripple. "Tell her I've started home. She can catch up."

The judge continued through the door and down the path under the arbor. He started to cross an empty Main Street, walking into the glow of the street lamp. The piano music faded behind him.

Celeste steered toward the Gray Lady, ready to unload her burden on the parking attendant. Suddenly she saw the small man with white hair step out from under the arbor and into Main Street. Even from a distance, she easily recognized Justice Smoot. His identity was further confirmed as he became illuminated by the yellow arc of the street lamp.

Celeste's thoughts were her usual for the elderly jurist - *there's that rotten little homophobic son of a bitch*. She watched him walk into the empty street, suddenly realizing he'd be in the middle of the junction in a matter of seconds. Celeste reacted instantly, without forethought. She turned the wheel to the right and touched the accelerator. The Buick responded dramatically to Celeste's command. It seemed to leap across the square, trapping the old man in the field of artificial light.

No! No! I can't! Celeste's right foot slammed onto the brake pedal, too late. The squeal of the tires and thump of the contact were rolled into one. There was no doubt as to the effect. The Buick's front bumper whacked the judge's small frame and tossed him off to the right. He rolled, then came to a halt at the cement base of the flagpole.

Immediately after the impact, Celeste's muscles tightened, her hands squeezed the wheel, her elbows locked. Her passenger, the selectman, grunted, waking Celeste to the reality of her circumstances. Stopped in the middle of the road, her right foot strained against the brake pedal. Then she heard someone yelling, screaming. She jammed the accelerator pedal to the floor, then braked to negotiate the corner at Ocean Avenue, and sped down the waterfront street.

The parking attendant, Elton, had noticed the big sedan when it started to pull over towards the restaurant. Recognizing the Buick, he'd assumed it was Selectman Jeffries. He'd started to stand in anticipation of greeting Jeffries when the sudden and unexpected sound of the motor revving caused him to pause in a hunchback position. He had stared, open-mouthed, as the big car abruptly changed direction and sped diagonally across the road. He saw the judge stop and look at the Buick as it bore down on him. He would never forget the color of the green polo shirt illuminated in the headlamps. He'd noticed, for just an instant, an expression of amazement on the face of Justice Smoot. And then the thud - too loud for such a small, old person. Elton didn't think old people should thud like that.

By the time Elton raced across the square to the judge's body, the maître d' had come out of the restaurant, his curiosity aroused by the unusual noises. When he saw Elton kneeling by the judge's body on the other side of the square, he started to run across Main Street. Then, thinking 911, he stopped, turned and rushed back into the restaurant, brushing by a startled Rhonda Smoot on the pathway.

TRAVERS DAY

22

BOSTON - SATURDAY MORNING

Jeffrey St. James heard of Justice Smoot's death on the seven o'clock newscast from his bedside radio. Before rising, he placed a call to his longtime friend and prep school roommate, Sleepy Adams, now the CEO of Northeast Telephone Company.

"I won't bore you with why I need it, but is there any possibility of learning the unlisted number at the Justice Zachery Smoot summer home on Nantucket?"

After St. James agreed to pick up the tab at Lock Ober's after this year's Harvard-Yale game, Sleepy complied.

By nine o'clock, clad in khakis and a polo shirt, St. James was in his Boston office, docksiders propped up on a low file cabinet. The lawyer wondered if the widow Smoot would truly be mourning after the initial shock had worn away. Rhonda's fondness for socializing was no secret amongst attorneys with a Washington practice. Indeed, some members of the D.C. Bar were rumored to know Mrs. Smoot quite well. Having observed her at a number of social events, St. James could readily understand the youthful wife's reputation. Also, her apparent admiration, if not downright flirtation, of himself had not been lost on St. James. For whatever reason, he hoped that a possible lack of deep grief could possibly be to the benefit of his client on this Saturday morning.

He was also aware of Rhonda's legal credentials, as well as her rumored tendency to meddle in the judge's business. Maybe, just maybe, the judge had decided the case before what the newscaster had referred to as the "fateful nightcap." If he hadn't, maybe, just maybe, the judge's widow would take a hint and do the right thing.

As he waited for the phone connection to be made through the cable that ran across the floor of Nantucket Sound, St. James glanced out the window. He looked down at the elevated expressway that scarred the city and separated its historic, tea-flavored harbor from the downtown business area. St. James was comparing it to the remainder of a vicious switchblade attack when his call was answered.

"Justice Smoot's residence. This is United States Marshal Ryan. May I help you?"

"Jeffrey St. James, for Mrs. Smoot, please."

"Sorry, sir. Mrs. Smoot is not taking calls."

"Marshall Ryan, I give you my word, this is of the utmost importance. If I can ask you to tell her I'm on the line, I'm sure...Rhonda will be pleased you did so."

A minute later, Rhonda Smoot picked up the phone. "Hello?"

St. James held a copy of the proposed Preliminary Injunction and Order that he'd submitted at the hearing the previous day. "First of all, Mrs. Smoot, I join the entire country in offering my most sincere condolences. I am absolutely shocked and horrified by what has happened."

As Rhonda sat in an easy chair by the front window, she conjured up the image of the lawyer whom she had admired in the courtroom the prior afternoon. "I'm still a little in shock over what's going on, and all. I'm sure you can understand."

Rhonda recalled her husband's promise of a decision on the case by sometime this morning. She looked into the dining room at papers strewn across the table, and realized that the call may have been motivated by more than sympathy.

"Of course, of course. Mrs. Smoot, please consider my next comments to be in keeping with my obligation as a member of the bar to his client. In all honesty, there is a reason, secondary to offering condolences, for my calling this morning. It occurred to me that Justice Smoot may have decided a very important case involving a racehorse before the ... ah, accident." St. James decided to drop a hint, a heavy one. "Although it's a long shot (he silently cursed his unintended pun), the possibility also crossed my mind that he may have signed an order regarding the Logan Industries case."

St. James knew this was the defining moment for Irish Eagle. No further legal avenue could be traveled between now and post time for the Travers Stakes, just about eight hours away. The lawyer held his breath.

Carrying the long-corded phone with her as she stood and walked to the dining room, Rhonda responded, "It really is okay, Mister St. James. I was at the courthouse when you argued your case for the injunction. I know how important it is to your client. I also know the world doesn't stop because someone dies, even a Supreme Court judge."

Rhonda sat at the table. From the group of documents she separated a single sheet of paper. It was the last page of the emergency motion for an injunction that St. James had submitted on behalf of the Plaintiff, Logan Industries. The final paragraphs of the pleading read:

Wherefore, The Plaintiff moves that the racehorse known as Irish Eagle - country of origin, The Republic of Ireland - be permitted to reside in the United States of America through Monday, August 25th and be permitted to enter and compete in a thoroughbred horse race, specifically, the tenth race of the day as scheduled at the Saratoga Race Course, Saratoga Springs, State of New York, said race also known as The Travers Stakes and to be run on Saturday, the 23rd day of August.

The Plaintiff further moves that the existing order of the United States Department of Agriculture requiring the continuing quarantine of the above said Irish Eagle be declared void and no longer enforceable.

Directly beneath the paragraph there were two blank boxes printed on the page. Next to the first was the word ALLOWED. Next to the second, DENIED.

Rhonda picked up a pen. She thought back to the final comments her husband made about the case just before they left the cottage to walk over to the Gray Lady - *This so-called wonder horse is just another animal under the law. The import regulations are there to protect our livestock. They can't be ignored. I'm going to deny that petition. I'll do it in the morning, first thing.* They did not always agree.

Rhonda knew her husband's signature, and had signed bank checks for him over the last few years. On the line beneath the ALLOWED and DENIED boxes, the widow of Justice Zachery Smoot forged her husband's signature while she spoke into the phone.

"As it happens, the judge did decide the case last night. I know he planned to send you copies of his decision this morning. I have it right here. I'll have the marshal fax the decision to the court clerk's office, your office, and to the government's attorney, Mister, ah ..."

"Kirk," St. James impatiently filled in the name.

"Yes, of course, Mister Kirk's his name."

The newly-minted widow paused for a moment. She thought of her dead husband. She knew how he had decided the case, but he was gone now, no longer part of this world, and he had been wrong. Rhonda placed a heavy checkmark in the box next to ALLOWED.

"By the way, Jeff," Rhonda said, "congratulations. We found in your favor. I guess there'll be a big horse race today, after all."

Saratoga Springs

Jane Weeks arrived at the track administration office at eight o'clock, nervous and depressed, wondering what the day would hold for the historic racetrack. For the next ninety minutes of the cloudless morning, she and her assistant, Cindy, attended to the paperwork needed to get horses to the starting gate on this Saturday, the most important day of the meet. But the busy work could not get her thoughts far from the question that hovered over the track grounds: Would the great horse from Ireland be scratched from the Travers Stakes?

At ten o'clock, a dejected Oliver Chipps came into the office carrying a copy of the *New York Daily News*. He sat at the big wooden desk, softly uttered a hello without looking at Jane or Cindy, and opened the tabloid. The dramatic story of the Nantucket incident could barely hold his attention, except as it impacted his immediate problem - the strong likelihood that Irish Eagle would be denied the starting gate by a mistake in an Iowa laboratory. And now, with the only person who could have possibly resolved the problem the guest of honor at the Lewis Funeral Home on Nantucket Island, the morning sunshine and excited crowd already gathering on the track grounds seemed clearly out of place.

The clicking sounds from Jane's typewriter were replaced by the ring of the phone. She stopped and answered, "Track administration."

"This is John Grogan, calling, ma'am. I'm an undersecretary of the United States Department of Agriculture for the Eastern Region."

"Yes, Mister Grogan. What can I do for you?"

Chipps looked quizzically at Jane. She covered the mouthpiece and said in a loud whisper, "Department of Agriculture."

Chipps lunged out of his chair and reached across the desk, snatching the phone from his flabbergasted assistant.

"Chipps here. I'm the racing secretary. In charge!"

"Ah, yes, sir. My name's Grogan, sir. I'm an undersecretary with the Department of Agriculture. I'm calling about a quarantined animal identified as, ah ... Irish Eagle?"

Good Lord, Chipps thought, moving out from behind the desk, *quarantined animal! This man's a moron!* "What is it?"

"Well, sir, we've been served with an injunction by the U.S. Marshall's office. The animal is ordered out of quarantine. This court order also says the horse is permitted to enter in something called the, ah, Travers Stakes? Oh, yeah. That's a horse r..."

The dropped phone receiver bounced on the wood floor. Oliver Chipps pulled Jane Weeks from her chair, wrapped his arms around her in a bear hug and danced her about the office, all the while shouting, "Yes! Yes! Yes!"

From her alcove, although in the dark about what inspired them, Cindy grinned, happy for the resurrected Astaire and Rogers.

23

SARATOGA SPA STATE PARK - NOONTIME

In a guest room on the Gideon Putman's top floor, Ricky DePolito sat at a writing desk jotting a series of numbers onto a sheet of hotel stationery. Distracted by the noise from the television, he turned to the Boston mobster stretched out on the double bed.

"Can you turn that shit off, Carmine? I can't hear myself think."

"Yeah, sure." Carmine pressed a button on the remote, the TV went silent. "How are you doin' with the numbers?"

"The betting combos are all set. Now I've got a half dozen calls to make. I'll fill the boys in with the amounts to bet and the different combos. That'll take about an hour or so. Then, at four o'clock our time, I call them back with a last minute confirmation code. That's when all the money starts bein' bet around the country. There's no turnin' back then, you know, like the fail-safe guy riding that fuckin' bomb in that old movie.

"Then we wait and see if the Micks deliver and keep Irish Eagle off the board." Ricky shook a cigarette from a pack and lit up. "We've got the first three finishers down cold. We called in every favor we had, used up all our markers for this one, Carmine. It'll go down as the greatest fix ever, fuckin' ever." Ricky hesitated a moment, then said, "We get along okay, don't you think, Carmine?"

"Yeah, sure, Ricky." Surprised by the question, Carmine sat up, swinging his legs to the side of the bed. "Why you askin' that?"

Ricky stood from the desk. "I might have created a fuckin' monster problem yesterday after I left the track."

"Yeah? The afternoon delight?"

"I wish. Here's what really happened. When I left Miami early in the week, I told my broad I was heading out to the West Coast to visit family. I keep her pretty much in the dark about exactly what I do for a livin', you know?"

"Yeah?" Carmine stared at Ricky, his curiosity rising.

"She said okay, and I figured she was stayin' in Miami. Yesterday, all of a fuckin' sudden, I see her at the track...with a fuckin' guy! And I mean laughin' and smilin' and eatin' hot dogs and shit. I head over to see what the fuck is goin' down, when I notice her walkin' away from the guy and headin' for the exit. So I follow the slut and she gets in a cab. I grab the next cab and follow her to a local no-tell motel."

"She's alone? Leaves the guy at the track?" Carmine asked.

"Yeah, she's fuckin' alone. She goes into her room and I'm pushin' in the door right behind her. She almost shits when she turns around and sees me. Then she tells me she's here with her fuckin' brother! She never told me about no fuckin' brother. And then I lose it. Boy, do I ever fuckin' lose it." Ricky walked to the window, shaking his head. "Thought I fuckin' offed her, but the morning paper says she's at Saratoga Hospital. In a coma, intensive care. It says they picked up her asshole boyfriend and they're holdin' him."

"Geez Ricky, we gotta think about this. At least we got some breathin' room with the broad in a coma. Will she talk if she comes out of it?"

"She knows she better keep her yap shut, but who the fuck knows with a broad. But she's not the only fuckin' problem."

"Somebody see you?"

"A maid, when I was leavin' the room. I almost fell over her fuckin' cart that had all the towels and little shampoos on it. And the cab driver got a good look. He hears about the broad, he can probably add it up."

"You could be a million other guys at a quick glance."

"Yeah, but because of all the fuckin' noise when I slapped the broad around, I figured someone might have heard the ruckus and then I had no time to clean up. I know I left prints. The Feds got me in their computer.

They probably know by now I'm up here at Saratoga, and they know she's my broad. Two and two is four, even with those dumb fucks. They gotta be lookin' already."

Carmine stood from the bed. "Does your timing suck, or what?"

"It'll really hit the fuckin' fan when Mister S gets wind of it. I'll be in the trunk of a fuckin' Caddie if this fix doesn't go down. If the boys around the country don't hear from me, they don't bet a fuckin' nickel. The fix is for nuthin'. We're talkin' millions, Carmine. Fuckin' millions."

"You make the calls now, tell them they have the green light to start laying the bets down at five o'clock, but remember, Eastern fuckin daylight savings time. After the calls, we gotta get you the fuck out of this town. You got a place other than Miami to go to?"

"I can catch a flight out of Albany to New York City, then out to the Coast. Got a good pal in Long Beach. I could stay with him while I figure out what to do next."

"I can cover your leavin' with Mister S," Carmine said. "I'll tell him your mother died or somethin'. As long as the fix goes off as planned, he'll be okay."

Carmine stepped to the door and pulled it open. He looked back at Ricky. "Go and get your shit out of your room. I'll see you down in the lobby. We're gettin' you the fuck out of this place, now."

"To where, Carmine? I've got to make those calls."

"You can make 'em somewhere else." Carmine held the door open. "C'mon. They won't let you make your calls from the county jail. That's for fuckin' sure."

Downtown Saratoga Springs

Aidan pulled the borrowed Saratoga Race Course Jeep into a space in the front lot at the Holiday Inn. Moments later, he and Doc Flynn were intercepted by the inn's manager as they walked into the lobby.

"Ah, Mister McGuire, heartiest congratulations. The news is all over the inn that your horse can run today. I'm sure you'll win. We have extra champagne in our walk-in cooler, all set for a big celebration."

"We'll be sure not to disappoint you," Aidan said. "Would you be so kind as to ring Eddie McCauley's room? I believe it's number 202. Tell him we're on our way up."

Eddie McCauley pulled his room door open. His T-shirt tucked into the waistband of a pair of blue trousers, the little man turned back into the room, Aidan and Doc on the heels of his leather slippers. McCauley sat in the straight-back chair next to a small table, his hands pushing against his knees. The hair on his uncrowded scalp was slicked back with brilliantine.

"What took so long to get to the door, Eddie? You all right?" Doc asked.

"Yeah, I'm okay. Was on the bog. A little nervous is all."

"That's not like you, Eddie," Doc said. "You're the ultimate professional. Real cool. Nothing bothers you from what I've seen over the years."

"Must be the pressure from the Travers, and all the questions about whether or not the horse will run." Eddie offered the explanation while he wondered about the purpose of the visit, particularly why the veterinarian came along with Aidan.

Doc turned off the TV as Aidan walked over and stood by the picture window. He looked down at traffic-clogged South Broadway. "The town's bustling, Eddie. You've heard the good news, of course." Aidan said.

"Oh, yes, I surely have. I've been watching the telly. I know we won't be scratched."

"In case you're wondering, Eddie," Aidan gestured at Doc who had taken a seat in an easy chair, "Doc is fully aware of what's going to happen in the Travers."

McCauley stood quickly and stepped in front of Aidan, fists clenched by his side. His eyes darted to the veterinarian, then back to Aidan. "What the hell are you saying? It's bad enough as is. Have you gone and told everyone who cared to listen? Tell me, Aidan, if my situation is to be common knowledge, just what have I to gain by cooperating?"

"Cool down, Eddie." Aidan stepped to the side, away from the red-faced McCauley. "You're assuming things that haven't happened. Doc learned only today that Irish Eagle won't finish in the money. No one else at Empire Breeders has any idea of what we're up to. You were told in Scotland that your private life stays private as long, and only as long, as you do exactly what I tell you to do. Don't be concerned about Doc. He has no appetite for meddling or gossip. Bores him silly, he tells me."

Doc smiled from the comfort of the easy chair. "Tis the truth, Eddie.

Perhaps it's too often that I'll busy myself with a bottle of Jameson's, but I couldn't care less about the wayward habits of others."

The jockey sat gingerly on the edge of the king-size bed, looking even smaller than he was. He still found it hard to believe that this brilliant horse trainer and, he had thought, friend, with whom he had worked, socialized and celebrated, was the same person who had thrust this monstrous dilemma on him. His thoughts returned to the practical - how to handle the aftermath of losing the Travers.

"The bloody press will be all over me after the race. What in hell do I tell them?"

"You've been a beaten favorite before," Aidan answered. "Use the same reasons. The Eagle didn't feel right galloping, was fractious in the gate - you might create a little of that - the horse didn't ship well. Even the greatest is entitled to an off day. You know the answers Eddie. You've been there."

"Sure, but after an honest effort, damn it!"

Doc couldn't resist the opening. "I'm surprised at your devotion to candor, Eddie, considering the duplicity that got you into this spot to begin with."

Eddie sneered at the veterinarian. "I don't need your comments, Flynn." The jockey turned to Aidan. "I rang Scotland this morning. The Mrs. says strangers have been around the village the last few days. They've been driving by the cottage a lot. Seem to be doing nothing but waiting around. If anyone lifts a finger to my family ..."

"I don't know anything about that," Aidan responded, cutting off Eddie's threat. "Let's just play our parts over here in the States and everything will be all right. Nobody wants any problems, believe me." Aidan looked at his watch. "It's time to get moving. I'm going to my room for a change of clothing. Then back to the track. Eddie you've a mount in the sixth race?"

"Yes, for Mellon Stables. Horse named Nansham," McCauley answered quietly, without interest, much less enthusiasm.

"Favorite," Doc chimed in.

"That's right. Maybe I'll see the winners circle today, after all," Eddie said.

"I've been invited for a drink with Mister Mellon in the governor's box for that race," Aidan said. "I hope you get the money. Good luck."

Aidan walked to the door. Doc stood, noticed his portly reflection in the mirror with resignation, and pulled at the TV button to turn the set back on. Aidan looked back and spoke. "Post time for the sixth is three twenty-five. You have to check in with the steward an hour ahead of the race. We'll give you a lift out to the track. Be in the lobby at two o'clock, Eddie."

It wasn't a thoughtful gesture, McCauley realized, but rather, an order.

Aidan and Doc left McCauley sitting on the bed, staring at the wall. They started walking to their rooms off the adjacent hallway. "Imagine, Aidan," Doc said, "having to deal with two woman. If Eddie had two brains, he'd be twice as stupid."

Saratoga Spa State Park

The clock on the wall behind the Gideon Putman's front desk read one o'clock when the man in the dark suit finally found a name he recognized.

"There! Guanci, Anthony Guanci - room 304. DePolito's used that name before." The FBI agent stood at the computer monitor beside the hotel manager. "Do you know if this Guanci is in the hotel now?"

"That, sir, is highly unlikely. I presume he's at the racetrack with the rest of the world."

The manager was still more than a mite upset at not being at the track himself. But, mostly, he was bothered by the agent's suggestion that the "Put" could be harboring not only a fugitive, but, as had been explained to the horror of the young Irish desk clerk, a fugitive suspected of a brutal attack, perhaps even a murder. Gathering himself, the manager decided that a cooperative attitude would stand the best chance of bringing this matter, which was attracting attention from a group of elderly guests, to a conclusion. He tapped the computer keyboard. Then, accompanied by a smug smile, reported: "Mister Guanci checked out of the hotel just about an hour ago. Sorry."

Rushing to the hotel's front door, the federal agent could be heard shouting something about an APB.

The desk clerk, who had stood aside, biting her fingernails, during the computer search, waited a few moments until she was alone, then dialed the number of the office trailer at the Northway Mobile Estates. "Hello, Mister Gaffney. This is Johanna Hennessey at the Gideon Putman calling."

"What is it, Johanna?"

"The Guarda, sorry, I mean the FBI, were just here. They were asking after a Mister Guanci. That's one of the names of the men you asked me to call about if anything unusual happened. When checking for the FBI men, the manager discovered that Mr. Guanci checked out of the hotel about noontime. He seemed surprised about it."

"What of the others?"

"Two of the men are still here. The older one I just saw on the veranda with his lady friend. They have the appointment that I told you about, at Roosevelt Bathhouse today at five o'clock. The brute who must be the bodyguard is also still around, never far away. The other man left the hotel with Guanci."

"Thank-you, Johanna."

"Something else, Mr. Gaffney. The FBI said they were looking for this person because of an assault, possibly a murder."

"Really? Thank you, Johanna. Call with any new information."

Buzzy Flaherty had listened to Johanna's call on the scratchy speakerphone. "I don't like what I fuckin' heard. Those stupid guineas would fuck up a wet dream. You got a radio I can hear the race with in that cab?" he said.

"For sure," Gaffney said.

"Brendan," Buzzy addressed the third man in the trailer, "give me the shooter. We'll drop you at the track. Keep an eye out for Carmine and his hot-head friend from Miami. If they show up, remind them we're playin' for fuckin' keeps. I'm gonna follow the head guinea around for the afternoon."

Brendan took a handgun from his shoulder holster and handed it to Buzzy. "It's loaded."

Buzzy stood, bending forward to avoid the low ceiling. "Let's get the fuck outta here. It's like being in a fuckin' sardine can. C'mon Gaffney. Taxi time."

Saratoga Springs

Although only a few miles from the Gideon Putnam, in another sense, The Slice was about as far away as you could get. The scruffy free-standing building was across the street from the racetrack's main gate. In its front window, neon tubing shaped into curvy script invited ladies, a clear warning they might be better off avoiding the seedy bar and pizza parlor.

Inside it was hot and quiet, stale air hosting the aroma of the house specialty. The Travers Day crowd that jammed the gin mill from mid-morning had moved across Union Avenue to join their brethren in witnessing, at the very least, the second coming of Secretariat. They'd be back after the last race, some a little drunk, most a little poorer.

Mandy, short and heavy with close-cropped hair and a pair of chipped front teeth, slid two bottles of Budweiser and two squares of waxed paper bearing slices of cheese pizza in front of her only customers. "Chef thpecial," she said.

Carmine, who had just returned from the hallway phone, picked up the steaming slice of pizza and stared at it. "These fuckin' people'd be hung up by the balls, or whatever, if they ever tried to pass this shit off as pizza in Boston." He took a bite, reached for his beer and watched the back of the bartender's Grateful Dead tank-top as she disappeared into the kitchen. He turned to Ricky.

"I just called Mister S. Told him you had everything set for the fix, and nothin' could be changed now. Then I told him your old man just died and that you had to get out to San Fran right away." Carmine smiled. "He's real sorry."

"You're the fuckin' best, Carmine."

"Hey, like that Whitney broad's song. You know, Ricky. What are friends for? I called you a cab."

Five minutes later the bartender walked out of the kitchen carrying a case of Coors on a shoulder, a toothpick stuck in her mouth. She watched Ricky as he lit a cigarette, leaned his head back and propelled a stream of smoke in the direction of the ceiling. "Nathty habit," she said and glanced out the open front door. "Anybody waitin' on a cab?"

Carmine half stood and looked out the door. "That's ours. Time to go," he said. Ricky raised his right hand and Carmine grabbed it with his, twisting both fists.

"Good luck, Ricky. You need anything, you let me know."

Ricky picked up his garment bag laid across a barstool and walked to the door, through the threshold and across the wide sidewalk. At the curb, he turned back to Carmine who stood watching from the door, "Keep your hands off that bartender."

Carmine nodded and smiled. He watched as Ricky slid onto the rear seat of the cab, dragging his bag in after him. Suddenly, two well-built men were at the cab's rear doors. They leaped into the rear seat on either side of Ricky, pinning him between them. The taxi sped away.

The sound of the doors slamming and the squeal of tires caused Mandy to look up from the beer cooler she was packing with Coors. "What the hell?"

"Not your business, sweetheart," Carmine said. "Just that my boss doesn't like loose ends." Mandy shook her head, dismissing the comment that made no sense to her. Carmine walked to the bar and took a long pull of his beer, draining the bottle. "Time to head across the street. Who do you like in the big race?"

"The horth from Ireland, like everybody elth."

Carmine placed a pair of twenty dollar bills on the bar. "Do yourself a favor, sweetie. Take one of these double-sawbucks across the street and bet the five horse in the Travers. I guarantee you'll win enough to pay for a dentist."

The bartender watched Carmine walk out the door. "Athhole."

24

SARATOGA RACE COURSE - BARN AREA

"Only one scratch," Aidan announced as he walked into Irish Eagle's stall, ducking underneath red and white geraniums spilling from a hanging planter.

Georgie O'Malley looked up from beneath the thoroughbred's belly. He was going through what he dubbed his pre-flight check - examining every part of the horse for any imperfection that could affect its trip around the racetrack. "Who's out?" he asked.

"Canadian Mission."

Georgie stood and brushed some straw from his pant leg. That's bad luck. According to the Form, he can run a bit, seemed to have a decent shot at second money."

The assistant trainer walked out of the stall with Aidan. His spirits had soared earlier in the day when the quarantine order was lifted. He felt certain he was in on the making of racing history. He and Aidan stood beneath the sloping shed roof beside a stack of burlap sacks stenciled with *Erin Cove Oats* in green lettering.

"How's the champ?" Aidan asked.

"He's as fit as he's ever been." Georgie paused and shook his head. "I can't thank you enough for letting me be part of his team. I am honored, Aidan."

"Come on Georgie. You do all the work, I get all the credit." Aidan put his arm over his assistant's shoulder and walked him to the end of the row of stalls. "It's about fifteen minutes to post for the sixth race. I'm going up to the box to see how McCauley fares. He's on the favorite, Nansham. I like the idea of his having a trip around so close to the Travers. It should make him more comfortable with the track."

"Aidan, all Eddie has to do is make sure he doesn't fall off our horse."

Saratoga Springs

As Harry and Stephie were leaving their B&B to head off to the track, one of the inn's owners asked if they would be celebrity hunting, explaining that Travers Day brought a lot of well-known people to the track. Stephie's enthusiastic response brought the advice to dress up just a little to gain access to the box seat area of the clubhouse, where the rich and famous would be gathering. Stephie changed into an outfit of slacks and a decent blouse, both made presentable with the house iron. Harry took a loaner from the inn - a navy blue, linen blazer. Even though beer-stained and a miserable fit, the innkeeper assured him it would pass muster with the clubhouse ushers.

With the exception of a single puffy cloud, the only intruder in the blue sky over the racetrack was a biplane towing a rectangular green banner. Stephie pointed her cup of Coke at the airborne advertisement. "Look, that's sure appropriate for the day, a Guinness banner." She and Harry had managed to squeeze to the front of the aisle above the owner's box section at the Saratoga clubhouse. Stephie redirected her gaze to the long green tote board that dominated the track infield. She watched the small light bulbs flash periodically, changing the board's numbers to reflect the amounts being wagered at the betting windows throughout the track.

"Gotta be a zillion dollars being bet today, Harry."

Raising a pair of binoculars, Harry watched the entries for the sixth race as they came on to the track. "These are real good binoculars for a cheap rental. Hey, there's the jockey for Irish Eagle, Steph. He's riding the number 8 horse in this race."

Stephie's attention had shifted from the track to the box seats. "Hey!" she exclaimed, pointing down and to her left. "Is that Jack Nicholson?"

"He's probably here," Harry said. "He owns Meadowlark, one of the horses in the Travers."

Now on the lookout for celebrities filing in and out of the box seats, Stephie pointed to her right. "That's the governor right over there. I recognize him. He was on TV last night. I wonder who the other guys are?"

"The younger guy is Irish Eagle's trainer. His name's McGuire."

"Mmm. Not bad. Not bad at all," Stephie mused.

Aidan McGuire took a pair of field glasses from the shelf in front of his seat in the governor's box and focused them on Eddie McCauley. The jockey sat up straight in the saddle on Nansham as the nine starters in the sixth race, and a half-dozen outriders on ponies, paraded up the track in front of the grandstand. As the hoofs settled into the dirt, 50,000 pairs of eyes watched, anxious for the first nine races on the card to have their turn and clear the track for the magic of the Travers Stakes. Aidan turned to one of the two men in the box with him, a distinguished-looking older man wearing a Panama hat.

"McCauley looks right decent sitting up on Nansham, wearing your Mellon silks, sir. If he gets you the money, I don't want you luring him back across the Atlantic. He rides for Empire."

Harold Mellon chuckled at Aidan's comment and looked through his field glasses. The prominent banker checked the tote board and mentioned that his horse was holding at two to one. He then directed his view at the horses and riders strung out along the racing oval. He zeroed in on McCauley. The jockey appeared to be shouting at the outrider leading him up the track.

"Don't know why, but McCauley seems a might upset at Bonnie," Mellon said. "Hard to understand that, she's a real sweetheart. Everyone loves that old gal, and she sure as hell knows her job."

Aidan watched McCauley as he started to gallop his mount, post time now just a few minutes away. "Just pre-race nerves, Mister Mellon. You know all the pressure we went through just to get Irish Eagle into the starting gate today. Eddie will be okay. Trust me, he'll be okay."

The third man in the box, New York's governor, turned to his guests and asked, "Where's Mr. Logan?"

"Last I saw him," Mellon laughed quietly, "he was at the advance window with a wheelbarrow full of cash, betting his horse huge. They're ramming big money into the tote, Governor."

"Looks like the track is staring at a minus pool today," the governor responded. "But don't misunderstand me, Aidan," he continued, now directing his comment to the Irishman, "your entering Irish Eagle in the Travers is the biggest boost to New York horse racing than anything since Affirmed took the Triple Crown at Belmont in '78. It might cost us a little at the betting windows, but we'll be reaping benefits for years."

"This isn't going to cost the track diddly squat, and you know it," Mellon said to the governor, placing his binoculars back on the shelf. "Your win pool is made up of some big betters, but also hordes of small ones. The little guy's not going to cash in a winning ticket to collect two dollars and ten cents. They'll hold onto them for souvenirs, just to prove they were here today to see the great Irish Eagle run. Plus, you'll do just dandy in the exotic betting pools."

The Governor smiled at the two men, silently conceding that Mellon had made a valid point. "Can I interest you gentlemen in a couple of Saratoga Sunrises? A fitting libation for the big day."

After the sixth race, a grim-looking Eddie McCauley led Nansham to the clerk of scales enclosure and dismounted. Watching the jockey as he stepped onto the scale for the ritual post-race weigh-in, a dejected Harold Mellon turned to Aidan.

"Must have his mind on the Travers. We were lucky to get up for third. Looked like he didn't want Nansham to run. If I didn't know better, I'd say it looked like he was choking him down."

"Sir, Eddie's been riding for Empire for years. He just had a bad trip," Aidan said.

Mellon was instantly apologetic. "Oh, I'm sorry Aidan. Of course I don't mean anything. It's not the money. I just hate to lose. Was in Juvenile Hall once for beating the crap out of a kid because he whipped me in a foot race."

"You have no need to apologize to me, sir."

"By the way," the banker said, "what do you make of the late rider changes on Meadowlark and Sonion in the Travers?"

"Really?" Aidan replied. "I haven't been paying much attention to the rest of the field. McCarron is off Meadowlark?"

"Yep, and Pincay is off Sonion. Word is they're both ripped. No reason given for the changes. Just announced an hour ago."

"Interesting. They were on two of the horses I expect to be looking for second money."

"Just seems strange," Mellon said as he turned to leave the box. "Travers and all. You'd think they'd have figured out who the hell they'd want in the irons before race day."

On the day of a stakes race, the combination recreation and locker room for the jockeys, located close by the paddock saddling area, would ordinarily be bustling, charged with expectation. Now, just a half an hour before the running of the Travers Stakes, the usual electricity was absent in the white clapboard cottage housing the jockey quarters.

The jocks sat around the room in various stages of dress, some just back from the ninth race, others going through pre-race rituals. In contrast to the unusually somber mood, brightly colored racing silks hung in the open lockers assigned to the jocks. The camaraderie and wise-cracking that bridged the gap between races had disappeared. Even the constantly busy ping-pong and pool tables were strangely idle. Perhaps the presence on the grounds of Saint Patrick, as the Irish colt had come to be known on the backstretch, influenced the atmosphere, a sort of muted tribute to greatness. But, more likely, it was because two of the most popular and highly regarded jockeys at the Spa had been yanked off their Travers' transportation at the last minute, without explanation.

"Hey, Eddie," Charlie Leonard said, as he walked over to Eddie McCauley's locker area, "what happened to Nansham in the sixth? Plenty of horse. Plenty of racing room."

McCauley sat on a metal stool in front of his open cubicle. He looked up at the thin, rusty-haired reporter as Leonard pulled a small notebook from a pocket of his tan suit coat. The newsman, who seemed to personify his ever-present No. 2 pencil, set his black shoes squarely in front of McCauley. "Leonard, *Baltimore Sun.* I interviewed you over in England last June, after the 2000 Guineas. So, Eddie, what went wrong in the sixth?"

"Horse was off the bridle. It happens. I'm trying to get ready for the Travers now, if you don't mind. So I could use a little privacy." The jockey stood, turned to his locker and pulled on a green silk blouse. On the back there was a large white circle with a green L in the center.

"Sorry, pal," the reporter said as he turned to leave, "thought you might like the opportunity to explain a crappy ride. Cost a bunch of suckers, including me, a few bucks. I suppose there's no way you can blow the Travers now, is there?" Leonard walked across the room to a locker where another jock was pulling the knot of his tie up to his collar.

God, McCauley thought, is the bugger on to something? As he reached down for his boots, he heard the reporter asking a fellow jockey, "Hey, Laffit, how come you got taken off Sonion? What gives?"

Following the running of the ninth race, the buzz throughout the track grounds became louder and constant. In a half an hour, the horses entered in the Travers would be leaving the paddock for the racing oval. The huge crowd in the grandstand was restless, anxious to get Irish Eagle onto the track so they could admire him in the flesh.

"C'mon, Steph. Let's see if we can get close enough to get a look at Irish Eagle, Harry said. "I got that tip from Carmine and bet a hundred bucks against the wonder horse. I'm beginning to wonder why I ever did that."

"Okay, but do you think we'll get anywhere near the horses?"

"Never know if we don't try. Let's go."

After fighting their way through the throng on the second floor of the clubhouse, Harry and Stephie finally arrived at a landing for an outside staircase. Overlooking the mob crowding the paddock to the rear of the building, they realized there was no chance of seeing anything at ground level. Harry pulled Stephie from the crowd and into an alcove next to the landing. That vantage point provided a clear view of the cordoned-off saddling ring and path that ran from the jockey quarters, giving the appearance of a huge keyhole.

"This crowd is really wired, Harry."

"Yeah, Steph, this is pretty wild." He raised his binoculars. "They all look like winners. Here," Harry handed the glasses to Steph. "Take a look."

Stephie pushed her hair from her face and pressed the binoculars to her eyes. "They all look the same to me. Big and brown - except for the gray one."

Suddenly, the constant din of the crowd morphed into a low roar. It started trackside and, like a wave, washed through the building and onto the paddock area. Harry looked around but didn't notice anything unusual. He spotted a security guard caught up at the top of the crowded staircase and shouted at him.

"What gives, officer? Why'd the crowd get so excited?"

The guard, intent on reaching his destination, ignored the question, but a teenager behind him answered Harry.

"Last flash on the tote board. Somebody dropped a bundle on the five and nine horses. It looks like a bunch of money is goin' against Irish Eagle."

25

SARATOGA RACE COURSE

"Jaysus," Georgie O'Malley said to Doc Flynn. "It's like that movie where they parted the Red Sea for Moses."

The Irishmen were walking in front of Irish Eagle, through a throng held back by a phalanx of New York State Troopers. Georgie had a tight grasp on the colt's reins as he guided him on his trip from the barn to the paddock.

"He's perfect!" "What a beauty!" "Can see why he's the best!" and other such platitudes sprang from the crowd.

"Reminds me of the heavyweight championship fight I saw in the Philippines years ago, Georgie," Flynn said. "They called it the 'Thrilla in Manila.' Mohammed Ali was led into a huge stadium and the crowd couldn't get close enough to him. I wondered if he'd make it into the ring. I never thought I'd experience that level of excitement again, but, as I live and breathe, here it is, and for a horse, mind you."

"Well, don't worry, Doc," Georgie said, spying the paddock area. "Looks like we'll make it okay."

"Smile, Georgie," Flynn said, gesturing at a grouping of TV cameras staring down from a platform supported by iron-piped staging. "We're on the telly."

The spacious saddling ring was dotted with leafy elms, each surrounded by small groups of gaily, well-dressed men and women. Each horse stood in front of the elm with its number attached on a painted square of wood. As if sprinkled about the area for decoration, the tiny athletes assigned to steer the powerful horses around the track wore colorful silks representing the most famous racing stables of the United States and Europe. Wealthy owners, famous trainers and jockeys, their celebrity eclipsed for the moment by the Irish contingent, spoke in quiet voices, sharing that final thought or piece of advice that might possibly mean a length, a neck, a nose at the finish line. But on this third Saturday of August, they all knew they needed nothing short of a miracle to finish in front. This was the year of Irish Eagle.

The area around the elm labeled No. 11 was empty, having been reserved for Canadian Mission, a surprising scratch earlier in the day. The space around the tree wearing Irish Eagle's No. 2 was the only other vacant space. As the Irish troupe made its way into the ring further shouts rang out from the crowd. National bias apparently did not extend to the animal kingdom, as the Saratoga crowd had adopted the foreign-bred horse as its own.

"Where in God's name are Aidan and McCauley?" Georgie asked, looking around the paddock. "For God's sake, it's show time."

"Don't worry, Georgie. After everything we had to go through to get here, you can bet they'll show." Doc Flynn paused as he tied the horse's reins to a metal post. "That McCauley had better not be having second thoughts, the little bigamist."

Doc's comment mystified Georgie. He was never really comfortable with McCauley, particularly since he had discovered the false ID a few years back, a situation he'd never brought up again with Aidan. His guess had been that the jockey probably had some sort of secret sex life that he pursued under a phony identity.

"What the hell are you talkin' about, Doc."

Realizing that he had vocalized his concern, Doc scrambled for cover. "Oh," he laughed, "just joking. Nasty rumors floating around about Eddie's womanizing. Nothin' to them."

The track steward arrived, a clipboard tucked under his arm. "Open up," he demanded, walking over to Irish Eagle.

Doc grabbed the horse's snout and pulled it down, then exposed the upper inside lip. Although there was no doubt about the colt's identity, the track steward had every intention of treating the wonder horse in the same manner as every other Saratoga starter. He examined the tattooed numbers on the lip against the numbers on the official record attached to his clipboard. "Check," the steward acknowledged. "Where's your rider?"

Doc looked in the direction of the jockey quarters. He saw Eddie McCauley in the silks of Logan Stables come out of the door and walk down the two-step staircase, only to be lost in a sea of larger bodies. "He just came out of the jock's room. He'll be right along."

From their elevated perch next to the rear staircase landing, Harry and Stephie watched the excitement created by the arrival of Irish Eagle in the paddock. Binoculars glued to his eye sockets, Harry scanned the area to the rear of the grandstand, then zeroed in on the path leading from the jockey's quarters to the saddling ring. He watched the door to the white building open and a little man in green and white silks step out and down the two wooden stairs.

"What's so interesting?" Stephie asked.

"McCauley, the jockey for Irish Eagle, just came out. He's late. Everyone else is already in the paddock."

"Can I see?" Stephie took the binoculars from Harry and quickly raised them to her eyes. "Looks like he's lost his best friend. What a puss. Hey, there's the trainer we saw in the box seats. He's walking down the path toward the jockey. Now he's stopping to talk to him."

"Give em back." Harry reached for the binoculars.

Stephie held the field glasses tightly to her eyes. "No, Harry! Let me keep 'em." she insisted. "I can read lips. Remember?"

The jockey scowled at Aidan as they approached each other on the path. Eddie McCauley had listened to pre-race guidance from Aidan at tracks around the world, but he did not need to be reminded again of his instructions for today's race. He had thought of little else since the morning he was visited at his Scottish home by McGuire and his frightening companion.

The swarm of excited fans, anxious to get a glance at the jockey and trainer, tested the restraining cords stretched between state troopers. The clamor of the crowd actually provided a wall of privacy for the two horsemen as they met on the path. Aidan towered over Eddie and seemed to envelop him as he put his right arm around the jockey's shoulders, turned him toward the paddock, and walked him up the path. Eddie cringed at the familiarity that he had welcomed in the past.

McCauley spoke in a spiteful whisper. "Damn it, Aidan, I'm not exactly thrilled with our bloody relationship at this point. Is this where you remind me that your thugs are lookin' after my wife and kids? Both families, of course."

"No, Eddie, that's not what I've got to say. Not at all."

The two men walked slowly towards the grassed saddling ring. To the fans straining to get a look at the celebrities, they watched last-minute instructions from the trainer to his jockey in one of America's most important stakes races.

"You recall, Eddie, what you were told in Scotland," Aidan said, "to follow my orders exactly."

Eddie had to make a huge effort not to shout at Aidan. He tried to shake the trainer's hold on his shoulder, but was unsuccessful. "Of course I remember! What the hell is this, Aidan? I'm not an imbecile. Just a coward. We've made our deal. I'll keep my part. Now, fuck off."

Abruptly, about thirty feet from the paddock, Aidan stopped walking, his grasp halting Eddie alongside him. His arm still around Eddie's shoulders, he turned him inward. A good head taller than the jockey, Aidan faced in the direction of the red and white clubhouse awnings. The crowd clamor continued to insure a private conversation.

"Eddie, listen up. Your instructions have changed. You are to win this race. You're to take Irish Eagle on the greatest trip he's ever had around a race course. Do you hear and understand me? Win this race. Those are my orders."

McCauley looked at Aidan, wide-eyed. "You're," he hesitated, "you're serious, Aidan, aren't you."

"I've never been more serious about anything in my life, Eddie. You don't have to know why things changed, just thank God and do the only thing you've ever done with this great horse - win. The colt's never been sharper. Take him right to the lead and let him run, easy enough out of the two hole. Wire to wire, Eddie. The race is yours for the taking. I am ordering you to win the Travers Stakes aboard this great racehorse."

Aidan unwrapped his arm from Eddie's shoulder. They resumed walking, the jockey leading the way with a brisk, confident pace.

Stephie blindly handed the binoculars back to Harry. She continued looking in the direction of the trainer and jockey as they made their way into the paddock ring.

"Harry, you are not going to believe what the trainer just told the jockey."

"Why? What?"

Stephie continued watching the activity in the paddock. Directly behind her and Harry, on the staircase landing, the stream of fans seemed frozen for lack of room to move. "Well?" Harry insisted, taking Stephie's arm and turning her to him.

"Irish Eagle's trainer told the jockey to win the race. That his instructions had changed. That he had new orders. He kept telling him to win the race. That's what he told him. I saw every word, Harry. Every word."

The color drained from Harry's face. "Jeez, Steph, I think I just blew three hundred bucks."

Eddie McCauley, a few steps ahead of Aidan, strode towards his mount. Jockeys, trainers, and owners stopped and watched as the pair made their way to the horse. While grooms held onto the high-strung horses already saddled, the steward looked at his watch and bellowed, "Riders up!"

"C'mon Eddie. Let's go," A nervous and excited Georgie O'Malley instructed the jockey as he led Irish Eagle to the center of the ring. "Nice of you to show up, too, McGuire!" he said to Aidan, barely disguising the comment in jest. "You know, we do have an entry in this race."

"Sorry, Georgie, public relations." Aidan walked around Irish Eagle, eyeing every bit of the chestnut colt. "Looks perfect. Any problems since I saw you in the barn?"

"Nope, not a one. He'll toy with 'em."

McCauley placed his left foot into Georgie's cupped hands and was heaved onto the back of Irish Eagle. The mounting created another excuse for the crowd to roar its approval. The jockey, his crisp green and white silks glimmering in the late afternoon sun, beamed and waved his whip, acknowledging the crowd. The familiar feelings of superiority and confidence came over Eddie as he took the reins. He was bigger than all of them!

Doc Flynn made a final adjustment to the horse's halter, looked up and asked, "And what makes you so happy, McCauley?"

"Tis a beautiful day, Doc." Eddie ruffled Irish Eagle's mane, beamed and waved again to the crowd that cheered him out of the paddock. The colt calmly joined the string of horses parading down the bridle path leading to the racing oval. Thousands of fans followed, as if in a religious procession. Above the noise of the Saratoga crowd, the track bugler, dressed in the livery of a footman to nobility, summoned the horses with the familiar "Call to the Post".

Standing in an owners box, R. Jack Logan's eyes flashed anger and concern at Aidan when he finally returned from the paddock. Various members of the Logan Stable entourage quickly moved aside for the trainer as he stepped over and next to Irish Eagle's owner.

"Tell me what in hell's going on, Aidan!" Logan demanded.

"Sorry I'm so late in returning, Mister Logan. I never saw such a crowd as between the paddock and up here. It took forever to travel five feet."

"That's not what I'm talking about, damn it. Look at the tote board!" Logan stretched his arm straight out in the direction of the track infield, pointing an accusatory finger at the green board. The numbers flashed, triggering another loud round of disbelieving observations from the crowd. "Somebody's betting the crap out of the five, eight and nine horses. Look, we're at fucking even money. The morning line had us at one to nine. Why in hell are we being backed down like this? What the hell is going on, Aidan? What the hell does this all mean?"

The horses began to form a line behind the starting gate which contained twelve narrow, metal stalls. Anticipating the start of the race, a rumble made its way throughout the grandstand and clubhouse. The few in the crowd not already standing, rose. The track announcer's voice boomed through the facility: "It is now post time for the running of the Travers Stakes."

Aidan raised a pair of field glasses to his face. He ignored the tote board and zeroed in on the green starting gate straddling the track. He watched intently as an assistant starter led Irish Eagle into the No. 2 stall, just wide enough to contain the horse. Aidan noticed that McCauley was still smiling, actually beaming. Horses 3 and 4 were quickly loaded into the gate by the assistant starters.

"Well?" Logan insisted as the 5 horse was led into its stall.

Aidan, keeping the field glasses up to his face, finally answered the owner's question. "It means, Mister Logan, that a lot of people who don't know anything about horse racing are wagering on the Travers Stakes. I expect your horse to have a five to ten length victory."

From an open-front booth on top of the grandstand, track announcer Smiley Collamore had called over ten thousand races during his thirty-one Saratoga Augusts. Each a colorful spectacle, another opportunity to get excited, but he anticipated today's tenth race like no other. A surge of adrenaline rushed through his system as the flap doors behind the last horse loaded into the gate were slammed shut. Smiley stood and raised his field glasses to his eyes. Through the mike pinned to his collar he announced to the crowd: "The flag is up..."

The peal of the starting gate bell sounded throughout the track grounds. Eleven sets of green gates flew open, freeing the high-strung thoroughbreds.

"...They're off! Flying cleanly out of the gate to the lead and showing early speed, from the Emerald Isle, it's Irish Eagle!"

26

SARATOGA SPA STATE PARK - LATE SATURDAY AFTERNOON

The Gideon Putnam minivan dropped three passengers at the Roosevelt Bathhouse, then pulled away from the red brick building, spitting small rocks in its wake.

Franco Sparta and his lady friend walked up a short path to a set of doors held open by knee-high planters. A mixture of summer flowers overflowed the concrete bowls onto the foyer's floor. As the couple stepped into the tiled-floor lobby, Sparta's bodyguard, No Toes, lagged behind, standing by a pay phone in the entranceway.

To the couple's left and right, sets of swinging doors opened into corridors running perpendicular to the lobby. An unsmiling gray-haired woman in a white uniform sat behind a centered reception desk. A pair of bejeweled eyeglasses hanging from a silver chain broke her severe appearance. She was the only other person in the lobby.

Even though the sun had been burning throughout the day, the building was comfortably cool. A late afternoon breeze carrying the scent of newly cut grass from the rear lawn made its way through an open glass door behind the reception desk.

"Good afternoon, and welcome to the Roosevelt Baths. You have reservations?"

Franco pulled a card from his sport coat pocket and handed it to the receptionist. She placed her eyeglasses on the end of her nose, glanced at the card, then looked up and over the rim of the spectacles at a clock over the door.

"You're five minutes early," she scolded, "and who is the gentleman standing by the door, please?"

"He's with me. He's my helper," Franco explained.

"Your helper has no appointment. He's only allowed to stay in the lobby and wait. Women to my right, men to my left. Our attendants will assist you."

"We're paying for this little visit, you know. How about some courtesy, if it's not too much trouble," Franco said.

As the receptionist was deciding to ignore Franco's comment, a thin man with floppy blond hair seemed to materialize out of nowhere. He also wore all white, his trousers topped off with a short-sleeved polo shirt. He smiled at Franco, then walked across the lobby to the men's wing of the building and disappeared through the swinging doors.

The receptionist glared at Franco. "Women to my right, men to my left, *sir*." She returned her attention to the romance novel open on her lap for a moment and, smiling, looked back up at Franco. "By the way, no radios allowed. You can't listen to the big race."

"Lady," Franco responded with equal glee, "I don't have to listen to the race. I already know who's gonna win." He turned and spoke to his bodyguard. "It's okay, Toes. Just hang out with this lady here. Nobody else around but us, anyhow. Everybody and their brother's at the track to watch the Mick horse. I'll be out in about an hour," Franco paused, "maybe sooner." The gangster turned back to the receptionist. "How long for the tub and a rub?"

"You were correct, *sir*. Just about an hour."

Franco's lady friend gave him a peck on the cheek. "Have fun, Honey, and watch out for that attendant. He looked kind of interested in you." She slipped out of her linen jacket, tossed it over her shoulder and strutted towards the women's wing of the old building.

Franco walked across the lobby and through the swinging doors into the wide corridor of the men's wing. Immediately to his right, a set of tall doors pulled in against white walls were open onto a cement portico. At the far end of the hallway, a large, wide-open window created a draft. It was quiet. The only sound was of leaf-laden branches shifting at the urging of a friendly wind traveling through the park. There was an outdoor feeling to the clinic-like atmosphere. Franco turned to his left. A pair of rolling carts heaped with towels, sheets and a variety of bottles hugged the wall. The half dozen or so doors on each side of the hallway were closed. There was a light bulb over each door on the left-hand side. The two toward the end of the hallway were lit.

The last door on the left of the hallway opened and the bulb over the door went out. A white-uniformed attendant left the room and walked briskly to the door directly across the polished floor. He was followed closely by a middle-aged man who was naked. At the same time, the breeze in the park picked up, shaking the leafy branches and pushing a gust of air through the open window and down the hall. For a moment it seemed to Franco as if the men were out of doors, in the woods, and the man in white should have been chasing after the naked man, not vice versa.

"Mister Sparta?" Franco was shaken from his strange illusion by a soft voice calling his name. The attendant from the lobby stood in a doorway on the left, halfway down the hallway. "This way, sir. Your bath has been drawn here, in room six."

The Boston mobster hesitated a moment, then followed the attendant through the doorway. He looked around the square room that was naturally brightened by a window facing onto the rear yard. Just inside the door, a free-standing cast iron tub took up most of the space on one side of the room. A clothes rack on rollers stood next to the window.

"My name is Roger, sir. Now, if you'd care to strip down, I'll settle you into the bath."

"Just strip, with you standing right here? I don't think that's going to happen."

The attendant produced a knowing smile. "I've had bashful bathers before. I'll step across the hall and tell Jocko you'll be in for your rubdown in thirty minutes or so. Just make yourself comfortable in the bath and I'll be back to check the water temperature in just a minute."

"Wait a minute, Roger. How do I lock the door?"

"If you could lock the door, sir, I couldn't get back in to check the temperature of the water, now, could I?" Roger said, as if to a child. "Anyway, you can't lock the door. It's against the rules. What if we had an emergency? I'll be back in just a smidgen. In the meantime, if you need anything, just pull the cord hanging over the tub."

Roger stepped into the corridor and pulled the door closed behind him.

Leo Gaffney's Green-Stripe Taxi was parked in the small lot across from the Roosevelt Bathhouse. The cab faced a set of tall doors open to a portico. In addition to the view of the inside corridor straight ahead, Gaffney and his front seat passenger, Buzzy Flaherty, enjoyed a clear view of the main entrance to the building. It was from this vantage that they'd watched the hotel van deposit its three passengers about twenty minutes earlier. Later, just after five-thirty, through the open doors beyond the portico, Buzzy observed Franco Sparta walk into the building's wing from the lobby. He saw his Boston nemesis, after a slight hesitation, enter a room on the left side of the hallway. The two men in the cab waited in silence. After a couple of minutes Buzzy said, "Something's not adding up. Where the fuck is the muscle?"

The question brought a quizzical look from Gaffney.

"Bodyguard." Buzzy said. "The fuckin' bodyguard."

"He came with Sparta and the lady. We saw him walk into the building with them," Gaffney said as he opened his door. "I'll go into the lobby and take a look around."

The taxi driver returned within a minute. "The bodyguard's the only one in the lobby. Just sitting on a bench, he is. It's funny, like the place has been deserted."

Buzzy scratched his chin a moment, looked at his watch and pointed to the dashboard radio. "Turn it on. The race is about to go off."

Gaffney, who had done his best to stay in the dark about the flurry of out-of-town gangster activity, was mystified by the next comment from Buzzy.

"That fuckin' Irish Eagle better get stuck in the fuckin' gate."

No Toes stood, trembling, at the pay phone. The receiver dangled toward the floor, swinging from the end of its metal cord. He went over the words that Millicent Feinstein's roommate had just spoken to him from her Boston apartment: "I don't know why she left, or where she went. She said Boston was too weird and dangerous for her and she was leaving for good. She paid me her half of the rent through next month. Just who are you?" the voice had demanded angrily. "Are you the reason she had to leave? Are you the one who always calls? I can't afford this apartment by myself. What do I do now? Move back to goddamn Podunk?"

No Toes muttered words of disbelief. He recalled what Mister S had said about Millicent, particularly what seemed to be a threat to tell her about the "real Toesy." Maybe he did talk to her. He must have. What else could it have been? That's why she's gone. His feelings turned to quiet rage.

The hulking bodyguard walked slowly back into the lobby. Except for the chirping of birds heard through the open glass doors, the reception area was quiet. It was also empty. Fifteen minutes ago, the receptionist had stepped into a room off the lobby, saying something about watching the big race. Then, the man with the cap had come in, looked around, and left. It had been then, alone in the lobby, that he excitedly decided on the long-distance call to Millicent.

Oblivious to the sudden, excited chatter coming from the TV room off the lobby, No Toes walked without hesitation into the men's wing. He turned to his left, noticing the closed doors lining the corridor. There was no one about. He walked to the first door on the right hand side of the corridor and opened it without knocking. Beyond the threshold was an unlit, narrow room. It held an empty cot covered with a white sheet, a pillow at its head. He turned back to the hall, not bothering to close the door. The only burning bulb was across and up the hall, over door No. 6. No Toes crossed the corridor and opened the door. Narrow shadows from waving trees swayed against the wall, beyond the cast iron tub. Franco Sparta's head was nestled onto a small rubber pillow on the near end of the tub. The body that No Toes DeLicata had devotedly protected for the last eleven years was covered with water filled with little bubbles, its temperature having dropped slightly from the 98.6 that Roger had achieved. No Toes stepped into the room.

Leo Gaffney wanted to get out of his taxi, away from his passenger, but was afraid to move. The man from Boston had become angrier than anyone he had ever seen. The call of the Travers Stakes ending with Irish Eagle's easy victory had just been broadcast over the car radio. When the race concluded, Buzzy had slammed his head back against the headrest, closed the eyes in his reddened face, and actually howled like a wolf.

Gaffney looked straight ahead, afraid to turn toward Buzzy. His view was through the open doors beyond the portico and into the bathhouse. He saw the bodyguard walk into the men's wing corridor.

Still fuming, Buzzy opened his eyes, sat up straight in the seat and reached into the glove box for the Magnum. "I don't know what the fuck happened with that race, but that guinea bastard Sparta's the reason. I'll find the bastard. Pull this fuckin' cab in front of the fuckin' building and keep it fuckin' running!"

Buzzy flew out of the car and sprinted across the road.

Following instructions, Gaffney started the taxi. He watched Flaherty slow down to a fast walk as he crossed the lawn and portico and entered the men's wing through the open doors. Then it hit him - Flaherty doesn't know the bodyguard's in there.

Franco's eyes were closed, but he sensed a presence in the room. The Mafia chief spoke in a quiet, relaxed voice. "Roger, this is great, just fucking great. I could stay in this tub forever."

No Toes took a narrow metal instrument from his pocket. It fit comfortably into his hand. He pressed the tiny button embedded in the chrome cap. The switchblade spring mechanism worked smoothly and quietly. A five-inch finger of steel surged out of the knife's jacket. In two steps the bodyguard was at the top of the tub, staring down at his employer's naked body, surrounded by a sea of bubbles.

Franco started to ask if it was already time for his rubdown. Immediately after he uttered "rub" the blade sliced deeply across his neck, its honed edge scoffing at any hint of resistance. The length of razor sharp steel slashed the trachea and severed the carotid artery. There was a single, raspy quest for air before Franco's gray eyes opened and rolled to the back of his head. His final earthly awareness was of his bodyguard. He saw tears running down No Toe's face, was confused, and died.

Buzzy's sneakers were silent as he moved quickly down the corridor. Like a moth, he was drawn to the only light, the bulb over door No. 6. He slowed, walking almost on tiptoes to the open door. With his gun in hand and back pushed up against the door jamb, Buzzy turned slowly and looked into the room. He stopped, eyes wide. No Toes stood next to the tub. The bodyguard held the barrel of a handgun in his mouth. He pulled the trigger.

Saratoga County Airport

The busiest four-hour window of the year was opening at the county airport. The far side of the airfield was lined with parked private jets that had arrived within the prior twenty-four hours. The Lears and Gulfstreams had toted the rich and famous with an interest in the horseracing world, or who simply liked to be seen at Saratoga, to upstate New York and the Travers Stakes. Ninety minutes ago this year's race was logged into the record books as belonging to Irish Eagle. Now, anticipating their returning passengers, the flight crews had the powerful engines beginning to whine, and the cabin attendants were making sure adequate provisions were cooled or warmed. Inside the terminal building, the shirt-sleeved airport manager smoothed back his hair as he handed a laminated ID card back to a middle-aged man in a brown suit.

"Pretty damned unusual, to say the least, Mr. Scott, but, as you know, the FAA "...says 'jump' and we say 'how high?'"

"You can be sure your cooperation is noted, sir. We know that requests for special treatment are always tough, and cause a lot of belly-aching. The Lear's gassing up as we speak and its passengers are in the parking lot. They're waiting for my okay to head for their ride. If it's no problem, I'll have them board right at the pump. If you just open the security gate on the right side of the building, I'll take it from there."

Ten minutes later the airport manager watched through a second-floor window as the side door of a black van slid open near the jet fuel pump. A heavy-set man in casual clothing hopped onto the tarmac, followed by a man seemingly half his size. Immediately, another large man followed out the side door and a fourth man, also heavily built, from the passenger door. The three big men surrounded the smaller one. The four then walked fifteen yards and boarded the fueled Learjet 55C.

As the private plane carrying the passengers from the van took a position at the front of the departure queue, the airport manager shook his head, wondering what in hell was going on. He knew that ZK preceding the tail numbers meant a New Zealand registration for the Lear and that the flight plan listed Kennedy International on Long Island as the destination. He had heard the FAA rep say something about Bermuda into his suit coat lapel. That was all he knew.

27

ERIN COVE - MONDAY AFTER TRAVERS DAY - NOON

Franny Coughlin raced up Dock Road from the harbor, through the rain, skidding to a stop in front of the Purple Goose. Seconds later, the regulars looked up from their lunches and drinks as the huffing and puffing Coughlin came into the pub. He stood between the bar and dining area, panting, beads of sweat on his forehead. He smoothed his wet hair back, gathered his breath and announced: "Eddie McCauley's dead! Killed in an auto crash leaving Heathrow. Goin' like a bat out of hell. Slammed into a light pole. It's all they're talking about down at the betting shop. He's just come back from the States a hero, and now, he's dead!"

28

ERIN COVE - TWO WEEKS LATER

Outside the sitting room window of St Columbkille's rectory, the early September evening turned to darkness. Inside, an electric timer clicked a discordant note and advanced another notch, causing the lamp next to the window to light.

"Look at that," Father Mulligan said from his chair, surprise in his tired voice, even though he had witnessed the occurrence countless times. "No need to even know it's getting dark on you. Everything happens by itself nowadays." The priest was silent for a moment. "Well, most everything." Cigarette smoke curled lazily toward the lamp under the pleated shade. "Did you ever notice how smoke seems to drift to the light, Annie?" He took a drag on his cigarette, blew a stream of smoke and continued, "I wonder why that is."

"I wonder about a lot of things, Uncle." Annie sat back on the couch, her jean-covered legs tucked under her bottom.

"The Lord must have had his reasons for this mess, Annie. But he seems to be going to great lengths to keep it secret from us mortals."

Annie pointed to an old copy of *USA Today* on the floor, halfway into the empty hearth. "According to the American press, even though Irish Eagle won easily, so much money was wagered on other horses in the race there's an investigation to see if the American Mafia tried to influence the outcome. Add in a pair of Boston gangsters found murdered in Saratoga on the day of the race and you can be sure they'll be kept good and busy. But I doubt they'll ever discover exactly what happened."

"It's not surprising to see hoodlums killing each other," the priest said. "I've read they do it all the time in America. And with millions to be made - our millions - there was plenty of reason. Amazing, though, that jockey, McCauley, welshing on us. You would think we could have counted on him."

"Then he goes and gets himself killed driving his fancy sports car," Annie said. "No chance to ask some pointed questions. It would be interesting to find out why he changed his mind about losing, or if he ever intended to lose. He must have known it meant the end for him."

"But I can't understand it, Annie. I talked with Doc Flynn after Sunday Mass. He told me that when McCauley saddled up for the race he looked like he had the world on a string. Absolutely beaming, he was. That's a funny attitude for a famous jockey who is suppose to lose an important race on purpose. Very strange. It makes me wonder."

"Who can say? Maybe his ego ruled the day. Some put their reputation, their legacy, above all else. He could have thought it through and decided he'd be discovered if he lost on purpose. Decided to do his thing and take the consequences. The Americans have an expression - 'In your face.' Maybe McCauley was saying it to all of us. Maybe."

"Could this fiasco be a message? I've always felt we were on the side of the angels, but maybe God was telling us to take a closer look. Could there be, Annie, after all this bitter misery, a middle ground, each side giving a little?"

"I don't think there's a God caring one way or the other Uncle. We've discussed my skepticism often enough."

"You never felt that way 'till you were off to university in Dublin. I think the professors brain-washed you, Annie."

"No, it wasn't my professors in Dublin. It was a British bullet shot into my nephew's heart. You go and ask your all-powerful, compassionate God how he lets that happen to a pure and perfect five-year-old, and ruins the life of his devoted uncle at the same time, then get back to me."

After a moment, the priest shook the remote control he held in his hand. "How in blazes do I turn off the telly?"

"Point it at the set and press the button on the bottom." Annie instructed her uncle.

Father Mulligan did as told and the raucous applause of a TV studio audience was silenced.

"Trying to get as much nicotine as possible into your lungs before Millie returns from holiday?"

"At my age, there's little to lose." The priest took a final drag before he stubbed the cigarette out in the ashtray next to the lamp. He reclined his head against the lace doily spread across the chair back.

Annie shifted nervously on the couch. "I've the house under agreement for sale, Uncle. Closing escrow by the end of the month."

"I'd have been surprised to hear of your staying here in Erin Cove, now that all you have is Aidan, and him being out of the country half the time. Off to Dublin, Annie?"

"Actually, at least for the time being, it's London. There's some work for the Cause there, if they'll have me after this. It's cost them a fortune they can ill afford. Then, probably, back to Dublin. Maybe I'll finally finish up at the university."

"I'm sure there's a young man to capture your heart, now that it's available to leave our village."

"Actually, I met a fellow in Boston who seemed a half-decent sort. Maybe I'll see him again. Maybe not."

"Don't be too cavalier about your future, Annie. The years come and go at high speed. I'd hate to see you wasted away. You'll make someone very content."

Annie looked beyond her uncle, through the window, into the night. She thought back to her youth, and how this gentle priest would listen to a little girl's nervous voice in the darkness of the confessional booth, her freckled face whispering at the silhouette beyond the screen. Her uncle would calmly assure her that Mister Rooney's grocery could handle the loss of a piece of penny candy and, no, Annie, there'd be no good served by having to go and tell him all about it. A penny in the poor box at the back of the church would find its way to the storekeeper, without a name attached to it. He had always been there for her.

She had determined to keep her thoughts to herself. By doing that, she hoped, they would fade away. She kept telling herself they were woven of gossamer, flimsy enough to merit no longevity. Yet, she was obsessed by them. Perhaps just once more, her uncle would have exactly the right words of comfort. She took a deep breath and spoke quietly as she stared out the window.

"What you heard from Doc Flynn about the jockey, McCauley, is interesting, and troubling, Uncle. I've been trying to make something into a dream, but the truth is I overheard some talk just before the Travers race that has cost me sleep ever since. When I think of it, I'm all confused.

"On my way up to Empire's box to watch the race, I was part of a crowd so dense it moved like molasses. At the top of a staircase, I noticed a young woman talking to her beau. Perhaps I was drawn to her because I was thinking maybe she was having the life I was missing, would have the future I wouldn't. While I was held up on the landing, I overheard her excitedly saying that Aidan - our Aidan - had just told McCauley that things had changed, and his new orders were to win the race. Win, Uncle, not lose as planned, as we counted on, as the Army's money was wagered on. She was quite specific with what Aidan had said. I know it sounds unbelievable, and I don't know how she could have heard anything, but that's what she told her friend. I know I didn't dream this. It happened right in front of me.

"But that's not all. Just after the race, as Aidan left the box seats to go down for the winner's circle picture-taking, he walked right by me. Our eyes met, but for just an instant. He was quick to look away, and not a single word to me. He didn't come back to the seats, and I never found him back at the hotel after the race. He left a message that he had to fly right off with one of Empire's clients. He hasn't been back to the farm, and I haven't seen or heard from him since. What could it mean, Uncle? What could Aidan have possibly been doing?"

Without warning, the television set sprang back to life. Game show contestants jumped and shouted. They were wearing strange costumes. Numbers were flashing in front of them on the telly screen.

Annie looked over at her uncle. His hand was locked onto the remote control unit. She watched the priest's head roll forward, leading his body to the floor.

London - Monday Night

George Barron, deputy director of MI5 for Northern Island, gathered the five sheets of paper, folded them in half and placed them on the desk next to a crystal ashtray, dropping his reading glasses on top. He was in the second-floor study at the Hillman House, the only room being used tonight in the exclusive men's club. The ships clock in the dark, adjacent room rang a single bell. "Eight-thirty," the ex-Royal Navy commander said as he swiveled from the desk. "McGuire's due in half an hour."

Across the room, Gerald Appleyard leaned against a mahogany bookcase. "I'm sure he'll be prompt. This operation has shown, in spades, Aidan is most reliable in every way."

"He's made a believer of me, Gerry. We could not have asked for more from him." Barron gestured toward the papers on the desktop. "The report from the debrief of my favorite veterinarian is right to the point. Flynn confirmed that what appeared to happen, did in fact happen. He filled in some details that only someone on the spot could. A couple of hitches, but all handled. McGuire never flinched. Got the bastards' money delivered to the U.S. version of the Mafia - never to be seen again. Never to be used by Mr. Donnelly and his terrorist thugs to buy a single bullet."

"Having dealt with Aidan on a number of difficult situations at Empire, I am not one bit surprised." Gerry sipped from a gin and tonic, then continued. "I guess I understand your wanting to have an eye kept on him, George, but I never thought it was necessary. Aidan's commitment is genuine."

"Agreed, but we did not know that. This was his first assignment, and of his own making. One with enormous consequences. Unusual security and actual eyeballs made sense." Barron smiled. "I am convinced of McGuire's allegiance, but, at least for tonight, I'll still be Mr. Brown to him. Understood, Gerry?"

"Of course." Appleyard moved to an armchair set in front of the bookcase. "I'm curious, George, no pun intended, can you tell me how you got Doc Flynn on board? I've known him as an Empire Breeders employee, and a key one at that, for years. Never had a hint of his MI5 connection until this operation."

Barron packed tobacco into his pipe as he considered Appleyard's request. After a few moments he responded. "Of course, Gerry, you're entitled to know some background. You will be interested to learn that, for many years, Flynn has been a relatively important volunteer with the IRA." The MI5 officer paused to let that information sink in with Appleyard, whose mouth was agape. "A few years back, he filleted an informant in a pub up in Cardiff for the IRA. The Crown prosecutor had him six ways to Sunday. We offered Flynn his freedom in exchange for his Republican soul. He accepted without hesitating, knowing that if he changed stripes again his IRA comrades would be sent all the proof they'd ever need of his touting for us Brits. We add a few quid every now and then to keep him in Jameson's. He's been very useful to us the past few years."

Knowing that Appleyard liked to consider himself important enough to MI5 to have access to virtually every bit of classified information, Barron tried his hand at mollifying the respected businessman and occasional spook. "You appreciate, Gerry, our philosophy of pigeonholing information. Limited access, even with our most essential friends. Consider that McGuire was also in the dark about Flynn. Still is. If we thought you needed this information earlier for our purposes, you would have had it."

Hiding his pique at being kept ignorant for years of an Empire employee's terrorist credentials, Appleyard said with a small smile, "Of course, George. Wouldn't want it any other way." He drained his G&T.

A hundred or so yards up St. James Street from the Hillman House, Padric Hughes straddled his moped, parked up close to a phone box. The IRA soldier settled onto the seat of the motorized bicycle. He waited just a few minutes, and then watched as the green BMW he was expecting pulled into the curbside in front of the private club's fancy building. Padric reached into the pocket of his black leather jacket and confirmed that he had a number of coins for the phone box, as well as the slip of paper with the number he'd be calling. While fingering the coins, he discovered a forgotten wad of twice-chewed khat, which he quickly popped into his mouth. He hoped there were a few kicks left. Chewing the bitter paste, he wondered how long he would have to wait in the soft rain for the expensive sedan to pull back away from the curb.

At five minutes to nine Aidan McGuire stepped out of his BMW in front of the HiHo. The only visible light in the club shone from three narrow windows on the second floor. To his surprise, no footman greeted him. Aware it was just about nine o'clock, he decided to leave his car in the no parking curb zone. Aidan crossed the pavement and ascended the marble steps to the glossy black door, then remembered that it was the first Monday of the month, and the club was dark. But the message from the courier who found him at lunch on Saturday was clear – be at the Hillman House Monday night, at nine o'clock sharp. Before he could reach for the brass handle, the door was pulled in by a tan-suited bulldog of a young man with close-cropped hair. Tommy, who normally tended the entrance, was absent. "I'll keep an eye on your vehicle, sir," the pit bull face assured Aidan. "Please take the lift to the second floor and go right into the study. The door is open."

Once in the room, Aidan followed directions from Gerald Appleyard and took a seat on a leather settee, across the small room from an older, bald man dressed in an out-of-season tweed suit. Appleyard introduced the man, who remained seated at a desk, as Mr. Brown. Aidan recognized Brown's voice as being that of the person who had interviewed him in early summer at Berkhamsted. Thirty minutes later, Aidan answered the last in a series of incisive inquiries. Brown seemed satisfied, in fact, delighted, with the responses. As he dug at the burnt tobacco in his pipe with a pocket knife pick, he asked Aidan if he had questions, or any observations he could volunteer.

"Well, sir, I'll admit to a high degree of anxiety when it appeared that Irish Eagle could well be scratched from the race. I was seeing all these well-laid plans headed straight for the toilet."

"We were also concerned when we first heard about the problem with the horse's blood testing. But once we learned that the money being wagered by the IRA had been turned over to the Italian thugs, we relaxed. Even if the colt never got to the starting gate, I can't imagine Donnelly asking for a refund." With effort, the portly pipe smoker reached to the desk and tapped tobacco into the ashtray, then continued. "I'm sure the Mafia would have hung the blame for any cock-up right around Donnelly's neck."

"Well," Aidan said, "I can tell you that Donnelly was enraged. He insisted it was the Italians that somehow caused the problem with the colt's blood work, which I'm convinced was not what happened. I'm sure it was botched at a laboratory. In any event, when he heard that Irish Eagle was likely to be scratched, I received a call from him that must have melted the phone wires."

"Yes, yes." Brown put a stick match to the remaining tobacco in his pipe and puffed away laboriously. "Used some words I'd rarely heard."

Aidan stiffened slightly and moved to the edge of his chair. He looked at the face behind a haze of smoke. "Sir?"

The man in tweed realized his indiscretion. Suddenly defensive, he responded, "We could not be too careful, Aidan. We covered every possibility. We had to watch and listen everywhere. Our American friends were most cooperative in arranging to tap phone lines at your hotels. They despise terrorists as we do. It's the way it has to be. I'll not apologize."

Aidan was silent for a moment and then eased to the back of the settee. "I understand, sir. No objection taken."

A slight smile, a lighter tone, "Is there anything else, Aidan?"

Aidan had agonized over the death of Eddie McCauley, guessing the single auto crash could not have been accidental. He knew Eddie did not drink, and he had ridden with the jockey at the wheel of his Porsche. McCauley handled his sports car like he handled the horses he raced, with skill and care. Aidan despised the thought that the scheme which he had devised and promoted had now taken an innocent life, particularly one not involved in the conflict. He did not expect to soothe his conscience, but wanted an explanation.

"Just one thing, sir. Eddie McCauley's death. It is difficult to understand why."

"I anticipated you'd ask about the jockey," Brown said. "We considered the easy way out, telling you that his death was accidental. But you need to be able to trust us. You're entitled to the truth and will have it, even if it's not what you want to hear at times.

"We've shed no tears over McCauley. He was not without sin. You told me in July he accepted a bribe to do the IRA's bidding - to strengthen those brutal murderers. Since the day he agreed to participate in the IRA's scheme, in our eyes he's been an enemy combatant. In any event, we had no real choice about his living or dying. If there's one thing the IRA does a splendid job of, it's bleeding information. Once they had McCauley in their clutches, and they would have, he'd surely have exposed you, explained that he won the race because you ordered him to. Without that knowledge, the IRA has no reason to suspect you had any involvement in the jockey's change of heart.

"I expect they have concluded that McCauley made a deal with the Mafia, and that it was the American gangsters deciding which horse won, which lost, in that race. It's not a leap for the IRA to conclude that the Mafia controlled McCauley through God knows what kind of threats, or perhaps it was simple greed - they offered him a bigger bribe."

"You could be right on, sir. As I told you at our July meeting, when Donnelly and I visited McCauley in Scotland, he initially seemed to balk, not at the idea of the bribe to hold the horse back from winning, but at the amount the IRA offered."

"Yes, I remember well, Aidan. You said it was only when Donnelly also threatened to break his hands and end his career that he came around. American gangsters aren't known to be polite when they don't get what they want, either. Yes, Aidan, I do expect Donnelly will believe Mafia threats to McCauley equaled or surpassed IRA threats of broken bones, and that they also threw in more money to sweeten the pot. The IRA's millions had already been delivered to them. It's not complicated, Aidan. The IRA thinks they were had by the Mafia."

Aidan nodded. "Makes sense. A good theory, sir. When Donnelly asked me what happened with McCauley, I had no explanation. I reported that I simply did not know why he chose to ignore my orders to lose, and he seemed to believe me."

"Authorities in the States have been on board from the beginning, Aidan, including polishing this Mafia theory," Brown said. "We have been working with their State Department and they understand how important this mission is to us. They have their FBI investigating possible Mafia activity connected with the race because of the unexpected betting patterns at the track. Also, there were a couple of murders in Saratoga on the day of the race they think are probably connected.

"I am confident you have escaped IRA suspicions," Brown continued. "You had no actual control over McCauley once he got on that horse. Only he knew his final instructions from you were to win that race. We had to be sure he was silenced. You are now a critical asset to us because your bona fides have been accepted by the IRA. We could not risk McCauley exposing you and losing that advantage. Simply put, McCauley's death will save many lives. Just this one project you created has cost the terrorists dearly in both funds and, perhaps even more importantly, their confidence. They have been dealt a body blow they won't soon be over, if ever."

"Yes, sir," Aidan said. "I now understand Eddie's death was unavoidable. I never thought of all the ramifications if he lived. Perhaps that was deliberate on my part. Maybe I just didn't want to know. "

"If it helps, Aidan, remember that the IRA would certainly have murdered him, but only after brutally torturing him. It was imperative they did not get their hands on him at all. We did not let McCauley out of our sight following the race. As soon as he left the track grounds, he had two or three of us for an escort, admittedly without his cooperation. You should know he had a quick, painless death. He was given something on a private flight back to London. He went to sleep and never regained consciousness. Don't know how they did it, but operations centre staged a violent auto accident and made the injuries gory and savage enough to seem the obvious cause of his death. No autopsy was necessary.

"Incidentally, we've done a financial analysis. McCauley's assets will provide handsomely for both of his families. We'll see to it that some of his assets won't make it to his estate balance that favors the English family in Cambridge, but will rather be diverted to establish substantial accounts for the Scottish clan. The deserting husband will let mother know of her windfall by way of an anonymous message." The portly man chortled. "Both mothers, and all the sprogs, will be all right financially."

Appleyard, who, except for introductions, had remained silent, answered a soft knock on the door. A bent over, white-haired waiter held a silver tray carrying three snifters and a bottle of Courvoisier Four Star Brandy. William, mostly retired, was gifted the use of a small room on the club's top floor. For that privilege, he was available for special duty, such as this evening.

"Right over on the side table, by the Tiffany," Appleyard instructed. William set the tray down next to the lamp, backed away from the table and silently left the room.

Appleyard poured the brandy and handed snifters to Aidan and Brown, who set his pipe in the ashtray and pushed up from his chair. Brown stood beside Appleyard, their backs to the bank of three windows, and raised his glass to Aidan.

"To you, Aidan McGuire, for heroic service of incalculable value to the Crown. Your efforts have undoubtedly saved lives and prevented the savage maiming of innocent persons."

"Hear! Hear!" Appleyard endorsed the toast to his employee. Glasses touched lightly, and the three men sipped the smooth brandy.

Delighted with the approval of his protégé's efforts, Appleyard raised his glass again. "On a much lighter note, Aidan, I am pleased to report that the membership committee has voted. Welcome to the HiHo."

The delicate glassware touched once more, the chime of the crystal salute drifting to the corners of the room. Aidan sipped from the snifter as he looked beyond the two men and watched late summer rain trickle down the windows.

In front of a grocery a quarter mile down the street from the Hillman House, a blue Toyota waited by the curbside, motor idling, wipers sweeping light rain from the windscreen every few seconds. At an intersection seventy-five yards ahead, a blinking red traffic signal halted the occasional vehicle. Inside the grocery, a burly man slammed a public phone back on its cradle and hurried out the door. In moments he was across the pavement and into the drivers seat of the Toyota, sitting next to Liam Donnelly. "He's just left the building. No one following. Be along in a minute."

"Excellent," Donnelly enthused. He raised the brim of his flat cap, adjusted the rear view mirror and looked at the length of street behind, and then straight ahead. "And no bloody traffic."

Aidan's BMW pulled away from the Hillman House and streaked down the street, headlamps shining on the wet surface. He touched his foot to the brake pedal as he skirted a blue Toyota beginning to pull away from the curb. Shortly, he came to a stop at the intersection. Moments later, the Toyota pulled alongside Aidan's driver-side window and stopped. Donnelly removed his hat and looked across and into the BMW, at Aidan. His hand went to the window button. Silently, the glass slipped into the well of the door.

At the same time, Aidan turned his head towards the Toyota and lowered the window in his BMW. He looked Donnelly in the eye, then raised his right arm and, thumb up, smiled and reported. "It went like a Swiss watch, sir. They've even made me a member of the club."

"Aha! You're safely tucked away in the viper's nest. Congratulations, Aidan." Donnelly beamed. "Wonderful! Wonderful! Finally, at last, we're inside! The Council will be thrilled. Worth every penny, every bloody one. It was brilliant, played out perfectly."

Donnelly looked again to see that the two cars had the road to themselves, then scrambled out of the Toyota and into the backseat of the BMW. "Take me for a little ride, Aidan. We'll have a minute to talk."

Aidan turned the BMW to the left, followed by the Toyota. His answers to a few questions about his meeting with MI5 more than pleased Donnelly. Aidan then said, "Sir, I'm very concerned about my sister, Annie. I've been avoiding her. I don't know what to tell her. I'm sure she's wracked with doubts, that she's confused..."

"Aidan," Donnelly interrupted, "it pained me to have to keep the real purpose of this scheme from your sister, and I realize the personal sacrifice it was for you to deceive her. But we had no choice. Everybody this operation touched, inside and outside the Army, had to be convinced that our effort to fix that race was genuine, or someone would surely have slipped up - an inconsistent comment, the wrong reaction to something overheard. From the charade of doing business with a grotesque gunrunner we know brags about his dealings, to our personal phone calls, everything had to appear genuine, down to every little detail, for we know the Brits have eyes and ears everywhere."

Aidan nodded, accepting Donnelly's logic.

The IRA commander continued, "But now, Aidan, the play is over, and it's time to reap the benefits. We've no one more courageous or dedicated than Annie. I'm meeting with her come Thursday. She'll be told of your skill and bravery on behalf of the Cause. She'll be rightfully proud of her brother, as well she should."

Aidan dropped Donnelly at the curbside, then turned a corner and accelerated, thinking of William Upton. He would contact the American journalist within the week. His message would be clear, to the point. He had gained the trust of both sides to the conflict. Now his goal was to get as close to the top of both chains of command as possible. He expected to provide Upton with information from each - the strengths, the weaknesses, the goals, the methods, the willingness to sacrifice, the breaking points. Perhaps it would help, perhaps not. He would do what he could.

As Aidan slowed for a gentle curve, his eye caught a floodlit billboard. It featured a giant chocolate biscuit with a creamy white center. Timmy's favorite.

Acknowledgments

Without the support, encouragement and patience of my wife and daughters, this story would not have been told. I also am indebted to my editor, Syd Lewis and publishing designer, Kevin King, both indispensable in this effort.

This is a work of fiction. Names, characters, businesses, places, events and incidents are either the products of the author's imagination or used in a fictitious manner. Any resemblance to actual persons, living or dead, or actual events is purely coincidental.

About the Author

In order to balance the mundane fact-filled documents he has authored over many years in his general law practice, Tom Kenny chose to create his own stories and fill them with characters and situations of his own choosing. He has written three novels, including *The Morning Line*. He lives and practices law on Cape Cod. Like many so situated, he seldom goes back "over the bridge" to return to the mainland.

JUN 2017

71194625R00145

Made in the USA
Columbia, SC
24 May 2017